Johnny Scarface

JOHNNY SCARFACE

STONE WALLACE

FIVE STAR
A part of Gale, a Cengage Company

Farmington Hills, Mich • San Francisco • New York • Waterville, Maine
Meriden, Conn • Mason, Ohio • Chicago

The publisher bears no responsibility for the quality of information provided through author or third-party Web sites and does not have any control over, nor assume any responsibility for, information contained in these sites. Providing these sites should not be construed as an endorsement or approval by the publisher of these organizations or of the positions they may take on various issues.

LIBRARY OF CONGRESS CATALOGING-IN-PUBLICATION DATA

Names: Wallace, Stone, 1957– author.
Title: Johnny Scarface / Stone Wallace.
Description: First Edition. | Farmington Hills, Mich. : Five Star, a part of Gale, a Cengage Company, 2020.
Identifiers: LCCN 2019018304 (print) | ISBN 9781432858018 (hardcover : alk. paper)
Subjects: | GSAFD: Suspense fiction.
Classification: LCC PR9199.4.W3424 J64 2020 (print) | DDC 813/.6—dc23
LC record available at https://lccn.loc.gov/2019018304

First Edition. First Printing: January 2020
Find us on Facebook—https://www.facebook.com/FiveStarCengage
Visit our website—http://www.gale.cengage.com/fivestar
Contact Five Star Publishing at FiveStar@cengage.com

Printed in Mexico
1 2 3 4 5 6 7 24 23 22 21 20

My love and most appreciative thanks along with a tip of the
Stetson to the grand gal who's been beside me
on all of these dusty trails: my life pardner, Cindy.

★ ★ ★ ★ ★

PART ONE:
HEADING BACK

★ ★ ★ ★ ★

CHAPTER ONE

Riding long, lonely, and often treacherous trails plentifully occupied with all manner of predatory critters and poisonous vegetation and lacking those resources necessary to sustain life, and heading to destinations from which I could never be sure I would return, would soon be but a dusty memory. A part of my life I could say without regret I was forever putting behind me.

I was returning to *her.* The gal who called herself J. C. Montgomery, named after a newspaperman who was her mentor, but whose real name sounded like a sweet dessert to be savored on a warm and enticing summer night: Berry Dale. It was the relationship I hoped to have with Miss Montgomery that solidified my decision to give up the profession I had known, the occupation that for better or mostly for worse had become ingrained in my spirit—but other motivating factors had been at work even before she came into my life.

Out of a sense of obligation I'd completed my last assignment. It was finished, and, as far as I was concerned, I was done. No longer would I be called upon to act as a witness seeker. While we'd succeeded in what we had set out to do, it had come at a cost.

Those dead, both the good and the bad, the innocent and the deserving, were left to the elements of the earth or whatever other procedure would be afforded them, and with only the one exception I felt little remorse. The body of the sheriff I carried back with us to Chesterfield City, where he would receive a proper burial, which was his due. A good man, and I felt sorry that he'd met the end he had, but that emotion would soon pass. I carried no guilt. I only had to remind myself that his riding along with us had been his decision. Neither me nor my *compañero* had encouraged it—or even wanted it. A good man, a brave man, but a stubborn cuss whose pride led him to attempt to revive a faded reputation. The lawman named Austin Briggs had long since passed his prime but still sought that final glory that ultimately led to his death.

If not for the bravery of one man, it was a sure bet that the three of us riding the trail into Chesterfield City—a man and two children—would have shared the same fate. My own death would have been swift. Brutal, true, yet in the end merciful compared to what those *bandidos* had in mind for the girls. Each time I contemplated that abominable cruelty I found myself suppressing a cold shiver that would run up my spine like the gliding of the sharp edge of a knife. The chill would stay with me, despite the damnable and oppressive heat that seemed to never let up.

The sheriff's death was regrettable, but my most lasting sorrow would be for the little Mexican, Francisco Velasquez—the one who had prompted me into this adventure, the man who had given his life to save us in a bold, courageous gesture . . .

Or was it a deliberate sacrifice? I had started to question if that might have been his purpose all along. He fulfilled the obligation he owed his murdered sister, and, with that accomplished, had he willingly surrendered his own life?

I couldn't quite make up my mind if that had been his intention or not. Either way, it was a noble act. I hadn't been able to penetrate the brain of Francisco, and that still left me with a question that would follow me all the days of my life. I contemplated it a lot as I rode my mount with the two dirty and disheveled girls keeping a slow pace perched atop their own horse behind me. The elder of the two, Lorraine, handled the reins, while her little sister, Bethany, kept her tiny body snuggled protectively against her back. As I saw it, they were the rewards of this journey. Silvano Ramos, their tormentor, the scourge of west Texas, was dead. Without their leader, his outlaw gang would soon disband and scatter and ultimately be killed off or at least be forgotten, their individual crimes likely not even recorded as footnotes in history. Second-rate villains, and ultimately of no account. The real future sat upon the horse that once had belonged to Francisco and that obediently followed my own horse's lead.

But back to Francisco. It never left my brain, that question of whether he was my friend or my enemy. I realized he had reason to look upon me as both. Because of the work I was hired to do as a witness seeker, he could hold me responsible for the tragic death of his sister at the hand of the brutal Ramos. But he also could regard me in friendship, appreciating and respecting me in my decision to ride alongside him while we tracked the wife murderer-turned-outlaw. I knew that I could never reach a satisfactory answer and so concluded that his feelings toward me were ambiguous. I was his friend, but likely it was a friendship tinged with resentment.

Would he eventually have killed me, perhaps in fulfilling a promise he owed both to himself and his family—particularly a commitment to his mother, who demanded vengeance for what had befallen her only daughter? That secret he took with him to the grave. In those final moments of his life he could have cleared up that question, but he chose not to and left me without an answer to the riddle. And, while I knew it would continue to haunt me, might even on occasion torment my dreams, in the long run maybe it was better that I didn't know. Nor was it better for me to know that if that *had* been his intention, his killing me would have stemmed more from a sense of obligation than a personal desire.

It made little difference now. And maybe sometimes mysteries were best left unanswered.

Perhaps it was a little cruel, but such contemplation could be tempered with the reminder that Francisco was dead—and I wasn't.

I've always been a man drawn to his own thoughts. Thoughts and reflections that traveled with me on my long journeys— riding alongside me not so much as my friends, but rather as companions. Sometimes welcome, other times not.

The girls and I shared a few campfire nights on our ride back to Chesterfield City. There wasn't much talk between us—hardly any, as I recall. The girls kept themselves close to each other, particularly the little one, Bethany, who kept her small body pressed tightly against her sister. While I didn't doubt they both trusted me to bring them to safety, on occasion I caught the older girl, Lorraine, casting a wary eye at me. I always responded with a smile—nothing too overdone, mind you, just enough of a smile to give her confidence that she was protected and had nothing to dread.

I reckon the most difficult part of our ride was Lorraine's knowledge that the third horse I was guiding along our trail with a lead rope carried a corpse. I'd managed to wrap Sheriff Briggs's body in sufficient blankets so that no part of him would be exposed, but that didn't hide the truth from the girl. I don't think her sister had quite the same comprehension, though after what she had endured courtesy of the Ramos gang I couldn't swear by it. Both girls had been witnesses to a violence that no young eyes should ever be subjected to. I caught Lorraine on more than one occasion shifting her focus toward the packaged body draped over the back of the horse, only to then swiftly avert her gaze. A disturbing sight for the child, and I often wished I could simply have buried the sheriff next to Francisco.

Laid them beside each other at the location where they had both so gallantly died. The best I could do before setting up camp each night was lead the horse away from our site and secure the animal someplace where the girls would not have to be reminded of its tragic cargo.

I prepared our evening meals by the campfire, but neither of the girls had much of an appetite. I understood, though I also realized that, for the two of them to keep pace with our travel, nourishment was essential. Both Lorraine and her sister had pale complexions, and the older girl had dark circles framing her eyes. Besides her hardly eating, those shadows also indicated that Lorraine wasn't getting much sleep. And, because I had to remain at least somewhat vigilant, my own periods of shut-eye were limited and all too brief. I wondered if Lorraine was afraid to close her eyes because she still held an uncertainty where I was concerned. Maybe she was fearful of bad dreams. Or, more likely, that if she were to drift into slumber she might awaken and find herself and her sister abandoned. In any case, she never confided in me, and I didn't prod. Instead, I tried to keep her spirits boosted, even though I'd had precious little experience dealing with children or their wants or needs or what might be troubling their little minds. Especially with girls. Out of necessity we traveled slowly, but I reminded them often that soon we would be riding into town.

Not that Chesterfield City would have any particular meaning to the girls. At least not to my knowledge. I had no idea where their family had come from. Only that their parents and a cowardly uncle had tried to build a country homestead before they were come upon and savagely butchered by Ramos and his men.

Finally, the last night we camped, I knew we would arrive in Chesterfield City the next day. Much of our ride had been through monotonous flatlands dotted with sparse vegetation mainly consisting of yucca and cholla. Occasionally we'd pass a lonely and almost haunting Joshua tree, but the overall deadness of the landscape seemed to make our travel that much slower. We had passed through much the same country when we'd set out after Ramos—Francisco, Sheriff Briggs and I—but as strange as it seemed to me now, recalling the periods of doubt and trepidation that accompanied me at least, there also rode with us an adventure that kept our spirits alive. Now that it was over, and with my two companions dead and only myself guiding two traumatized children to safety, it just seemed a long, dreary journey back to where it had all started.

With our destination close at hand, I confess my main thought was resuming my acquaintanceship with Miss J. C. Montgomery. But the funny thing was that after all I had endured, and with my concerns shifted to the welfare of the two children, I found it hard to even remember what Miss Montgomery looked like. Heck, as I considered it, I couldn't rightly remember if I'd made the decision to call her by her proper name, Berry Dale, or her newspaper alias.

After supper that last night on the trail I sat on a log by the fire, my eyes settled on Lorraine and Bethany as they huddled together under their blanket, warm against the night chill. Lorraine looked about ready to fall over but, as usual, was putting up a gallant fight against surrendering to shut-eye, her intent to provide comfort for her younger sister. My focus of sight might have been on the girls, but my focus of concentration was elsewhere. Namely on my soon-to-be reunion with this lady for whom I had formed a great affection. My imaginings were deep and pleasant and perhaps reflected in a relaxed and contented expression, because, without my even being aware of it, in the next instant I felt a hand rest upon my wrist.

I turned my head and saw Lorraine sitting next to me. Her soft, slight fingers pressed delicately into my skin, but her features, still smudged and dirty, were blank. Empty. Neither of us spoke a word; we just looked at each other for what seemed a long while but likely was just mere seconds. It was a peaceful night. The skies were wide and clear and dotted with a sprinkling of stars. The valley where we had set up camp was so still and quiet that the echo from a gunshot could probably be heard from miles away. A quiet that was broken only by the snap and crackle of the wood charring on our campfire. And so, in a dark lighted only by the flickering flames of a small fire and an air that breathed in silence, the two of us sat side by side. Eventually our eyes separated, and we both set our gaze on the flames that licked skyward, setting loose sparks that glowed briefly before dying and returning to ash. Much like the future of the Ramos bunch, I couldn't resist thinking.

And then Lorraine spoke. Her voice was young, gentle, but the words she said expressed a worry that obviously had been troubling her.

"Where do me and my sister go, mister?" she asked.

I glanced down at her. She hadn't been looking at me when she asked her question. Her eyes peered straight through the campfire over to where her sister lay sleeping in the bedroll I'd laid out for them. My thoughts had been preoccupied, and I wasn't prepared to respond. Yet it didn't take me long to recognize her very real concern.

"Our folks are dead," she went on, speaking her words in a blank, unemotional tone. "And—we don't have no other family, 'ceptin' Uncle Henry."

Henry. That was a man for whom I'd formed an unhealthy opinion. A cowardly coyote who allowed his sister and brother-in-law to be murdered and stood by and watched their killers snatch his little niece, most likely with the intention to eat her flesh should their food supply run low. My back teeth clenched as I recalled our encounter with "Uncle Henry" and how, if ever there were men I could gun down without provocation, he'd top the list.

"Don't think you'll be seeing your Uncle Henry for a while," I managed to say in a calm, even voice. "But I don't want you to be worrying. I'm going to see to it that both you and your sister have a good home."

Lorraine went silent and looked a little sad. I reckon she was remembering what she had lost. The child never really had the chance to properly mourn with all that had happened. I expected to see her cry, but, while the expression on her face was pensive, no tears rolled down her cheeks.

"There's a lot of good people who'd be pleased to give you and your sister a home," I said. "Might even consider it a privilege."

Lorraine thought for a moment. Then her eyes squinted, and she said, "Why'd they see it that way?"

I looked at her with an inquisitive cocking of my head.

"As a . . . privilege?" she clarified.

She tossed me a good question. I hadn't thought I'd have to explain my remark; simply wanted to provide some words of encouragement to ease the stress from her mind. But I got the distinct impression Lorraine wasn't going to let me off the hook that easily. It suddenly dawned on me that I wasn't dealing merely with a child, but a young lady of some wisdom.

I turned my gaze toward the fire and sought an answer that she might not only understand but accept. Instead I found myself asking *her* a question.

"Where was your family from?"

She regarded me with a bewildered look. "From?"

I nodded.

"You saw where we were from," she said tensely, the corners of her mouth pulled down in a frown.

I didn't want to distress her, as, naturally, that wasn't what I meant by my question. I wanted her to tell me where her family originated, before they tried to establish their homestead, to learn if there might be someone who knew the family and who might be willing to take in the children.

The girl sighed. "I—I don't remember us ever having a home."

I sat quietly, waiting to hear if she might say more.

It took a while before she offered, "Seems we always lived in wagons. Don't remember ever staying put for long. Pa . . . seemed he just could never put down roots. Finally, Mama said we had to settle somewhere; then Pa got it in his head to start a settlement. Clear the land and build a place where others could come to live. Like a town, with a church and a school." She smiled wanly. "Mama said that Pa was dreaming big, like he always done when he got an idea in his head. But she was happy, because for the first time we was gonna know a real home."

Lorraine's face brightened in that moment, only for her expression to fade darkly as she likely recalled the tragic outcome of what had been her family's hopes.

I confess I felt my heart ache for the girl, yet there was nothing I could say. What words of comfort could I provide—especially with me not knowing what was going to happen to the sisters now that they were alone? No kinfolk, no friends to call upon. It appeared as though an orphanage might be the only choice. And that was an idea that simply didn't sit well with me. The girls deserved better than that.

I only hoped that when we got into Chesterfield City my newspaper lady friend might offer a more agreeable solution.

CHAPTER TWO

Reckon I should have expected no less, the three of us riding into Chesterfield City just before sunset, our third horse packing a dead body. Citizens out and about stopped in their tracks, folks on horseback or riding in buckboards slowed or came to a halt, and eyes fell upon us as a collective hush descended over the main street. Only faint murmurings disturbed the funereal quiet, and that provided an apt setting. The slow clip-clopping of our horses' hooves across the hard, dry turf seemed magnified in the silence, and I was overcome with a queer sensation. Yet all the while, as I observed the crowd, searching faces that I wasn't really seeing as they all seemed to merge together in a blur, I only hoped to discover one person. She would serve as a reminder that the worst part of my ordeal was truly over, and that I could finally seek a new way of life, away from lengthy travel and the never-ending uncertainty of threats to my well-being.

Her office was just ahead, the building that housed the *Chesterfield City Chronicle*. But I did not see her joining the others who watched us proceed into town, many regarding our strange trio with wrinkled brows and curious and inquiring expressions, and I felt a heaving in my gut as my brain started to work against me. Maybe I'd felt too confident about how things were between my lady friend and me. Since riding out from Mexico with Francisco to my now ending the journey here in Chesterfield City, there had been a lot of things clouding my

18

thoughts, and I couldn't say for certain that much of what I perceived was even real anymore. Maybe what I wanted—what I had hoped for—was only something I'd conjured up for my own benefit. A pretend reward for surviving our run-in with Silvano Ramos. Heck, maybe Berry Dale didn't even exist. After all, that was one helluva odd name. One that might even have been picked from a flight of fancy.

I gave my head a brisk, deliberate shake, almost knocking my Stetson off onto the road. I told myself I was just tired. I couldn't see my imagination being that colorful—leastwise as far as that name was concerned: Berry Dale. No, I was just starting to recover from an eventful adventure, a long, slow ride back to civilization . . . and now had to face the problem of what to do with two girls whose futures I somehow felt responsible for and yet had no idea how to manage. More than enough for a man alone to handle.

I heard a sharp cry come from behind me. I turned my head and saw Lorraine look on in horror as some men rushed forward to pull at and remove the blanket that covered the corpse of Sheriff Briggs. He'd been dead for many days, and his body was already rigid and in a corrupted condition not too pleasant to behold. Seeing the dead man was bad enough, but the girls did not need to be exposed to this vicious, insensitive behavior by the citizens.

I reacted instantly and instinctively. I leaped from my horse, loosened my grip on the lead rope, and thrust myself into this cluster of questionable humanity, pushing and shoving them away from the dead sheriff, readily prepared to plant a fist into the face of anyone who might try to stop me. I was met by loud voices of objection and even accusations, and, as several of the men started to move in on me and I heard both Lorraine and her sister start to cry out, another voice cut through the din:

"Stop it, you people! Let him alone!"

I recognized that voice. The words were strong, the tone determined, if issuing from a female . . . belonging to the girl I had ridden back miles to see.

She broke through the crowd that had gathered 'round the horse, and soon she came full and welcome into my sight. Our eyes met, yet the only words I could find to say were: "J.C."

She stepped toward me, and, as corny as it might sound, time stood still. My recognition of her came instantly, and I can say in all truth that at that moment she looked even more beautiful than my mind's eye remembered, even dressed in her rather stiff, professional outfit and with her brown hair piled high as it had been that first time Francisco and I had met her. Our time apart had not been that long, but the picture my brain retained of her blurred at times, especially during our ordeal, when it seemed as if I might never see her again. But now she was standing before me, her smooth, attractive features seeming to express a combination of relief, joy, and maybe even a touch of astonishment at seeing me alive. Had we been honest with each other at the time, neither of us could have held out much hope that I would return alive from the Ramos manhunt. But—at least where I was concerned—that was an outcome I could not allow myself to dwell upon.

A smile soon widened across her lips as a sparkling came into J.C.'s eyes. The crowd surrounding us grew quiet, but even if it hadn't I doubt I would have paid it much mind. The world beyond this small intimacy—for the present, at least—had ceased to exist.

But reality once again set in as J.C. turned her focus toward the body draped over the horse. Then she looked back at me with a more collected and troubled expression. I simply nodded.

"Sheriff Briggs," I said. I added, "He wasn't the only one. My *compañero*, Francisco, too."

"And Ramos?" she then asked, tentatively.

The crowd remained silent and appeared to listen intently, each citizen eager to hear what I would say. I gazed about at them, all still indistinct faces.

I answered, and my words came more as a pronouncement. "Silvano Ramos is dead."

There were gasps and quick mutterings among those in the crowd. Then again there followed a silence so heavy one could almost hear the faintest whisper of a soft breeze. I noticed some of the women and even a few of the menfolk making the sign of the cross over their chests, not for the soul of the dead outlaw, but rather a blessing of thanks that the murderer would threaten them no longer. I had to resist surrendering to the sudden burst of pride that threatened to overcome me, because, although I survived the bloodshed that occurred that night, I was not the real hero. I'd just been a lucky sonofabitch. The truth of the matter was that, although I was grateful to whatever fortune had spared me, I had yet to understand its reason for doing so. I wasn't one given to false modesty, but it was hard for me not to acknowledge that better men than I had perished on this journey.

In the next instant a big, heavyset but well-tailored man pressed forward. He was about fifty, I reckon, clean-shaven, had neatly-groomed gray hair that flared back over his brow and ears in a straight comb, and smelled a lot better than I'm sure I did. Despite this, I detected an oily presence, which was confirmed once I noticed the harsh, disapproving look J.C. thrust at him.

He was grinning broadly, flashing teeth so white they were almost blinding, as he handed me his card. I glanced at it:

Mister Theodore Sherwood
Publisher
Chesterfield City Leader

The *Mister* preceding his name seemed a mite pretentious, I thought. But it would soon make sense to me. What did seem odd to my eyes was that this gentleman had more the appearance of a prosperous gambling hall proprietor than newspaper publisher, with an attitude to match, which I was quick to deduce. I hadn't been aware of it the last time I'd been in Chesterfield City, since time was short, and there were other more pressing matters to tend to, but shortly I was to learn that J.C.'s newspaper had a rival, the *Chesterfield City Leader*, a publication that boasted a wider readership and generated larger advertising dollars from businesses throughout the county. The paper was run by this "Mister" Theodore Sherwood, and from what I was also to learn his main purpose in his professional life was to run the *Chronicle* out of business.

Sherwood had made his fortune in publishing back East. Possessed of a combination of restlessness and downright greed, he sought new opportunities in the West, where prospects for expansion were promising and where his journalistic and business principles could be exploited in a new direction, enticing readers by writing about—and frequently embellishing—colorful characters and exciting incidents. J.C. had her own ambitions, but she would not compromise her integrity and insisted on reporting the truth as it actually happened, refusing to pander to those cowboys and trail hands who wanted their stories generously sprinkled with some old-fashioned gunplay and saloon ruckus, like that depicted in dime novels. An admirable quality, but J.C. soon discovered that many readers preferred adventure over accuracy, and that put the *Chronicle* in a distant second place to the *Leader*. Needless to say, there was no love lost between J. C. Montgomery and Mr. Sherwood.

Sherwood was quick to say in a most unctuous manner, "Would consider it a privilege to buy you a drink, son."

Well, first off, I'm nobody's *son*. Least not since my parents passed on. Second, I could figure what Sherwood was really after, and while at that time I was ignorant of the rivalry between his and J.C.'s enterprises, I wasn't ready to speak to anyone about what had happened, or to satisfy morbid curiosity by giving out the bloody details. Ramos was dead, so were others, and that was about all I was going to offer at the moment. Most particularly I had to take care of the two sisters. I politely refused his offer of a drink and noticed that J.C. looked pleased.

"Why don't we go to the office?" she suggested, at the same time piercing Sherwood with a narrow-eyed glare.

That was fine with me. I was uncomfortable with all the looks of . . . well, reckon it was admiration that I was receiving, coupled with words of congratulation on a job well done and more offers of drinks at the saloon. Hell, if I were so inclined I likely could have stayed drunk for the next six months. I looked over my shoulder at Lorraine and her little sister, both of whom still appeared nervous and uncertain amid all the excitement.

I helped the girls down from their horse and, carrying the little one in my arm and taking Lorraine by the hand, moved through the crowd that seemed to part respectfully as we passed through. There were still whispers and murmurs, and finally I heard a strong voice speak and then falter as it said, "Let's take Sheriff Briggs inside his office one last time."

And for the time being that was where the town's attention was rightly focused.

I was relieved to be away from the crowd. My head was spinning. We walked through the front shop with the heavy smell of printer's ink permeating the air, an odor that Lorraine responded to with a tight wrinkling of her nose. J.C. told us to wait inside the office while she took a moment to explain to her two shop workers that no one was to be allowed inside the building; that facts were being gathered, and all information would be released in an exclusive edition of the next day's paper.

Yep, J.C. was a pretty shrewd businesswoman, I determined with no small admiration. As I say, I didn't know at the time, but she had one up on her competitor, Sherwood, courtesy of yours truly.

I took a chair across from J.C.'s desk, sliding it back so that it made a scraping sound against the dusty hardwood floor. Little Bethany clapped her tiny hands against her ears at the harsh sound before she settled onto my lap while Lorraine stood next to me, for some reason refusing the chair that J.C. offered her. J.C. looked at the girls, especially Lorraine, appraisingly yet kindly. I hoped that seeing another female might elicit a smile or some similar reaction from Lorraine, but the girl's expression was stiff, the look in her eyes maybe a mite suspicious, making it evident that she wasn't ready to give her trust too freely. With all the tragedy and distress the girl had experienced, I wasn't about to try and coax a different attitude from her. That would take time, and she would likely have to come around in her own way. The little one, Bethany, seemed content just to snuggle into me, the first show of affection I'd gotten from her. Well, maybe not affection—more a familiar protection. In any event, I was not about to discourage her wanting to be close to me.

J.C. took the chair behind her desk and smiled at the girls. Then she shifted her attention toward me.

"You look as if you could use a drink," she said. "I have some bourbon in my desk."

I gave J.C. a slightly curious look. *Bourbon?* Outside of some of the Mexican senoritas I'd come to know—most admittedly not of the highest character—I didn't come across many hard-drinking gals. And J.C. certainly didn't seem to fit that bill.

She read into what I was thinking. "Rarely for myself," she explained, her words deliberate. "But I have a lot of thirsty visitors who come into my office."

The truth was I could have appreciated a swig from that bottle, was sorely tempted, but I looked at my little companions, uncertainties and innocence and all, and decided to hold off until later.

I declined her offer with a short wag of my head, and J.C. gave a smile that told me she understood. And I think she admired my restraint, especially suspecting how thirsty I must have been.

She turned her attention back to the girls. I knew she had questions, yet at the same time she probably felt it wasn't appropriate to ask about the two children, at least not in front of them, though she had to suspect that their being with me had something to do with Ramos.

Instead she asked in a casual tone, "Do your friends have names?"

I turned to look at Lorraine, who had inched a little closer to my chair. She still had her eyes fixed on J.C., and her expression remained unsure, doubtful. When she didn't offer J.C. her name I spoke for her.

"This here is Lorraine," I said. "And the little one is . . ." I had to stop to think for a moment; the child's name had slipped my mind.

That was when Lorraine said in a voice barely above a whisper, "Her name is Bethany."

"Thank you, Lorraine," I said, tossing the girl a wink in appreciation.

Now it was my turn to reciprocate. "And this here is J.C.—or you might call her Miss Berry Dale. She's a good friend of—"

And then a remarkable thing happened, completely sudden and unexpected. Little Bethany, from whom I'd heard not so much as a peep, giggled and said in her tiny voice, "Fairy tale."

J.C. and I looked at each another. Even Lorraine seemed surprised to hear her sister speak.

"Fairy tale," the little one said again, this time with a happy grin on her chubby face. At first, I didn't understand, and then it dawned on me that she likely had interpreted J.C.'s name, Berry Dale, in her own childish way, and that encouraged her to repeat what she'd heard. It was a wonderful, innocent moment that I saw as an encouraging sign.

Bethany fell silent again. She laid her head back against my chest, and I stroked her hair.

Lorraine explained quietly, "Mama used to read Bethany fairy tales."

Neither J.C. nor I said anything. What Lorraine told us was a reminder of the sadness those two girls would have to live with—and hopefully someday recover from. My lips drew together in a tight smile. J.C.'s own smile appeared tentative.

It wasn't long before the children began to show signs of sleepiness. Bethany had already nodded off several times, only to briefly come awake before drifting off again. Lorraine looked exhausted on her feet and finally accepted the chair that J.C. offered, only to soon have her own eyes become heavy-lidded. When J.C. suggested it might be time for bed, both girls were too exhausted to protest. I carried Bethany in my arms while Lorraine walked with wobbly steps beside me as J.C. took us upstairs to her living quarters above the office and print shop. She put together a comfortable sleeping arrangement for the girls, and, once they were snug in bed, nature took its course, which took scant moments. The two of us then crept from the room and went back downstairs to the office.

"That's your bed you gave them," I said to her.

"Mm-hmm," J.C. purred. "But tonight, they need it more than I do. I can make myself comfortable elsewhere."

I didn't comment but thought it a fine gesture.

J.C. again invited me to have a drink, and this time I accepted. She pulled the bottle from a side drawer of her desk, pushing it toward me, then handed me a clean glass from the bureau shelf behind her. I poured myself a generous portion of Kentucky bourbon, taking a moment to admire the clear copper color of the liquor before taking my first welcome swallow. Normally I wasn't a bourbon drinker, but those first slugs of whiskey were the best I could ever remember tasting.

I noticed J.C. probing me with a peculiar gaze. I waited to hear what she was about to say.

"Before we go any further, there's a little matter we have to clear up." She sounded solemn.

I didn't know what she meant, and the expression on my face must have reflected my vagueness.

I saw the start of a smile start to creep across her lips. "You promised that when you came back you'd tell me your name."

My head bobbed in a slow nod.

"And do you intend to honor that promise?" she asked in a rather formal tone.

The way she phrased her question almost sounded as if she were requesting a verdict from a jury foreman. Anyway, I hesitated. I recalled how Francisco and I had tried not very successfully to suppress our amusement when we'd learned that J.C.'s birth name was Berry Dale. Now it might be her turn to get back at me. My name possessed its own peculiarity.

Still, fair was fair, and I ventured forward. "Name's Gambel. Chance Gambel."

I waited for a reaction. But instead she looked to consider. And then she nodded.

"Was your father a chance gambler? Poker or faro player?" she said with a subtle humor.

"No," I said with a wry smile. "In fact, I don't think my father ever set foot inside a gambling hall. So, I can't give you the answer you're looking for. Because I don't know. Never asked how my folks came up with 'Chance.' "

"*Hmmm,* interesting choice of name," she mused. "But no worse than Berry Dale," she said, with just a hint of amusement in her voice, letting me know she *did* remember that night at the restaurant. But at least we were now on common ground.

Her manner turned more serious. "I am curious, though, why you felt it necessary to keep your name a secret."

I gave a succinct reply. "Professional reasons."

J.C. waited to see if I would offer more. I reckon out of a long-time habit I was reluctant to reveal my reasons. But, after some thought, and with the realization that my life would now be heading in a different direction, I decided to educate her on why very few people knew the name Chance Gambel. I told J.C. how in my work as a witness seeker my efforts to bring people in to testify at trials did not always end well, and how there was always the likelihood that I could end up with a price on my head. Lots of people from the accused to kin to the witnesses themselves didn't take kindly to what I did. With an uncommon name like mine it wouldn't be hard for someone with a grudge to track me down. Just a few questions to the right people, and I could end up with a bullet in my chest. Better that I keep my identity a secret.

"But . . . doesn't seem to matter now," I concluded. "Face might be familiar—can't do a thing about that—but the name shouldn't mean nothing to anyone. Just so long as I don't advertise it too freely."

"Maybe you should call yourself something else," J.C. suggested.

"Like you did? Thought about it," I admitted. "But somehow it doesn't seem right. When it comes time for my burying I'd like my stone to have the name I was given inscribed on it."

I gestured toward the bottle on the desk, and J.C. nodded.

She said, "Before you get yourself too drunk, why don't you tell me what happened with Ramos—and how you came to be in possession of those two adorable girls."

"Talking about Ramos is the easy part," I said to her. I spoke more softly. "It's the girls that are the problem."

"Why is that?"

I frowned. "Because they're orphans. Their parents were murdered, their uncle was a no–good chicken-shit, and now I've gotta find 'em a home."

My words were deliberately expressed. I could already feel the liquor start to compromise my sobriety. Too much, too fast. I had to slow it down a bit. I looked at my near-empty glass and prudently put it aside on the desk.

J.C. changed the subject. "I'm sorry to hear about what happened to your friend."

I looked directly at her, my expression at first uncomprehending. "Friend? Francisco?" I paused, wore a subtle smile. "Don't know if you could rightly call him my 'friend.' "

"But the two of you seemed . . . well, like partners."

I nodded. "We were companions. *Compañeros.* Complicated to say more. But I'll remember him as a good man."

"What happened?" she asked tentatively.

To hell with restraint. I needed to pour myself another drink, which I swallowed back swiftly. I then felt sufficiently braced to tell her the story of Francisco's sacrifice.

When I was finished, J.C. appeared a mite pale. She didn't say anything at first, but when the words came they were spoken in admiration. "He was a brave man. He . . . had to know he was going to die. Even with him killing Ramos he couldn't have known that the others wouldn't kill him."

"I reckon he was ready to die," I told her. I didn't know why I said that. But I shouldn't have been surprised by the puzzled look J.C. gave me, a restrained urge to have me say more, reveal those suspicions that I personally held about Francisco's death. But I resisted. Those weren't pertinent to the story—not how I saw it. Some things were meant to stay personal. My face twisted into a troubled expression that J.C. noticed and respected.

"If you prefer, we could talk later," she suggested, emphasizing, "whatever it is you feel comfortable about offering the readers."

"No. Better just to get it out now."

"But there are some things that you're not ready to discuss?" J.C. said.

"Just . . . that I'd rather keep to myself. For now."

J.C. appeared to understand my reservations. Someone with less compassion would be picking at my bones like a vulture.

But the newspaperwoman did make her presence known when she said, "There's a lot of anxious people waiting to hear what happened, including my competitor. Naturally I'd like for them to read it in the *Chronicle.*"

"I won't talk to anyone else," I assured her. Truth be told, I had an ace to play. "But if I give you that 'exclusive' . . ." I held back the rest.

J.C. eyed me slyly but didn't speak.

"Well . . . just pondering if there might be something in it for me," I said, punctuating my words with an inquiring lift of my shoulder.

J.C. remained patient.

I went on, hoping to further my advantage. "After all, once the story comes out you'll have the most famous newspaper in all of west Texas."

J.C. settled back deeper in her chair. "And what would you ask in return?" she said matter-of-factly.

I spoke outright. I was feeling the bourbon enough not to feel the need to beat around the bush any longer. Truth is, under other circumstances—such as total sobriety—my request might have been humbling for me.

"I'd like a job."

J.C. leveled me with a studious expression and the arching of an eyebrow.

"You . . . want to work here? Work for me?" she presumed.

Again, I spoke with boldness. "I was thinking more of working *with* you."

J.C. looked amused rather than offended at the audacity of what I was proposing. "It's certainly an *interesting* offer," she said. Her tone, though, was noncommittal. She wasn't quick to give an answer, likely unsure whether to take me seriously or not, figuring that my words were lathered with liquor.

If that was the case I hastened to erase her doubt. "I'm the only one who can tell the story." I added with emphasis: "As it happened."

J.C. shook her head perplexedly. "I know that. But why would someone with your background want to work on a small city newspaper? You're used to freedom and open country, not to spending a good part of your day cooped up in a small office breathing in the smell of printer's ink."

I didn't hesitate with my reply, pride be damned. "Because I need a job."

J.C. furrowed her brow, as if she couldn't quite accept so basic an answer—or maybe she was puzzled by my straightforwardness in presenting it.

"I've run my course," I explained, making my voice sound weary. "The time's come to take the saddle off the horse and settle down."

J.C. looked thoughtful as she nodded.

It was then that I found myself elaborating, and oddly it was as if I had no control over the words that passed through my lips. "I've come close to dying twice in the past while. I've ridden with men who did get hit by that bullet with their name on it. This last time . . . with Ramos, it was only through luck . . .

31

or destiny that it was me who came back alive. Yeah, I've changed some, and in ways I'm not quite ready to share or talk about. Of the three of us who rode out, I had the least reason for being there. Francisco had his mission or his obligation, whatever it was that drove him on. Briggs had his pride. Me—I was coerced into going along. Also, I can't deny I was motivated by my own guilt, a guilt that I'd never acknowledged, because I remained blind to the consequences of a duty I'd performed, a sort of responsibility I had to be reminded of. And if things hadn't ended as they did . . . with Ramos being killed . . . if my *compañero* Francisco also hadn't been killed, it still might have ended badly for me, because I never knew what Francisco's intentions were for me. He might even have willingly gotten himself killed because he knew that, if he didn't die, he would have to kill me, and maybe he couldn't bring himself to do that. I've questioned that and likely will go on questioning, but I'll never know."

I went silent for a moment before I carried on. "But for fate or fortune or God . . . it wasn't meant to be. Sure, I've come out a winner, if you want to call it that, but do I risk another round at chuck-a-luck or play another hand against the house? Chance Gambel. Yeah, you asked me about my name. Well, that aside, I figure I've gambled long enough against the odds. Can picture the devil sitting across from me at the table just daring me to try my luck one last time. And I'm not ready to let that sonofabitch win."

Had I not been feeling the swift effects of the bourbon against my fatigue I might have regretted expressing myself as openly as I just had. In fact, I realized I'd just made a speech. I wasn't a man prone to baring his soul. I'd spent a great deal of my life riding lonesome, making my own decisions and living solitary with my own triumphs along with my mistakes and regrets. I watched as J.C.'s features took on a sympathetic expression, and I might have grimaced in reflex, as I did not want for her to offer that sort of reaction. Whether I'd intended to say those words or not, I'd been speaking a truth and had not been seeking compassion. The facts were the facts.

But there was more I *did* have to say. This confession was personal and concerned not the mysteries of my past, but the two of us: J.C. and me. I only hoped I had the right to speak these words and wouldn't regret them.

I smiled wearily. "I'm tired. Maybe a little drunk. Hell, I *am* a little drunk but not so much that I don't know what I'm saying. But I want you to know this: pretty much all of the time I was on that trail after Ramos I held you in my thoughts. Reckon that's what kept me going, kept me from dwelling on that uncertainty of what might happen once we found him. Maybe I thought about you too much, because there was one point before we had our run-in with Ramos where I made the decision to pack up Lorraine and Bethany and ride back to you. As far as I was concerned, it was over. I'd just had enough. And that was because I finally knew I wanted something more in my life."

J.C. looked as if she were about to say something, but I wasn't ready to allow an interruption.

"No—let me finish," I said with an upraised hand. "Until I met you I never knew that I'd been carrying an emptiness. And a yearning." I halted in my words to give J.C. the chance to digest what I was saying. I couldn't tell by her expression what she was thinking—if my words had any meaning to her. I finally gathered up the courage to say, "I know we made no real commitment, but I reckon what I need to know is if you still have those feelings I thought we shared that day."

J.C. looked almost about to blush, though her features displayed little other emotion. She was slow with her words, but when she spoke her voice was laced with tenderness. "I worried about you every minute that you were away; I want you to know that." Her lashes lowered. "But I have to be truthful: I never expected you to return. I prayed that you would, but I knew that if you found Ramos chances were none of you would come back alive." Tears began to glisten in her eyes. "After a while I had to make myself believe that would be the case, that I would never see you again, and the only way I could deal with that was . . . I had to pull my heart back."

Her words were honest but painful; they dug deep into my own heart, but, even with the bourbon swimming around inside my head, I retained enough clarity to understand the concern that had troubled her. Or maybe I simply pretended to.

After several moments, she smiled weakly. "I chose to be in a tough business, and a lot of people see me as having a strong, maybe even rigid, backbone, and I suppose I do. But that's only part of who I am. Most people here don't see the other side of me—and that's deliberate. I've built on that, especially when I have to deal with the likes of Theodore Sherwood. But the woman in me has dealt with my share of hurt. I guess that's because I'm also a romantic, have been ever since I was a little girl. Raised by a loving family. Quick to give my heart and my affections freely." She paused, sighed, and spoke reflectively. "There was another man once. We courted, and soon we were in love. At least I was. Deeply. We had what people saw as an ideal romance. We talked of marriage and building a family . . . and then one day he just left. I don't know where to, only that he never said a word or even left behind a letter explaining where or why he'd gone, only that he never came back. When you care that much for someone, and he betrays you like that, it's hard to want to give of yourself again."

"I never left you," I solemnly reminded J.C.

She again offered a fragile smile. "Not the way Andrew did, no. Even though I wasn't seeking it, when I met you that day I felt something I hadn't experienced for a long time. And to be honest, after that hurt I was still carrying, it wasn't something I really wanted to feel, that I wanted to put myself through again." She exhaled heavily. "But sometimes things happen, and there's not much you can do about it. I found that I was attracted to you; the romantic in me was urging me to open up my heart again. And I didn't fight it, not even when I learned of what you were setting out to do. Maybe it's foolish, but, until I saw you ride off with the sheriff and your Mexican friend, I held onto the hope that you would turn back. I knew I couldn't tell you to do so; I had no right. But . . . I hoped that if you truly had the same feelings toward me as I had for you, that you might make that choice. That's why when you didn't . . . and I saw what I determined was going to be another loss in my life . . . that's why I had to let go."

"But I came back," I said, stressing my words. "And I came back because of you. And now I want to share my life with you. I want to be a part of *your* life."

Yet I felt it wasn't going to be that simple. J.C. might have admitted she had a romantic nature, but that toughness she also confessed to having and the "inflexibility" she said she possessed could be difficult obstacles to overcome. And not just for me . . . but for J.C. herself.

I thought it best not to go on with this conversation. It was disappointing and not what I'd expected to hear when I returned to Chesterfield City. But the situation would have to work its way to its own conclusion, and the best way for that to happen was just to give it time. As impatient as I was for a commitment, I wasn't going to force my intentions upon J.C.

Instead I poured some more bourbon into my glass. I figured the least I owed myself was the opportunity to get drunk.

"Why don't we get back to discussing business," I suggested after ingesting a good, stiff swallow of the potent liquor.

J.C. was agreeable and likely relieved to respect my request.

"Listen," I said. "I don't care if I have to work in the print shop. I'll take the smell of printer's ink over the stench of gunfire any day."

It took a few moments for J.C. to return to her professional conduct. "But . . . you mentioned coming in as a partner."

"You might as well know I can't invest," I told her outright. "Least not financially."

She responded with a neutral nod.

"I do have money," I said. "Money that was owed me, and then some. But that money is earmarked."

J.C. sat silently.

I spoke earnestly. "It has to go toward taking care of those two girls. Can't be any other way."

J.C. lowered her eyelids. She rocked her head slowly. "Of course," she murmured. "I can appreciate that."

I swallowed the rest of my bourbon and immediately felt another heady rush. "For now, what I *do* owe you is a story." I glanced at the clutter on her desk. "Find some paper, and get your pencil ready."

CHAPTER THREE

When I awoke the following morning, I had an awful aching head, the likes of which I hadn't suffered with in a long time. I immediately and correctly attributed it to the booze I'd drunk the night before, which had slammed the inside of my skull with the wallop of a bullwhip. I hadn't consumed that much from what I could remember but had tossed back the liquor too quickly and likely not in the right state of mind. Instant drunk leading to an instant hangover.

Now I had to clear the fog from my brain sufficiently to figure out where the hell I was. Didn't recognize the room that was dark with the curtains drawn, but why would I when I couldn't even remember passing out? Wherever I was, the lack of fresh air that I'd become accustomed to by spending so much time taking my shut-eye outdoors on the trail intensified the pain in my head. My mouth was dry and tasted bitter. My stomach was queasy. I could have made a vow right then and there to swear off booze, only I knew I'd never hold true to it.

I could smell that faint odor of printer's ink with each breath my nostrils drew in, and that finally told me that I hadn't left the *Chronicle* building.

I had fallen asleep in an upholstered chair in the parlor of J.C.'s upstairs living quarters. No idea how I'd got there. As I struggled to remember the details of the night before I recalled J.C. and I putting the girls to bed . . . and then she and I having a talk in her office and my going generous on her bourbon.

That's when I started to remember. And, as my head cleared, what slowly returned to me was not a particularly pleasant memory. Still and all, my recollections were fragmentary.

The smell of printer's ink, though not so overpowering in the upstairs room, was still enough to aggravate my hangover, and so I lifted myself from the chair and on legs that felt as wobbly as two strips of uncooked bacon maneuvered my way through the room, down the stairs, through the print shop, and out onto the sun-bright street. The sudden exposure to daylight pierced my eyes with an abrupt and consuming brilliance that I needed a few moments to adjust to. I stepped back into the shade of an overhang until I could tolerate the sunlight and even how it reflected brightly off the white-framed buildings. I didn't know whether J.C. was awake or not, since I wasn't sure of the time, but my main concern was finding a restaurant where I could grab a cup of strong, black coffee to clear my head and maybe a biscuit to settle the tidal wave in my belly. The streets were pretty quiet, so I assumed it was still early in the day. Keeping watchful that I would not be accosted by the curious, I started along the boardwalk.

Yet hardly had I started to walk when I heard a youthful voice call out, "There he is. The man who killed Silvano Ramos!"

That was all it took. The excitement quickly gathered, surrounding me as if in a swarm. Where most of these people came from I didn't know. But now I realized I'd made a mistake leaving the protection of the newspaper office and venturing out onto the street where the citizens considered me a "celebrity" and remained eager to pry from me details of my recent adventure.

Well, whether contending with a hangover or cold sober, this situation placed me in somewhat of a dilemma. For the life of me I couldn't remember what I'd told J.C. the night before and if any of what I had said was print-worthy or just drunken ramblings, maybe even colored with some exaggeration. Yet I did recall that I had promised her an exclusive. These people were clamoring for details of my run-in with Silvano Ramos and his gang, and this was information I gave my word to J.C. that I wouldn't share with anyone until after the story was printed in the *Chronicle*.

Through all of their pleading and downright demanding I remained firm in my commitment. "Wait 'til the paper comes out, folks," I told them as politely as I could and only hoped the story *would* be featured in today's *Chronicle*, or else we might have an anxious mob on our hands.

I decided to forget about the restaurant and started back to the *Chronicle* building, where I'd brew my own pot of coffee. I knew I'd be shot-gunned with questions if I sat myself in a public place and that I just might grow frustrated enough to start talking.

The small crowd of citizens gradually if reluctantly dispersed once they saw I was not of a mind to share my story with them. As I expected, they were disappointed, and some appeared downright angry. I heard some nasty comments spoken behind my back and ignored them. Yet, at the same time I had the uncomfortable realization that, once the story of my experience with Silvano Ramos and his outlaw band came to print, I, as the last adult survivor, would be portrayed as a hero, whether justified or not. The people of Chesterfield City had already come to look at me in that regard, and it was unlikely I would be able to change their opinion. While in the past I'd always worked in relative anonymity, I had come to see that, as towns and settlements expanded in the West, people found comfort in their heroes. Reckon it helped them to sleep better at night, knowing that, although there was always the threat of lawlessness, there still existed those individuals determined to see that fairness and justice prevailed. I never put myself directly into that category, though I suspect my work had some value in that regard. But now that all that was behind me I did not want to be considered as someone of importance; I wanted simply to settle down to a quiet life where I could blend in as just one of the townsfolk.

But if I were to be tagged not only as a survivor of Silvano Ramos's last raid but as the man responsible for sending him to his grave, I'd never be allowed to enjoy the anonymity I now sought. And, of course, that could lead to other problems. I knew the West well. If you were regarded as a gunslinger—even if undeserving of that recognition—chances were good you'd be tracked down and challenged by some young buck eager to prove his own worth. I planned to retire my guns, two attractive if deadly ivory-handled, single-action, .44-caliber Colt Dragoons, but, once word started to circulate about my so-called accomplishment and my whereabouts, I might not have the opportunity to embrace that quiet life.

Reluctantly, my guns would have to stay strapped to my sides until whatever heroic deed I had tagged onto my reputation could be forgotten, and I could just be regarded as an ordinary citizen of the town.

I came back into the newspaper building and was met with the pleasant aroma of freshly brewed coffee, a smell much more inviting than the printer's ink that soon would flood the front shop once the workers arrived to prepare the daily in which I expected to be the main feature. I noticed that the door to J.C.'s office was partially opened, but I still tapped against the glass instead of inviting myself inside.

J.C. told me to come in. I saw that she was at her desk busily editing the copy for print. The pot of coffee was brewing on a small stove off to the far side of the office. J.C. didn't look up from her work as I entered.

"Help yourself to some coffee," she offered vacantly while her hand stroked a pencil across words jotted down from our previous night's talk. She looked to have lines of concentration drawn across her brow. I got the impression that she might have been up for a good part of the night going over what she'd written during and following our talk.

I eagerly and gratefully accepted her invitation and poured coffee into a clean porcelain cup, then stepped over to the chair opposite the desk. I didn't relax myself in the chair; in fact, I sat a little aggressively, my posture leaning forward, as, truth be told, my mood was anxious. J.C. still didn't acknowledge my presence with so much as a lifting of her eyes.

I took a slow sip of my coffee before I said something to stimulate a conversation: "Seems you're cutting out a lot of words."

"Just trimming the fat, as it were," she replied, attention still deeply focused on the copy.

"Looks as if I might have given you plenty to trim," I remarked. I took a quick swallow of coffee. When she didn't answer, I spoke outright. "You might as well know I can't rightly remember all that I told you last night."

J.C. finally raised her eyes at me. A faint, questioning look appeared on her face.

I cleared my throat, still plenty arid from last night's imbibing. "Reckon what I'm saying is . . . well, you saw how it was, with my having those few drinks kinda hitting me like the kick of a mule, not having slept much over the past while and all. Maybe I . . . well, maybe I said things I shouldn't have."

J.C. put her pencil down and straightened in her chair.

"Are you saying that you might have embellished your story?" she asked—though not quite thrusting an accusation at me.

I looked directly at her. "That's what I hope I *didn't* do."

J.C. then picked up the copy and began reading out loud what she'd written—all that I had told her the night before.

When she laid the copy back onto her desk and met my gaze with a look seeking approval, I admit I was relieved. What she'd read to me was the account as it really happened. I hadn't been emboldened by the bourbon to the point where I might have tried to impress J.C. by giving a grandiose account of my part in the adventure. I'd made it clear in my telling that I wasn't a hero, only a survivor. Francisco and Sheriff Briggs were the two men who deservedly were accorded that honor, with only a possible slight embellishment regarding the fate of the sheriff.

The fact is I never knew for sure what had happened to Briggs. He might have been come upon without warning and killed suddenly. But he might also have put up a struggle against the *bandidos* and, despite a courageous effort, lost. My telling had him portrayed as the latter, if for no other reason than to inspire kids to the true nature of a frontier hero. I was at peace with that aspect of the story. As for myself, my primary contribution came with escorting the two children back to town. I knew people would still be wanting to corner me to hear my side of the story, and I had to be prepared for that, but over time curiosity would fade, and whatever notoriety I possessed would likewise fade into desert dust.

I sighed and allowed myself to settle back into the chair.

"Are the girls still asleep?" I asked.

J.C. nodded. "Wouldn't surprise me if they slept right through most of the day. They must be exhausted."

"Yeah," I said. Then I frowned. "Yet after what they've gone through, I'm surprised they can sleep at all."

"Children are resilient," J.C. remarked.

"Maybe. But I still see some rough roads ahead. That's why I've gotta get them placed somewhere as soon as possible. Get them into a safe, stable situation. The quicker they're in a warm home being properly looked after, the better." I gave J.C. a direct look. "Don't figure you know of anyone who could provide . . ." I saw no need in finishing my sentence.

J.C. thought for a moment. She looked a little despondent. Lowering her head and the long silence that followed supplied me with the answer.

"Yeah, reckon we'll have to figure that out," I said with a weak nod. No offense against J.C., but I was hoping that, as a woman, she might have some worthwhile suggestion as to the welfare of these girls. Reckon I was somewhat disappointed, especially when she abruptly changed the subject.

"In the meantime, we never did finish that talk we had last evening."

I furrowed my brow and tried to stimulate my memory. With my recollection of last night still a mite cloudy, I wasn't sure exactly which of our talks she was referring to. And what precisely had been said between us.

Adding to my frustration was that J.C. didn't look willing to refresh my memory, preferring, or so it seemed, to let me muddle it out myself. Was it in punishment for my having gotten drunk? Or, did it have to do with that "personal" conversation we'd had, which, while I could not recall specifics, likely had to have been awkward if not downright embarrassing as were most overtures of that nature when in a liquored-up state.

Finally, I surrendered to my ignorance. "All right, you win."

"You were pretty straightforward about it yesterday," she said, appearing to enjoy my struggle at remembering.

"Well . . . last night I could have damn well told you I single-handedly took on Santa Ana's army," I replied.

"Nothing that dramatic," she said. "But you did make it quite clear you had a business proposition in mind."

The fog clouding my brain lifted just enough. She was referring to my somewhat brazen request that I come onboard at the *Chronicle* as J.C.'s partner.

"Damn bourbon," I said in a mumble.

"I don't think it was entirely the bourbon," J.C. said shrewdly.

"No, not really," I confessed. "Just loosened my tongue so I could present myself like a fool. Speak what was on my mind, but not too wisely."

"About changing professions?" J.C. ventured. "Working on a newspaper?"

"Yeah, that." I hesitated briefly before my words skipped ahead of my brain, and I added, "And more."

I searched J.C.'s face, and she didn't seem offended at what she must have suspected I was again about to propose. And, for the life of me, I don't know what in hell prompted me to once more tackle the subject, only that, although I was coping with a horse-heavy hangover, I was more sober than I had been the night before—and that maybe *that* would make the difference in her reconsidering where our relationship could be headed.

"Likely said a lot last night that I'm not having an easy time trying to remember," I said as I fidgeted slightly in my chair. Then I held myself steady, tried to control the slight alcohol-induced tremors in my hands by bracing both against the arms of the chair, and spoke with as much sincerity as I could muster. "Can we put aside whatever gibberish I might have said to you before? I'm sure I didn't express myself as well as I intended. But from what I've got clear in my head . . . well, reckon it's easy for a man who considers his future a doubtful prospect to make promises he knows he'll likely never have to honor. But whatever I told you when we sat in this office last night . . . just know that now, today, the truth is I meant it back on that day we set out after Ramos, and I mean it now: that I want us to be together. If it can't be in a professional way, well, I'll find myself something else . . . another line of work if need be. That's not important. What *is* important, what I want to be saying to you, J. C. Montgomery, is that I'd like you to be my wife."

There, I'd said it. Sober or semi-sober I'd gotten out the

words that I'd been carrying inside me since the day I'd left on the Ramos manhunt. Now I only had to see whether I'd opened myself to acceptance or mortification.

J.C.'s eyes narrowed inquisitively, giving the impression that she thought she might not have been hearing me correctly—though I couldn't have made my intention any clearer.

"I'm telling you I want us to be married," I blurted.

J.C. looked a little melancholy, her attitude suddenly somber. She gave her head a mild shake. "You really can't remember what we talked about last night. What I told you about why . . ." Her words faded as her gaze lowered to her desk.

No, I couldn't remember—*much*. But, if I hoped to get anywhere with her, I had to stay committed, and, since I'd taken the gamble to again open the door on this, I decided it had to be all or nothing.

"I won't be saying this again," I told her. "I *know* there's a future for us, and I think you know it, too. You've just got to decide where you stand. What you need to know is that I want to be with you; I want to work beside you—help this newspaper grow—and together we can do it. But if that's really not what you want, tell me outright. I'll pack up those children, and we'll ride away someplace where I can find them a home. And don't be worrying about me. I've always been a man of my own means."

I didn't know what J.C. was thinking. Only that she seemed hesitant if not outright afraid to acknowledge my question, and naturally I didn't take that as a hopeful sign. After several moments subjected to an uneasy silence, I decided to make it easy for her. And also for myself—and the girls. I started to rise from my chair, turning to leave. As I stood, I heard J.C. exhale what sounded like a deliberate breath.

"I haven't just been working on the Ramos story. I've thought about it for most of the night," she admitted in a quiet voice.

"The girls . . . and us."

I turned back to face her.

J.C. appeared to have difficulty getting her words out, her fingers fussing with the copy she was editing.

I was patient.

"The girls need a home," she said. Then a pondering pause. "I don't know if I'm ready for that. To take on that kind of responsibility." She breathed out a sigh. "But I also know that I'd always worry about what became of them. And trying to keep this paper running and contending with Sherwood's efforts to put me out of business, I have worries enough." She paused long enough to eye me critically. "I suppose in one respect I should resent you . . . for bringing them here."

"Maybe," I said. "But I didn't know what else I could do."

"I know," she said, easing my guilt with a faint smile. "You didn't have much choice."

"But that was never my intention—to expect you to be the one to care for them," I told her honestly.

J.C. still looked uncertain. I understood and appreciated her attitude. But there remained that other question that I was hoping to have answered. The right answer to which could settle the whole matter.

"And that's it?" I asked in a gentle voice. I did not want to put any pressure on her.

"No," she said delicately. "I also know you came back here . . . because of me."

I slowly rocked my head from side to side, and she gave me a bewildered look. Of course, she was right. But I wanted her to know there was another reason for my returning to Chesterfield City.

"Not entirely because of you," I said. "I figured Sheriff Briggs deserved a decent burial in the town where he'd served."

"Yes, of course," J.C. said quietly, with a respectful nod of her head. After several moments, I noticed as a look of frustrated concern creased her features, and she spoke with determination. "But something definitely has to be done for those girls."

I held back a smile. I suspected what J.C. might be contemplating. I hoped I was right in my thinking and not merely jumping the gun given the need of the situation. Still, if I was correct in my presumption and J.C. was considering providing a home for the two orphaned children, I had to wonder if she was possessed of a maternal nature. In truth, if hard pressed, I had to say I doubted it. J. C. Montgomery prided herself on being a professional woman, dedicated to her career. Motherhood, even if on a temporary basis, just didn't quite seem to fit in with who she was. Or maybe I wasn't giving her feminine side enough credit.

And I couldn't deny I still had my own doubts, not the least of which was having the girls raised in Chesterfield City. The town had a reputation for lawlessness that did not promote a safe or beneficial environment for two children who had just undergone the ordeal Lorraine and little Bethany had. And the situation could become worse, now with the sheriff gone and that office needing to be filled. There were a lot of towns with a dubious reputation in the West. Until laws were firmly established and enforced in most of these territories, there was always the threat of violence. The only sure recourse would be to ship the girls out East. But where . . . and, more importantly, to whom?

I spoke my piece in a slow, thoughtful voice. "The girls need a family. Parents. Or at least a couple who can see that they're cared for properly. Doesn't have to be a permanent arrangement. I'm sure eventually an appropriate home could be found for them."

J.C. must have suspected where I was headed with my words. While she didn't respond directly, it seemed obvious that she had already made her decision—at least where the children were concerned.

For myself, with my hangover starting to lift I almost could have used another glass of bourbon. The truth was I found myself dealing with a dilemma. I'd grown fond of the girls and, because of what I'd shared with them and brought them through, felt it my obligation—No, that wasn't the correct word. I felt it my *responsibility* to make sure they were properly cared for. And, with no ready alternatives at hand, that meant I should be the one to take on their guardianship. I naturally had uncertainties that I was prepared to take on a ready-made family at this stage of my life, especially after all my years of living close to a solitary existence. But unless a miracle came along in the form of a good family willing to take charge of raising Lorraine and Bethany, I couldn't accept the alternative, which, of course, was turning the girls over to an orphanage. I found that an objectionable proposition.

Yet if J.C. were willing to share that responsibility with me—as my wife—I believed we could make it work.

Her own feelings toward me still seemed vague; at least that was how I interpreted it. I wasn't sure if J.C. intended something more when she acknowledged her belief that I had come back to Chesterfield City for her. It was hopeful on my part, but I wanted to believe that she truly and with heartfelt honesty wanted us to be together—and that it wasn't just her concern for the girls that would encourage her decision.

She seemed to be struggling with herself. Reckon that was understandable given that so much had suddenly been thrown her way: a marriage proposal and a couple of children who, at this time yesterday, were completely unknown to her and for whom she might now take responsibility. I felt a sort of regret for heaping these complications on J.C., who, as she said, had enough to contend with running her newspaper business and fighting off the competition of Mr. Theodore Sherwood.

Finally, after long consideration she pulled her thoughts together and said, "It's wrong for you to leave. I can't push you away anymore than I could cast aside those two girls. But for the time being let's make the children our priority. As for us . . . we'll give it some time. But, until then, stay on in town; work at the *Chronicle* . . ."

"As an employee?" I interjected.

J.C.'s answer to me was firm—and fair. "For now. First let's see how you take to the newspaper game."

She was playing it safe. Not exactly what I was hoping for, but I had to appreciate she was being guarded both in professional matters and with her affections. For now, I had to accept what she was offering.

I considered her terms for about a half second. "Fair enough," I said. I stood up and we solidified our deal with a handshake. That, too, would have to do for now.

Chapter Four

It was decided that Lorraine and Bethany would stay with J.C. in her living quarters above the print shop, while I'd find boarding down the street. I was counting on this being a temporary arrangement. And, the more I thought about it, the more I was in favor of this setup. I'd been restless, and coming so close to death with Ramos only increased my impatience to settle down and find permanent contentment in my life. Maybe that rush hadn't been fair to J.C. I understood that allowing time to get to know each other better was necessary if we hoped to share any kind of a future together.

I was curious how Lorraine would take to J.C.'s offer. (Bethany, of course, was too young to have any say.) J.C. wanted me to be present when she talked to the girls. I was happy to oblige. After all, depending on how things worked out, I might have a permanent stake in this.

At first Lorraine seemed tentative, perhaps not completely understanding the arrangement we offered her and her sister. But J.C. was wonderful. In fact, she surprised me with how genuinely she expressed to Lorraine her desire to have her and Bethany stay with her and how I, too, would be around to help care for them. Both J.C. and I understood that Lorraine in particular needed to establish a renewed trust. I'd gotten both her and Bethany through to safety, and so she was comfortable with me. It was close to that way with J.C., as well, because of the gentle nature she displayed to the girls. But I could see that it was as a couple where we would offer the most advantageous situation to the two children.

I took a liking to family life—or at least to how it was managed during that time. The arrangement that J.C. and I had was kept appropriate and respectful so that no gossip would get started around town. That had been a concern to J.C. Knowing most of the town's citizens as well as she did, she also knew of that clique most prone to questionable chatter. We had to walk cautiously where that group was concerned. And I think we succeeded admirably. I did my work at the paper, shared the occasional meal with J.C. and the girls, and then left at a respectable hour for my own lodgings. All entirely innocent. If any talk happened to be spread around the streets, it was nothing that J.C. or I had learned about.

As for the newspaper employment itself, neither I nor J.C. were getting rich, but nor was there the stress and strain and uncertainty of my former occupation as a witness seeker. I recalled too many daybreaks where I questioned whether I'd waken to another.

And, so, this was the way it went. I reckon for about the first time since I was a young'un I felt a real contentment. After the *Chronicle* had printed the story about our encounter with Silvano Ramos in a week-long series of chapter articles, which inevitably boosted the paper's circulation (much to Theodore Sherwood's displeasure), I did find myself frequently sidled up to by a citizen eagerly wanting to know if I'd held anything back . . . if there was more to the adventure than was printed—some detail I'd deliberately left out—but I replied that everything that had happened had been published exactly as I had told it in the paper. No facts had been kept away from the reader. And soon my answers were accepted, and the town started to grow quiet where I was concerned.

But, before I could draw that last "It's finally over" breath, there came an unexpected surprise. One afternoon I received a telegram from an editor from Boston, who wanted me to tell my story as a book. While the telegram did not mention a specific payment, it was noted that I would find it to be a generous offer. Frankly, I was tempted enough to sit down for a long talk with J.C. But in her practical wisdom she pointed out that it would only bring a new and wider notoriety to me. In short, did I want to perpetuate the myth that I sought to avoid?

Nevertheless, I spent a few sleepless nights mulling over the pros and cons of this publishing offer. The money would certainly help to keep the *Chronicle* running—not to mention provide added security to the girls and their future. My reservations aside, I was almost ready to agree to the offer . . .

Until I met face to face with the fellow.

The establishment itself was pleasing: the dining room of Hornsby House. It was a large, corner-built structure with a front awning supported by two ornately-carved pillars anchored to the planking of the boardwalk. The awning proudly proclaimed the establishment's name in bright-gold script. The dining room itself had an elegant decor with the primary colors being gold and red. For a town with such a rough and tumble reputation as Chesterfield City, the prestige of Hornsby House seemed out of place, like a diamond embedded in a spittoon. But, on the other hand, it did provide the town with some needed class. It catered only to the finest folk, most of whom lived on prosperous ranches outside of town.

"We need a hero," this Mr. Frederick Brandt said to me almost right off the bat as we sat ourselves at a center table among the swells who were enjoying lunch. He was an Easterner all right—proper dress, fancy manners, and all. He also had a subtly enthusiastic way of expressing himself. While I'd had only limited dealings with Theodore Sherwood since I'd "insulted" him by giving the story of my adventure exclusively to the *Chronicle,* I'd still formed an opinion of him, and it was enough for me to put Mr. Frederick Brandt in the same category. A man with a surface charm but likely a not wholly reputable individual.

He'd ordered a specialty lunch of oysters and a bottle of expensive house wine, a glass of which he poured for me that I gently pushed aside. Neither my palate nor my dining etiquette matched his. I could instantly tell that Mr. Brandt was trying to impress me, but, being who I was and the type of life I'd led as a trail-driven witness seeker, I wasn't much taken in by propriety or pretense. A nice hunk of beefsteak and potatoes with a side order of greens was presented to me by the waiter.

After he'd digested his first forkful of oysters, washing it down with a gentlemanly sip of wine and then dabbing around his mouth with a napkin, Brandt repeated, "As I was saying, the book we're proposing needs a hero."

I didn't wait for him to say anything more. "There were heroes, two of them." I spoke up solidly.

Brandt looked a tad ill at ease. "Well, yes. Of course. A lawman and . . . a Mexican." A slight but detectable look of disapproval shadowed his face when he mentioned the "Mexican."

We both could see where this conversation was headed, and Mr. Frederick Brandt of the Bryce Publishing Company out of Boston suddenly discovered that he had a worthy adversary in this dusty and denim-clad cowboy. And unshaven, to boot. I'd felt that if there was any worth to his offer he would accept me as I was, and I didn't put any effort into grooming myself for this meeting. I could have felt as out of place as a mule at a cotillion if it weren't for the fact I'd deliberately chosen to come dressed as I had. J.C. sided with my decision. The restaurant had a strict dress code, but, being who I was with my "reputation," the maître d' made an exception—probably the only time

I appreciated the preferential treatment due to how people saw me.

Brandt took another drink of his wine, though this time it was more than a sip. He appeared not only uncomfortable but worried that he might be losing his advantage over our friendly talk. I took a liberal swallow of the whiskey I'd ordered and wiped off the residue with the back of my fist. We both looked at each other, him studying me over the rim of his wine glass. I didn't feel intimidated; in fact, I found the situation rather amusing. I dare say my companion found it frustrating. He couldn't know that he had about as much chance of getting me to agree to a deal as Silvano Ramos had of returning from the grave.

Brandt cleared his throat and shifted the bulk of his body forward in his chair as if readying himself to make a deliberate point. Which he did.

"You must understand that our readers don't want to read about dead heroes," he said, speaking formally. "Deceased heroes are for history to glorify. They're not relevant to a story that is still fresh in everyone's mind. Silvano Ramos had a reputation for evil that was known clear across the country; he was no regional outlaw. The fact that you were there when he was finally killed—the only survivor, as it were—makes you an important character in documenting this story, a character we can build upon—through the publication of the book and tours we can arrange throughout the country." Here he hammered home his point: "But it would mean so much more if you were presented as the real hero: the man who ended Ramos's bloody reign. The man who lived to tell about it."

He spoke those final sentences with the exaggerated passion of a sideshow pitchman. And I didn't much care for him referring to me as a "character."

"I already told the truth in the newspaper," I argued—and

without much emphasis, as I was confident in my position. "I'd be looked at as a liar if suddenly I turned around and said that I was the one who killed Silvano Ramos."

Brandt had a ready if convenient answer. "Well, let's say that you were speaking modestly; you didn't want the notoriety at first. You were honoring the two men that were killed, felt it proper not to downplay their involvement. Out of respect, of course."

"Of course," I returned, with barely hidden disdain.

It was all attractive talk, and, if I had to credit Frederick Brandt for anything, he was an admirable salesman, practiced and adept at delivering his pitch. But his arguments weren't going to work on me. I'd started to lead a regular life around Chesterfield City, which suited me fine. And, more than that, I could never bring myself to take credit for the act for which Francisco gave his life. To my way of thinking, that was akin to grave robbing.

I finally hoped to end this discussion with a blunt, terse comment. "I'm no Bob Ford."

Brandt regarded me almost incredulously. And once again he came at me with a ready answer. "Bob Ford's made a fine living with his tours."

"Bob Ford also lives each day with the knowledge that someone might put a bullet in *his* back," I said in return.

Brandt frowned. "Is that your concern?" he asked with a questioning tilt of his head.

"You can't help but think about it," I said, settling back in my seat and folding my arms across my chest. "Worst part is, would be a damn misfortune to wind up a dead hero when you were never a hero to begin with."

Brandt looked like a man clear out of options, and he spoke in a low voice that was almost a mumble. "Well, can't offer much argument to a man who fears for his life." Muttered talk or not, it was not difficult to detect the insult intended in his words. But I ignored it.

"My life is fine as it is, Mr. Brandt," I said with complete composure. "With a couple of small exceptions—like my being permitted to dine in this fancy restaurant dressed like a trail hand—people have come to accept me as just another citizen. I really don't want to promote any more notoriety."

"Two thousand dollars, cash!" Brandt suddenly said in a booming voice that attracted the attention of the other diners. It was his last-ditch effort—and, dammit, a mighty fine offer it was.

I don't know what my face expressed, only that I noticed a gleam come into Brandt's eye, as if pleased that his offer had exposed a vulnerable spot in my resistance. It hadn't—not at first; he'd just startled me with the abruptness and largesse of his offer.

"And that's just for starters," he went on. "It's what we call in the publishing business an advance. We'll also pay you royalties on book sales—those we can negotiate; cover the expenses of your tours; and, yes, even provide protection, if that's truly a concern."

I nodded my head, slowly. "Very generous."

Briefly, the notion of living a life without money worries swam around inside my head like a freshwater fish suddenly set free. J.C. could give up the headaches of running her newspaper and she, that is *we*—and, of course, the girls—could leave Chesterfield City and settle on a ranch someplace where we could raise crops or livestock if we chose and spend each evening sitting on the porch watching a magnificent sunset. Money . . . struggling to make a living might never again be a concern.

Temptation aside, it still wasn't an easy decision. I felt torn between living with financial comfort and living with my conscience. If I was swept into his offer I'd still be living a lie, and it would be hard to enjoy all those pleasures with a guilt forever gnawing at you, a reminder that you'd placed yourself on a public pedestal, taking credit for something you never did.

Damn, I never could have guessed I was possessed of such integrity.

I'm sure by now Mr. Frederick Brandt could see that I'd started to be swayed by his terms. He was quick to push his offer a little further, like prodding a stubborn steer to cross a creek with the promise of prime grazing pasture. "I think we could safely say that all told—with the proper promotion and distribution, which we would naturally provide—you'd earn in excess of ten thousand dollars. And, if the book itself is a problem . . . well, we have writers who could do the work for you. All you'd have to do is sign your name to the finished product. Give your personal endorsement to the reader."

I reckon that was what decided me and permanently made up my mind.

Sign my name . . . that would give permission—*my* permission—for a book of lies to be written and published and read by people who would never know the truth. I'd reap the financial benefits, but so also would a shady publisher who'd be able to lay his guiltless head on a pillow each night.

Even though I felt myself growing heated I kept my temper in check. "Reckon once a man signs his name, like his handshake, it should be his bond. If he's not completely comfortable doing it, feels it's in some way dishonest, best for all if he just steps away."

"You're a man of stubborn principles," Brandt said.

"Some of us have to be," I replied pointedly.

Brandt looked properly offended by my questioning his integrity. He was about to speak, but I raised my hand to silence him, at the same time I started to rise from the table.

I spoke my piece with a measured politeness. "I thank you for the lunch, sir, and apologize that I had to disappoint you. Know I'll likely never again receive so tempting an offer, and, fact is, I'll probably have moments where I'll regret having turned you down." Here my tone turned solemn. "But I'd have a lot more regret if I accepted your offer under those terms you just explained to me."

"Is it your pride that's holding you back?" Brandt then asked, making "pride" sound like a dirty word.

"Not altogether," I replied. "I'm just not going to take the credit for something another man gave his life for. You have a good afternoon, Mr. Brandt."

If I'd given in wholly to what I was feeling I would have punctuated my statement by heaving my untouched glass of wine into Brandt's face. But, while I prevented myself from causing a ruckus, I did hope that my words were overheard by others in the restaurant. I spoke with enough emphasis and clarity so that these diners could once more hear that I not only rejected but *resented* being looked upon as the slayer of Silvano Ramos. Those patrons present would most likely spread the word among their friends and neighbors of what I'd told this big-shot book editor—no doubt adding how I was probably loco for turning down such an attractive offer. Yet, how I saw it, if I could so blatantly refuse this proposal, it might stand as further proof that my account of the events as printed in the *Chronicle* was the truth.

J.C. knew that I would be having lunch with Mr. Brandt and was eager for my return to the paper. She was in her office, standing behind her desk, that perpetually worried look on her face, and, by God, she was actually wringing her hands in anticipation of hearing what I'd told him. Her two print shop workers had their gazes steady on me when I entered the building, but, not to be rude, this was personal, and so I walked right past them and shut the office door behind me.

It was funny, but suddenly I was unsure of what I should say to J.C. She'd encouraged me not to accept whatever offer Mr. Brandt presented if it meant compromising my principles, but she also didn't know how "generous" that offer was. I even debated downplaying the compensation and other tempting terms he had laid out. But I couldn't lie to her.

I spoke to the point. "He promised me a lot of money." I then smiled crookedly, and the words poured out of me expansively. "Fame, fortune, a life away from Chesterfield City, and a good future for the girls." I paused for effect, just for the hell of it. "And . . . I told him no."

J.C. stared steadily at me for a few moments, before her lips that had been only slightly parted widened in a grin.

"We're not doing so badly," she said.

"You mean that?" I said. I had to know her honest feelings. I didn't want for her at some later point to regret or condemn my decision.

J.C. held her grin, which gradually softened into an approving smile.

I stepped over to her, and at that moment I didn't give a damn if she'd respond to my advance with resistance or even a sharp slap across the face. I couldn't restrain myself; I just had to take hold of her and pull her into my embrace. Sure, that passion had been building for a long time, but with what she'd just said to me . . . well, what it told me about this gal was that she had a right appealing true and honest character. And that just broke down the barrier of resistance that I'd been struggling to keep in check when it came to my physical want to be near her.

She didn't strike me—nor did she resist the locking of my arms around her waist. Instead, when I pulled her body close to mine she gazed up at me with the purest look of love I'd ever seen. At least that was how I interpreted it. I'd known many girls through the years, but my eyes had never met the soft sparkle that was reflected in J.C.'s gaze.

"So why have we been beating 'round the bush all this time?" I asked her.

"I had to be sure," was how she answered, quietly but with a truthfulness I couldn't fault.

"Be sure," I said to her, speaking with a confidence meant for us both. "Because where I'm concerned nothing's going to change. Put aside whatever has been holding you back; that's all in the past. We all deal with pain and hurt, and it's never to anyone's benefit. Time to move forward with your own happiness. Don't deny yourself that . . . if you're sure that's what you want."

J.C. lowered her eyes and gave a slow if still mildly indecisive nod.

I spoke my next words gently yet deliberately. "And together—let's give those girls a real family."

J.C. looked back up at me. Then her eyes shifted, and she spoke as if bewildered. "Never could have seen myself in a situation like this."

"Nor me," I was quick to add, tempering my words with humor: "My God, nor me."

And then we both surrendered to a sputtering of laughter.

We didn't wait long. Now that we'd cleared up those stumbling blocks J.C. started the preparations for our wedding. And that was when I saw a different side of this tough businesswoman. To my delight, she seemed to transform into an eager bride-to-be—though her stubborn determination occasionally was put into effect when it came to certain negotiations.

Our nuptials looked to be a pretty big deal. Whether it was because of the respect people had for J.C. or from my own momentary celebrity, or most likely a combination of the two, the town of Chesterfield City seemed to be in a festive mood in the days preceding our nuptials. I confess I still had reservations about us settling permanently in the town, with its penchant for lawlessness, yet to see so many folks wanting to participate in our happiness gave me a confidence that there could be a bright and prosperous future for us in Chesterfield City.

Lorraine served as J.C.'s flower girl, and she was excited to be asked. I wasn't sure how she would take to her new family, but if she'd had any doubts J.C.'s request that she be a part of the wedding ceremony seemed to take those uncertainties away. In fact, it strengthened a bond between her and J.C. And that delighted me.

But just before the wedding could take place I moseyed down to the saloon one hot July afternoon for a schooner of cold beer, and it was then that a cloud appeared, with the potential to darken the upcoming proceedings.

I was enjoying my beer in solitude, since the saloon was fairly quiet at that time of day, and the few patrons were minding their own business. It was one of the first times where I felt I was accepted as just another citizen, no one of special importance. And that was a damn good feeling. Especially now. With all the activity going on with the last-minute planning of details for the wedding that were being organized by J.C. and what seemed were half the women in Chesterfield City, I appreciated having this opportunity to get away from all the fuss and chatter and have time just to settle back with my thoughts. Besides, the way I figured it, a wedding was mostly a woman's affair— certainly the planning of it. I justified my absence by convincing myself that my participating in discussions of flower arrangements or reception cuisine would be looked at as an intrusion.

The "intrusion" that was to come was aimed at me, and not particularly welcome. Two gentlemen named Roscoe Cutler and

Amos Tyde, aldermen who represented the city council, along with rival newspaper publisher Theodore Sherwood, appeared at my table, standing in a semi-circle, their exaggerated smiles and outgoing friendliness immediately causing my suspicious nature to surface.

"We'd consider it a privilege to buy you a drink, Mr. Gambel," Theodore Sherwood said.

I'd rejected his offer once before and would have been perfectly prepared to do so again, only I thought it inappropriate if not downright rude considering that he now was presenting himself in such distinguished company, two of the town's leading merchants and most prominent citizens, not to mention men of a strong political affiliation.

That wasn't to say I felt privileged at having this eminent trio ask to join me. I wasn't a particularly brilliant individual, but my perceptions had been honed quite fine through my years as a witness seeker, and my instincts told me that motivations beyond mere hospitality were at work.

The three men seated themselves at my table before I could invite them to do so. A bottle of fine liquor was then ordered from the barkeep. I wasn't sure how "fine" that whiskey would be given that we were in a saloon, unless a quality vintage had been put aside for a special occasion. I would have been satisfied with just another beer. But I was being wined (not necessarily dined) with an ulterior motive to this generosity surely in the offing.

Each man wore a fragrance that mingled unpleasantly with the smell of stale liquor and tobacco already hanging heavy in the air, courtesy of the other patrons, who were more to my type than my three companions. I was grateful that preliminaries were kept brief and that they didn't beat around the bush getting to the point. I wasn't eager to spend any more time than necessary sharing their company. My dealings with men who smelled pretty and dressed fancy usually had disagreeable outcomes. Despite their finery and presentation of good manners I found these individuals to be quite vulgar.

Still, I was polite and kept my features flexible, not rigid with the suspicions I already had formed toward these men.

Next a cigar was offered to me. A fine, fat smoke packaged in a gold case wider than a cowboy's belt buckle that was withdrawn with precision from the inside coat pocket of Chesterfield City's rival newspaperman. I hesitated just for a moment before I accepted Mr. Sherwood's cigar. A matchstick was then hastily struck by Amos Tyde, who reached his arm across the table to light it for me. It was all very cozy and solicitous, and I still wasn't buying any of it. I regarded the cigar before I tucked it into my shirt pocket.

"If it's all the same to you, I'll save it for later," I said.

"Gambel," Amos Tyde began, leaning forward in his chair as if to dramatically emphasize whatever point he was about to make, "as I'm sure you're aware, Mr. Cutler and I are prominent members of the city council, and we, along with other members including Mr. Sherwood here, have engaged in discussions regarding the current problem our community faces." He paused to eye his two companions, as if to check whether he was presenting himself correctly in this concern. Then he resumed. "That, of course, is our selection of a new sheriff to fill the vacancy left by the tragic passing of Austin Briggs. To cut to the chase, we feel that you might be the right man for the job."

Well, that was downright peculiar. Sheriff Briggs had working for him two deputies as I recalled. I never met the men during my last time in town, though even J.C. had mentioned that they had handled most of the policing duties around Chesterfield City. I had to wonder what had become of the two, and why one of these apparently seasoned lawmen wasn't asked to step into the sheriff's duties.

I silently questioned, had they resigned or vacated their posts?

"You have qualified men," I then said.

I noticed an uncomfortable shuffling among my companions.

"I'm afraid that neither deputy is with us any longer," Mr. Cutler said, speaking rather hastily.

I sat quietly, waiting to see if they might offer more.

"Yes. Both have decided to move on," Amos Tyde explained. "And . . . well, neither man—while effective in their duties— was quite what we are looking for as a replacement for Sheriff Briggs."

I remained curious over what prompted their voluntary departure or dismissal. And I had to remind myself that, while I didn't know the specifics, they were competent lawmen with experience, whereas my background was of a decidedly different nature, my sole qualification simply that I seemed to hold some "name" value. But these gentlemen were not of a mind to satisfy my curiosity, and, since the whole of this conversation was of little interest to me in any case, I put my inquisitiveness to rest.

I managed to keep my expression neutral at hearing this fancy talk proposition, and that was no easy task. I was thrown another reminder that whatever supposed reputation I'd established simply would not fade. First a deal for a book to fictionalize my "heroic exploits" facing the Ramos Gang . . . and now the offer of a "position" maintaining law and order in a town that even I could recognize was badly in need of taming.

I spoke reasonably. "I made it clear that I really had no part in what happened to Ramos."

"Well, yes," Mr. Cutler said. "But what we're offering you is based only partly on that. You see, we also know of your background as a witness seeker."

I felt my jaw muscles beginning to squeeze. I answered

abruptly. "I've given up that work."

"But you've proven you're a man not afraid of danger," Mr. Cutler argued. "That's the kind of sheriff we need, and we're prepared to pay handsomely."

Money. Always the incentive and always the most difficult part of the deal to turn down.

"Let's say I've grown tired of facing danger," I said. "And, as you each know, I'm taking on a new responsibility that I don't want to jeopardize with potentially hazardous employment."

"Yes, yes, we know," Mr. Tyde said with an impatient edge to his voice. "But you must be aware that your employer's enterprise is competing against Mr. Sherwood's newspaper. It's been a struggle for Miss Montgomery to keep the *Chronicle* going—David against Goliath, if you will, but with a more . . . shall we say, realistic outcome."

That was a boorish comment. I cast a slit-eyed glance at Theodore Sherwood. He was sitting back in his chair, hands folded against his belly, smiling smugly. This situation was getting more unpleasant by the minute. I reminded myself that in this round of negotiations I had the upper hand.

"Still, according to the story, it was the boy who slew the giant," I presented, allowing my own smug smile to challenge Mr. Sherwood.

It was an impertinent comment and one not appreciated by these men.

"We're getting off topic here," Mr. Tyde said, and it was apparent he was struggling to maintain his professional demeanor. "The point is, Chance, that the sheriff's job offers stability; a good wage has already been mentioned, and there are other benefits. It's a guarantee for your future."

"But no guarantee when it comes to life expectancy," I countered. I then spoke candidly. "Gentlemen, maybe I should be flattered by your offer. But, whether or not you know, I recently was presented with a much more attractive and lucrative proposition that would have asked nothing more of me than signing my name to a piece of paper. And I refused it."

At that point, something gradually began to dawn on me. My suspicious nature was once more starting to take hold. At first I thought the offer put forward by this committee was genuine enough, but maybe there was a bit more involved than just capitalizing on my so-called reputation. Perhaps this was a clever ploy to assist Theodore Sherwood in his efforts to push J.C. out of business so that his *Leader* would corner the newspaper market in Chesterfield City and expand distribution into neighboring territories, which I'd learned from J.C. was also the goal of the *Chronicle*. I wasn't sure exactly how Sherwood's plan would be put into effect by installing me as town sheriff, but I suspected he had something up his sleeve. I didn't trust him any further than I could toss spit, and his partners weren't impressing me with their false integrity, either.

Anyway, I felt satisfied that my final argument had put an end to our talk.

The three wise men sat in silence for about another minute before each rose wordlessly from the table and started to walk away, not one turning back to look at me. To their credit, at least they paid for the liquor. I considered the half-full bottle, thought what the hell, and took it with me as I strolled from the saloon. At least J.C. and I could enjoy another celebratory drink. My conscience was clear. I had no regret.

Once more I'd declared my independence.

But that was only an independence of principle, as my personal independence ceased on the following Saturday when J.C. and I became man and wife. All of J.C.'s planning paid off in a beautiful ceremony, and I was especially pleased to notice the glow and beaming smile that presented itself on Lorraine that day. J.C. took special care to make sure the girl was kept a part of all the festivities. And even though tiny Bethany had little understanding of what was going on, she, too, seemed happy with all the cheer and attention given to her, and she behaved well throughout the day.

To J.C.'s credit—while I did not know of this—she even had invited Theodore Sherwood to the wedding, which he attended, though keeping a stiff back and tight, forced smile throughout the proceedings. The three of us remained cordial even though that air of resentment remained palpable, mostly emanating from Sherwood.

I reckon I'd never completely lost my capacity for cynicism, because even as I enjoyed the celebration I knew that, come tomorrow, things would start to return to normal, and whatever goodwill had been established on this night of drinking and dancing and merriment would quickly be forgotten over the next several days. As for myself, I now had a family to support. I'd willingly accepted that responsibility and steadfastly refused to regard it merely as a duty. Nevertheless, doubts still prevailed. I hoped that I could prove I was up to the task. Having turned down two offers that, as distasteful as they were, offered genuine security, I didn't want my pride to mistakenly hold us back from the potential for a promising life.

Little did I know that not long afterward two incidents would occur, the consequences of which would have a profound effect both on securing a future for my family . . . and my trying to bury my past.

★ ★ ★ ★ ★

PART TWO:
A NEW RAMOS?

★ ★ ★ ★ ★

CHAPTER FIVE

His name was Jacquin. He was of the Comanche tribe that dwelled in the hills of north Texas. Unlike most of his Comanche brothers, Jacquin was a young man with a sensitive nature and peaceful ideals, who decided to venture forth into the white man's world when he came of age. He wanted to explore the ways of the white man—to learn of their culture so that he might reach a greater understanding of the differences that existed between these two peoples.

Even as a youth Jacquin questioned many of the teachings of his people. As he grew into adulthood he often debated the wisdom of the elders, who were ancient in body and perhaps just as ancient in their beliefs. The white man was looked upon as the enemy by the Comanche. But maybe there was another side to this history. In this desire he was met with strong disapproval from the tribe. But Jacquin was determined to discover the truth for himself.

Jacquin possessed an advantage in his ambition. On one occasion when he left the tribe in contempt he came across an old white man who had been injured in a hunting accident. Being the compassionate youth that he was, Jacquin calmed the man's fears and soon nursed him back to health. While neither could communicate with the other, they soon developed a wary friendship. Even after Jacquin returned to his village he would often make secret visits to the old man, where he began to learn the language spoken by the white man. Jacquin possessed a quick mind, and by the time the old man died the young Comanche had mastered much of the language. This was never shared with his own people; neither were the books that had been given to him by the old man, which he kept carefully hidden outside the village.

I rarely had dealings with Indians during my years as a witness seeker. When a crime was committed by a native from one of the more aggressive tribes, there often was little need for fair justice. It wasn't worth the expense to set me on the trail of someone who might either help free or condemn an Indian prisoner, and so, guilty or not, the trial was swift, perfunctory, and the verdict sure and often predictable. These so-called "legal" proceedings were held in saloons where proper protocol was seldom observed and the smell of beer and whiskey hung heavy in the air. Often there wasn't even a defense presented, just angry shouts and jeers and a broken-down judge who put out only the most minimal effort to restore a sense of order to what could laughingly be called a courtroom. The trial would begin at around ten in the morning, and by noon the accused would be hanging from a hastily-constructed gallows or even dangling from the strong, solid branch of a tree so that celebratory drinks could once again start being served shortly after lunchtime.

This was known as frontier justice—and, to be fair, this "justice" was not only limited to the Indian offender. More than one white man also shared the noose when citizens demanded immediate punishment for a particular crime. Depending on the mood of the community, the sentence of hanging could be imposed for offenses ranging from murder to horse thievery to even stealing livestock.

While my services were not needed in these instances, I still sat in on some of these farces, and those random judgments as much as anything helped to erode my interest in my occupation. Maybe had I been hired to bring in a witness who could corroborate a defendant's story, an innocent man would not be sent to the gallows. Those were details I would never know, but I heard many a man plead for a witness to be brought into court who would prove that he was not guilty of the crime for which he had been accused, only to be cruelly denied that request in favor of quick justice. The authorities preferred to satisfy the demands of impatient spectators with no connection to the case at hand, or perhaps were just eager to return to the business of slopping back their mugs of beer or shots of whiskey, much to the delight of the busy barkeep. I saw those men dangling from a rope not long afterward, and the knot that snapped their necks could not have been any more constricting than the knot that squeezed against my gut.

What I was witness to wasn't justice; it was swift and cruel injustice.

But I'd come to understand that, in taming the frontier, the West had its own laws. And any man, woman, or even child had best abide by them.

But back to the Comanche named Jacquin. It would not be long before I pieced together his tale. His story was one of tragedy and shame—and a guilt that no one would come forward to admit. I reckon in retrospect it might have been more naiveté than curiosity that prompted the young man's decision to venture out and perhaps experience a different way of life.

One day, he wandered into a little town called Lone Creek, situated some miles southeast of Chesterfield City. A small community still in the early stages of development, claiming only a post office, saloon, and hotel as its main features, its settlers were concerned primarily with the expansion if not the permanence of Lone Creek as clapboard buildings and houses were hastily slapped together. It was the type of town that, at the time, a strong dust storm would have blown clear out of the county.

The day that Jacquin bravely walked down the dusty main street he was greeted with stares of fear and suspicion by those few citizens out and about. Young children were hastened into their homes by their frightened mothers. A small band of men gathered on the boardwalk outside the saloon, holding their positions but braced for a confrontation with the Indian stranger. Whether it was courage or ignorance, I can't judge, but surely Jacquin must have understood there would be obstacles to overcome and that these obstacles might present severe or even life-threatening consequences. Yet the first thing he did was set himself on the boardwalk outside the general store, not acknowledging but neither ignorant of the piercing, even accusing, looks that came his way from that gathering of men just down the way. It was like a standoff, both parties holding their ground until, finally, the men, perhaps confident in their ability to halt trouble should it arrive, moved back into the saloon. Jacquin likely felt a sense of pride, watching these men depart. And he then hung around town, just kind of lollygagging, seeming to have no specific purpose.

As time passed and it began to appear that his presence posed no threat, some of the townspeople began to share a word with him, often just a tentative greeting. His responses were always quiet and respectful. While he could not disguise his Indian features—the bronze skin with the flesh pulled tight so that his cheekbones were highlighted and what some discerned as a subtle fierceness to his expression that even the occasional slight suggestion of a smile couldn't erase—Jacquin attempted to cultivate a respectable image through his choice of clothing. He first arrived in town dressed in a gray suit and white shirt decorated with a bolo tie and had even purchased a derby hat under which he bunched his long hair.

Eventually, though, rumors began to spread among the fearful few that his intentions were not merely to pass through Lone Creek but that he could, in fact, be scouting the community. And if that were so . . . for what purpose? There were those—let's call them dissenters—who opposed an Indian, especially a Comanche, loitering about their town, seemingly harmless but likewise aimless in whatever his intentions.

In some respects, I could not rightly blame them for their doubt and suspicion. The brutality of the Comanche had yet to be pressed into the back pages of history. It didn't take long for those citizens who opposed Jacquin's presence to exert their influence over those of a more tolerant way of thinking, and uncertainties began to grow and fester among the people of Lone Creek.

Without skipping ahead too much, it was several months later that I had to go back and piece together the events that soon were to transpire. I shuffled through conflicting reports, differing viewpoints, and some outright hatred and prejudice to reach my own conclusions.

I remained ambivalent throughout the course of my research and eventually reconstructed the story of an apparently peaceful Indian youth named Jacquin, soon to be transformed through prejudice and brutality into the vengeful killer known as Johnny Scarface.

CHAPTER SIX

His face was smooth and unmarked when he came to the rescue of the girl named Bridget Ellen Colson. Jacquin had been out on a sun-bright, lazy Saturday afternoon, his makeshift fishing pole dipped into the calm currents of the creek, hoping to bring in a catch for supper with which he intended to surprise his boss. By this time Jacquin had found a job as a clerk with a town merchant named McNally. Jacquin had decided that, if he was going to settle in Lone Creek, he'd best make himself useful so as not to be looked upon with contempt or derision.

Daniel McNally was a kindly and tolerant fellow, though initially cautious about bringing a Comanche into his employ, even one whom he himself had regarded with what had to be a hint of narrow-mindedness as "tamed." But there was something about Jacquin that impressed McNally, and after some discussion he offered Jacquin a job in his store—though emphasizing that it was strictly on a trial basis. McNally was well aware of the suspicion and superstition inherent in some of the townspeople, yet he was a man of vision who believed that by employing the lad he might foster a greater understanding between the Indian and the white man so that further settlement in the West could be achieved without the threat of violence.

Naturally his efforts and intentions were met with voices of disapproval among those same folks who were against Jacquin being in Lone Creek in the first place, those who feared that, with the door for opportunity now open, other "savages" would soon come to populate their community.

Finally, a town meeting was called in the newly-erected congregational church where opinions and aggressions were given vent, and heated words were exchanged between two opposing factions—with the opposition having the advantage, since they were mainly the voices of the business community being established in town. But the tide turned as clearer heads recognized the ultimate wisdom of what Daniel McNally had in mind. They were prepared to gamble on supporting the store owner's decision. A kindness shown is a kindness returned, it was argued—though there remained many who believed that Indians, and especially the Comanche, were incapable of gratitude or benevolence. Doubt, suspicion, and apprehension hung heavy in the air at that church meeting. Whatever peace had been established with the Comanche was not strictly binding, and, with the nearest army outpost many miles from their town, the people of Lone Creek could be slaughtered if hostilities arose, because it would be days before the troops could reach them.

"You might not only be jeopardizing the future of your store, McNally," one voice rose in protest, "but maybe your own future as a citizen of this community."

The threat could not have been put forward more blatantly— the threat not of a Comanche uprising, but of an ousting from Lone Creek courtesy of McNally's fellow townspeople.

This comment was greeted with equal responses of yeas and nays.

Arguments went on throughout a good part of the night. By the time the meeting came to an end, the verdict by a slim margin was that Jacquin would be permitted at least a temporary stay in town and be allowed to continue his employment with McNally. Of course, should Jacquin suddenly resort to the ways of his people and cause a disturbance in town—no matter how minor that trouble might be—he would instantly be banished, and Daniel McNally would be held responsible.

McNally understood that he was taking on a heavy responsibility and may even have entertained second thoughts, but he agreed with the decision and conditions. He still believed that by looking ahead and casting aside prejudices the town, the territory, and eventually the country would benefit and perhaps even prosper. It wasn't a credit he sought for himself; instead he thought of the legacy a small, sleepy little town called Lone Creek could leave the nation.

What I found interesting, what I later learned, was that Jacquin was not excluded from this town gathering. In fact, it was insisted that he attend, though never once was he permitted to speak. He was basically put on display and expected to listen but to remain quiet. He was obedient and sat stoically throughout the lengthy and mostly turbulent discussions.

The ruling, such as it was, was settled. The opposition maintained their stand and made no effort to hide from McNally or his young Indian their disapproval. While their vote had been defeated, they made it clear they would be keeping a close watch on the town's "token Indian."

Their problem was that at present there was no other store in Lone Creek from which they could purchase their goods. So even these less-than-broad-minded individuals had no other option than to do business with *McNally's Mercantile*.

What surprised McNally and a goodly amount of his customers was how polite, accommodating, and efficient Jacquin proved to be in his work. Not one to initiate or prolong meaningless conversations with customers, neither was he rude nor abrupt. He seemed both dedicated and determined to satisfy his customers, whatever their needs. He'd also proven himself to be honest. Still working to establish complete trust in Jacquin, McNally would often pretend to be tending to other business in his store while actually listening to how Jacquin related to customers. He never once had reason to reprimand the young man, and if complaints were forthcoming, delivered by those whose grievances had no more significance than their own prejudice, McNally simply told them to purchase their wares elsewhere . . . which meant a long ride into Chesterfield City. The story goes that one day a customer deliberately overpaid for an item and played forgetful as he collected his merchandise and prepared to leave the store. He'd hoped to catch Jacquin in a trap so that he could accuse him of thievery, but before he could reach the door the young man called after him and was holding in his hand the amount still owed to the customer. The fellow harrumphed in disappointment, but, his attitude aside, word did circulate throughout the community of Jacquin's honesty.

While this didn't earn Jacquin a silver star, it did set those critical minds to thinking. And things started to happen. McNally scratched a furrowed brow more than once at how his merchandise seemed to move so rapidly with his young employee servicing his patrons.

But McNally wasn't entirely free of condemnation. He still had to deal with the ongoing protests from those who resented Jacquin working for a white man—and selling wares *to* the white man. While opposition to Jacquin gradually diminished, McNally was still pressured to fire Jacquin and give his job to "one of their own kind," meaning someone seeking work within the community. But the real intention was a little less generous.

To his credit, Daniel McNally stuck to his guns, and, while he inevitably lost the odd customer who remained firm in whatever his or her conviction, the store owner did not regret his decision, or his own mule-headedness when it came to honoring his personal principles of right and wrong.

And perhaps Daniel McNally was right, because, in an odd

sort of way, as time went on, not only a tolerance but a respect developed for Jacquin, even among some of those who had been keeping their distance from McNally's "redskin."

Jacquin was pleased, even as he understood that there still existed pockets of resistance to him living among the citizens of Lone Creek. He even occasionally had to put up with verbal abuse likely intended to provoke him into an aggressive response that would see him swiftly and not necessarily gently removed from town. But Jacquin could not be goaded into responding. It wasn't just his own strong personality and reserve that allowed him to ignore the hurling of cruel taunts; Jacquin also knew what an aggressive attitude would mean to the man who had put his trust in him, a man he had come to respect and admire as his example of the goodness that could be in all people: his employer, Mr. McNally.

And then the day came when his life was to change in a different way.

Bridget Ellen Colson was by all accounts a pretty yet spirited young girl, the daughter of a prosperous Texas cattle rancher and landowner named Ray Colson; a girl whose indulgences reached the point where her father, as stern and domineering as he was, was little able to fasten the reins on his only child's impetuous behavior. She could best be described as a rebellious young filly, prone to sudden outbursts of independence— oftentimes reckless, and to the devil whatever the consequences. In short, she possessed a nature that, if not entirely disobedient, was still difficult to corral. In some respects, hers was a personality not unlike Jacquin's, but youthful and spoiled and therefore less inclined to exhibit a mature restraint in her conduct.

Jacquin heard the scream—a sharp, sudden shriek really, the excited voice of a female—and, startled from his half-dozing reverie alongside the still waters of the creek, he tilted upward the battered straw hat from his brow, reflexively releasing his loose grip on his fishing pole, and craned his neck, then turned his head both ways to source the direction whence came the cry.

His eyes finally focused on what looked to be a horse galloping wildly out of control, the rider unable to manage the handling of the reins. It appeared that, despite her efforts and vocal attempts to steady the animal, the girl was headed for disaster. The horse was heading in his direction, and Jacquin reacted quickly. From a young age Jacquin had been trained to be skilled with a horse—not just in riding but also in communication. The Comanche treasured and respected the horse; it was essential for a brave to learn how to master his mount. Jacquin could see that the girl was in trouble, wide-eyed in fear that the animal would soon toss her from the saddle. At the rapid pace that the horse was galloping, should she be thrown, there was every likelihood she could be seriously injured, or even killed.

Jacquin determined swiftness was essential as the horse raced toward him, hooves pounding furiously into the ground, though still at a distance of several yards, and veering toward his right. He leaped to his feet and sprinted to close those yards in an attempt to either halt or at least slow the speed of the horse.

The horse began to steady its pace as it saw Jacquin approach. And then the animal reared, bolting upright on its hind legs, with the girl holding firm onto the reins with gloved hands so as not to be thrown backward. The young Comanche raised both arms in a slow, calming gesture, and the animal halted, though it still seemed agitated by whatever had spurred it into action.

Jacquin spoke some words in the Comanche language, and this, too, seemed to further soothe the horse. There seemed to be a unique understanding between man and beast, although whatever that might be was not immediately recognized by the shaken rider. What likely was foremost in her mind was that a potential tragedy had been averted by the young man's speedy intervention.

The horse, a handsome palomino, started to settle. It nickered. Jacquin stepped over to the animal and gently rubbed the open palm of his hand against its muzzle. Once more he spoke to the horse in words the girl could not understand. The animal relaxed completely, and only then did Jacquin allow his eyes to connect with the girl named Bridget Ellen.

Neither one spoke. Bridget Ellen was speechless in trying to regain her composure. Jacquin simply was silent, as was his nature. His expression as well as his demeanor were inscrutable. Despite his time living among white people, he still possessed many of the characteristics inherent in the Comanche.

As his dark-brown eyes settled upon the girl he determined by the expensive breed of her horse and her fancy riding wear that she was from a privileged background, a world unfamiliar to him, but that was of no matter. He satisfied himself with the knowledge that he had come to her assistance at a desperate moment. He set his gaze free from her and turned away.

Before he could walk off, Jacquin heard the girl call to him over her breathlessness: "Wait!"

Jacquin halted and stiffened slightly before he slowly turned to face her.

The girl held up a hand to indicate to Jacquin that she needed a few minutes to catch her air. And then: "Why are you walking away?"

Jacquin didn't answer.

Bridget Ellen eyed him speculatively. "I don't know you. I haven't seen you before."

Again, Jacquin said nothing.

"You . . . you're an Indian," Bridget Ellen next said, exhaling her words, though not as an indictment but an observation.

Jacquin still did not respond.

The girl's horse started to become unsettled again, and she

tightened her grip on the reins. That was when Jacquin finally spoke.

"Your horse was frightened," he said, "but he is a good animal."

"Ranger's his name." Bridget Ellen gave a nod of her head. "Yes, he is," she replied, explaining, "It was a snake back on the trail. Appeared suddenly. Spooked him. But how did you know?"

Only a faint enigmatic smile was his reply.

And then the girl smiled, and her own smile was just as difficult to decipher. She gazed at the young man more closely now that she had recovered sufficiently from her panic.

"You're just a boy," she remarked.

Jacquin responded with slight indignation. "To my people, I am regarded as a man."

"I didn't mean to offend . . ." she started to say.

"Age is not necessarily measured in years," Jacquin explained. "It can also be measured by experience."

Bridget Ellen merely nodded, vacantly, before she asked, "Do you have a name?"

"Do not all people have a name?" came the question to her question.

Bridget Ellen looked a little perplexed. She couldn't understand why he replied with rudeness to her simple question.

Jacquin was wearing a straw hat under which he had bunched his hair. In what was maybe an act of defiance—or perhaps pride, or a move just to startle the girl—he swept off his hat with a flourish and let his shiny, black hair fall long and loose over his shoulders. He stood waiting to see what she might do or say.

The girl surprised him. While she first reacted with a reflexive stiffening of her posture in the saddle, Bridget Ellen sighed, relaxed, and then, just as deliberately, removed her own headwear—an attractive cream-colored Stetson—and her long, strawberry locks fell free, looking almost translucent as they reflected the bright glow of the sun.

Once more there was a silence between the two of them.

It was Bridget Ellen who finally broke the quiet. "Seems we've reached an impasse."

Jacquin creased his brow. "An *impasse*?"

She lifted a shoulder. "Neither of us has anything to say."

Jacquin continued to stand stoically, legs separated, hands placed firmly on his hips, his face impassive.

"Is talk so important?" he said.

The girl released a breath. "Well," she said, "if you have nothing to say and are just going to stand there, I'd just as soon be on my way."

"To where?" Jacquin swiftly asked her.

"Does that matter to you?" Bridget Ellen said with a hint of haughtiness.

Jacquin didn't answer.

Bridget Ellen took the reins in both hands and prepared to depart. "Then step aside and let me ride on. I'm already late for lunch."

Jacquin squinted his eyes. "If I let you go, I might not see you again."

The girl regarded the young Comanche with a look of mild astonishment. "Pardon me?"

"Perhaps our meeting was meant to be," Jacquin said.

"I don't see how my almost being killed . . ."

"When I happened to be nearby to rescue you," Jacquin explained.

Of a sudden Bridget Ellen seemed timid, perhaps even a little fearful as to the Indian's intent. She shook her head slowly, doubtfully, her long, strawberry-colored hair floating like angel feathers from her gesture and the slight valley breeze that caressed through it.

"Go if you must," Jacquin said as he stepped aside.

But Bridget Ellen didn't ride away. Instead she held her horse steady.

"Why do you not go?" Jacquin asked her. "I will not try to stop you."

Bridget Ellen didn't give him an answer. But as she continued to look at Jacquin it appeared to the young man that whatever apprehensions she might have had were fading.

"What is your name?" she asked him once again.

Jacquin cocked his head. "You wish to know what I am called?"

"Yes."

Jacquin considered. "And why is that important if soon you will leave and likely our paths will never cross again?"

Just short of frustration Bridget Ellen said, "It's common courtesy."

Jacquin hunched a shoulder. "I know not such a thing as . . . courtesy."

Maybe he was just playing games with her, teasing her; Bridget Ellen could not know. But she wasn't in the mood to partake of such frivolities after what had nearly happened to her, and her patience was fraying.

"Don't you know anything about manners?" she said in a huff.

And then: "If it pleases you, I am called Jacquin."

"Jacquin," the girl repeated.

The young Comanche pierced the girl with his dark-brown eyes and inflated his chest; his physique was not muscular but well-developed for a boy of his age. "Yes, and I am a Comanche. For many years, my tribe has been at war with your people. Many a white man has fallen under the hand of the Comanche." When the girl responded with a sharp look of concern he added less dramatically, "And many a Comanche has fallen under your rifles."

Bridget Ellen was schooled and knew of the bloody history between the Comanche tribes and the people of her race. She also could not deny that if this boy named Jacquin had not come to her rescue—if she had just happened upon him on her own—she likely would have fled from him in panic.

"Why are you telling me this?" Bridget Ellen wanted to know.

"Because it is only fair," he replied. "I sense the fear in you. Fear because of who I am. What I represent."

Bridget Ellen straightened in her saddle. There was a slight wariness to her words. "And should I be afraid?"

"That is for you to decide."

Bridget Ellen shook her head and spoke with confidence. "No. You helped me when you just as easily could have turned away. Why would you rescue me if only to harm me?"

Jacquin cupped a hand against his chin and nodded. "You are wise in your understanding."

Bridget Ellen lifted herself down from her palomino. Jacquin watched as she dismounted and surreptitiously took his first thorough look at her. She was pretty, fair-skinned, slim and attired in a white blouse with vest, black leather pants, and expensive, bejeweled riding boots. Yes, there was no doubt she possessed wealth, he determined. Sadly, he also understood the reality. Wherever she came from, it was not a world where he would be welcome . . . or into which he himself was prepared to enter. The education he sought saw him living among the white man. With few dissenters, he had been accepted into their way of life. But his true spirit would always be part of the purity of the land—and that could never be changed. It was entrenched in him. And, yet, for perhaps the first time that disparity saddened him. Because, while he recognized that cultural and class distinctions were insurmountable obstacles when it came to courting between an Indian and a white maiden, he could not deny feeling an attraction toward the girl, especially once she finally introduced herself with what she had called "common courtesy."

"My name is Bridget Ellen."

Jacquin considered briefly. "Bridget . . . and Ellen."

"No, not *and*," she clarified. "It is my whole name: Bridget Ellen."

Jacquin crinkled his eyes and wrinkled his brow as he further considered her name. He then looked to accept it with a short nod of his head.

"Now that we've been introduced, Jacquin, I think it would be proper if I showed my appreciation for your gallantry."

Jacquin arched an inquisitive eyebrow.

"By inviting you to my house."

Jacquin's eyebrow remained lifted.

"To have you meet my father," Bridget Ellen made clear.

Jacquin responded with a vacant expression. He took hold of the long, black hair that slowly swirled around his face in the mild valley breeze and stuffed the strands back under his straw hat. While Jacquin did not want to refuse the girl's invitation, he was unsure about being introduced to her family.

"I do not know that your father would care to meet . . . someone of my breeding," he said in a dispirited tone.

Bridget Ellen spoke to ease his doubts. "Nonsense. He most certainly would want to thank the man who saved his daughter from what might have been a terrible accident."

Jacquin shrugged. "What I would do for anyone," he stated, his words spoken in truth.

"Yes, but today you did it for *me*," Bridget Ellen said, encouraging him with a smile.

"I expect no reward," Jacquin said emphatically.

"But you will accept a thank you," Bridget Ellen returned. "From my father."

Jacquin continued to hesitate with his answer. While he did not voice it, he found himself in a dilemma. But, because he did not want to separate himself from the girl, he finally sighed and said simply, "If you think it wise, we will go."

Jacquin did not own a horse. Since leaving his home with the Comanche tribe he had made his travels on foot, and he walked barefoot alongside the girl as she slowly guided her palomino toward her father's ranch. Bridget Ellen tried to engage her companion in small talk as they made the short journey, asking him questions that Jacquin mostly answered in brevity. She even tried to tease some talk out of him, but Jacquin would offer little more than simple replies. The truth was that Jacquin had never before spent time with a white girl who was close to his age, and he didn't want to say something that she might find offensive or objectionable. He'd learned to be cautious in his manner by working with customers alongside Mr. McNally, who only occasionally had to remind the young man to keep mindful of his words and especially his opinions—a rule that Jacquin had learned to obey.

"Never met anyone who had less to say than you do," Bridget Ellen finally said to him, sounding a mite exasperated.

Jacquin said nothing.

"*Well* . . ." Bridget Ellen said, in a tone finally demanding an answer.

Jacquin offered a clever riposte. "Often to speak without having something worthwhile to say is to take unfair advantage of the air we breathe."

Bridget Ellen drew her horse to a halt. Jacquin turned to look back at the girl but didn't question why she had stopped.

Bridget Ellen scrutinized him before remarking, "You talk almost like a poet."

Jacquin was amused by her comment and for the first time permitted himself the suggestion of a real smile. "I'm not a poet. I've never even read verse. Most of what I've learned and come to accept has been passed down by men much wiser than myself."

Bridget Ellen considered before she said in a tentative voice, "I was taught that your people believed only in war."

"My people." Jacquin's features twisted into an ironic expression. And then he sighed and spoke without taking offense to her comment. "Yes, I suppose that is the teaching of your schools. Perhaps that is why it is hard for us to live together in peace. From a young age, your children are taught that we only seek war with the white man."

"Is that . . . what *you* want?" Bridget Ellen asked cautiously.

"What *I* want?" Jacquin said.

"Yes. Peace."

"I do not want war," Jacquin said straightforwardly. "I have no grievance with the white man."

"Is that why you came to my rescue today?"

Jacquin felt a rise in his belly but expressed himself without rancor. "I told you, I would hasten to the distress of any living creature, be it man or beast."

He resisted telling her why he had chosen to come to be among her people, and, strangely, she never questioned where he was from, likely assuming he still lived among the Comanche and today had wandered from his village. As Jacquin saw it, she was either simply accepting or unwilling to ask, though he doubted the latter, as she seemed a curious girl with many questions.

Bridget Ellen rode on quietly for a while before she muttered, "No, you certainly don't say much."

Jacquin kept his eyes lowered as he walked on beside her. The grass beneath his feet was lush, like a carpet of emerald green.

"This valley is pure," he sighed.

Bridget Ellen looked curiously at him. "But when you do talk you sound like someone who's had some schooling."

Jacquin gave his head a wag. "Unlike you, my learning did not come from a classroom."

"You never went to school?" Bridget Ellen queried.

"No, not a school as you see it. Your idea of learning and mine are different," Jacquin said. "With my people, time in school is wasted when there is so much more to explore. If one wishes to learn, his education should not come from the confines of a classroom but from all that surrounds him." He then elaborated. "History is a teacher, but so is the history of the land. I have also looked into the stars and listened to the travels of the wind. If one listens with more than just his ears and looks beyond what the eye can see, there is much that one can learn. Nature in all of its elements is the real truth."

The girl seemed quietly impressed. She spoke softly, reflectively. "I've never heard it put that way before."

"No, as someone schooled the way you were, with most of your learning coming from someone also similarly schooled, I imagine you have not."

"I'll have you know I went to one of the finest schools back East," Bridget Ellen said, slightly indignant in her response.

"Yes, I'm sure it was an expensive education," Jacquin said with faint sarcasm.

Bridget Ellen sniffed in a deprecating manner.

The girl's horse suddenly seemed agitated and looked ready to perhaps bolt into another run. A momentary panic came over Bridget Ellen before Jacquin took the animal by the bridle and clucked softly, and once more the palomino quieted. Bridget Ellen was astonished and wondered what effect Jacquin had on her horse to calm it so quickly—an animal that even on its best days was prone to a display of orneriness, much like her own temperament, she had to admit.

She also had to admit that she found the young Comanche fascinating, if his attitude seemed at times to be a mite contentious. She was intrigued by his words describing a culture of which she had no knowledge. It was a life to which she had never been exposed beyond what had been taught her and, for the most part, as Jacquin had pointed out, in a negative light: lectures and studies given by big city educators who had no firsthand knowledge of how it was in the West, who were quick to paint Indians as bloodthirsty savages whose vicious attacks were proving a hindrance to the expansion of new territories where civilizations could grow and prosper. And she received little insight into the Indian way of life from her own father. That was a subject never discussed at the dinner table.

"I tell you now, I do not expect to be received warmly by your father," Jacquin confessed as they got nearer to her house.

"You're not being fair. You're judging him before you've had the chance to meet him," Bridget Ellen returned.

"I made my decision to come with you only to show that these prejudices between us need not be," Jacquin said. "Perhaps that is wise, perhaps foolhardy. But a good man has shown others who were against my being among them that our cultures and ways of living should not divide us so completely. I would like to believe this will someday be proven right."

Jacquin expressed his truth to the girl. He could not know how she would receive it. While she was showing him an acceptance, a kindness, might this only be an obligation? That possibility did disturb Jacquin, though he would not try to delve into her deeper feelings—not only toward him but all that might have been ingrained in her through ignorant teachings at expensive schools where parents expected their children to be taught what *they* wanted to have them learn.

Bridget Ellen exhaled a long, slow breath and spoke her own honesty. "I won't lie to you. I wouldn't be bringing you to meet my father if you hadn't rescued me. I don't know what his feelings are toward your people; he's never discussed that with me. Maybe he's protected me, and maybe that's why I can be the way I am, independent and a little willful. But whether he approves or not, I've disobeyed him many times before, and if I'm disobeying him now, he has to know I have a reason. I want him to thank you for what you did."

Jacquin mulled over her words. "You are a brave girl," he said. "Or perhaps foolish. Perhaps we both will regret this decision."

"I don't think so," Bridget Ellen said with a reassuring smile.

Jacquin took the halter of her horse and continued to walk forward and alongside her. The truth was Jacquin was not convinced by the girl's assurances. He could maintain his stoic outward attitude, but just a thorn scratch beneath the surface he possessed the insecurities of any human being faced with an uncertain situation. He did not want her to think poorly of him, and, if he was careful in his words and in his behavior, there was no reason why she would have to form a bad opinion. He'd made progress being accepted by the white man thanks to the kindness of Mr. McNally and his work in Lone Creek. He realized that prejudices still existed, but he was overcoming them and even earning respect from many in the community. He refused to become confrontational despite how viciously he might be provoked. Vile insults were directed toward him and his nation, usually by those who got drunk in the town saloon when copious amounts of alcohol set free normal restraints, and intolerance was given free rein. Yet those occasions aside, remarks and jests subsided as those people possessed of such ignorance to spit derogatory words at Jacquin saw that they brought no reaction from him. While those individuals might not embrace the young Comanche in friendship, they soon started to let him be and in their own way accepted his presence in their town.

What Jacquin could expect on this afternoon he could not know. The man he was soon to meet was a person of wealth, a man of position who likely wielded power and influence. Despite his rescuing Bridget Ellen from what could have been a crippling or even fatal accident, Jacquin did not foresee a favorable outcome once her father saw that the man who had rescued her was a Comanche, a member of a tribe considered to be a scourge of the West.

Jacquin's pace began to slow as they neared the sprawling, two-story, Spanish-style ranch house, which boasted a wide veranda with a sloping overhang that provided a cooling shade from the hot midday sun. The property surrounding the house was expansive, and Jacquin saw many heads of cattle grazing contentedly. It was a stretch of land that the young man had never before ventured into, though one with which he was not unfamiliar, hearing the stories from his people of how the land had been cultivated for just such a purpose, the breeding of livestock for profit. If he was impressed by what he saw he would neither show nor express it. He hoped to hide his disapproval from the girl.

"Your family owns this land?" he said.

"Yes. Only now it's just my father and me."

"You have no mother?" Jacquin inquired.

"No, she died many years ago," Bridget Ellen offered softly. "I was very young. I–I don't remember her."

Jacquin merely gave a slight nod.

Bridget Ellen pointed toward the big house. "And that's my home."

"Such a large dwelling for just the two of you," Jacquin mused.

Bridget Ellen hesitated before adding, "Yes. But we also have accommodations for the servants."

"Servants," Jacquin echoed, and there was a trace of derision in his voice. "These servants live with you . . . in your big house?"

Bridget Ellen felt her body surrender to a twinge of unease. She began to debate the wisdom of bringing the young Comanche to meet her father. She'd never had reason to view her father as a man of prejudice, and if he did possess such feelings toward the Indian it was never made known to her. Her concern was with Jacquin. He seemed to have a bitterness, subtle yet detectable, that might provoke troubling consequences if the situation were to suddenly become strained.

She abruptly halted her horse, drawing in the reins. She sighed and gave Jacquin a doubtful look. The boy waited for her to speak, even though he could guess what was coming.

"Are you sure you want to do this?" she asked with a tentative edge.

Jacquin didn't reply, though he lowered his head as if contemplating his answer.

"I–I just want to be sure that . . . that you're ready to meet my father," Bridget Ellen said, a halting in her voice. "That . . . you can accept this is how I live."

Jacquin's thin lips stretched in an ironic smile. "Now you are the one who has doubts?"

Bridget Ellen hesitated, then gave a hasty nod of her head.

"You forget it was you who asked me to come with you," Jacquin reminded her.

The girl blinked. "Yes. Yes, I did. I'm just a little concerned . . ."

Jacquin was not surprised by this shift in her attitude. While Bridget Ellen might have boasted to be a girl of her own mind, he concluded that, when it came to her father, in some respects her independence likely went only so far. He also could not deny that these doubts that had now come over her were the result of what he had said—comments that were critical and that she feared would be taken as an insult by her father. He inwardly resented his lack of restraint but realized that his heritage and his pride could not always resist expressing feelings that were deeply rooted within himself.

Jacquin collected himself and attempted to resolve her dilemma. "I will not make it difficult for you if you'd rather I go no farther."

Bridget Ellen gave no immediate answer. And Jacquin would never know if she would have accepted his noble gesture, as it was already too late. A proud, chestnut-colored stallion came galloping up the green, sloping ridge, advancing at a brisk, steady pace. Bridget Ellen gazed with recognition at both the horse and rider, the latter dressed in his favored ranch wear, white shirt and ornate bolo tie, tooled leather vest, and a Stetson with a decorative red band that she knew stood as his primary trademark. He was a big man who even at a distance exuded a large presence: the man who was her father.

He called to his daughter long before he reached her. She raised her hand to acknowledge him with a slight wave. Even while traveling across the still valley air the man's voice resonated strong and commanding—the voice of a man used to being in charge, rugged and uncompromising in his dictates.

Jacquin had endured enough bigotry and outright hostility not to be easily intimidated by any person of a mind to instigate trouble. And, while Bridget Ellen now seemed a mite doubtful of the invitation she'd extended—and this was made clear by the troubled expression she wore on her face——he intended to keep his mood disciplined, even if that might prove difficult. Because Jacquin had already determined that the girl's father was not only a proud and a stern man but doubtlessly possessed of stubborn principles. And those were values not easy to challenge, especially not by a Comanche boy.

The man rode up on his mount and pulled rein in a smooth, practiced gesture that glided the horse to a halt directly aside Bridget Ellen's palomino, a move that gave the impression he was a young buck trying to impress his gal with a fancy maneuver. He then stretched his bulky body over the saddle to give his daughter a hug. Jacquin stepped back from his view but took notice at how the girl seemed to stiffen at his embrace and how her expression seemed vacant at his affection. But she allowed her father this moment of physical greeting before she twisted free from his arms and in haste turned her head toward Jacquin, who was now behind her on the opposite side of where her father's horse was standing. Her father tracked her gaze, a smokeless pipe clenched between his teeth. At first it was as if he'd taken no specific notice of the young Comanche, but now as his attention fell fully upon him their eyes locked, and the man's gaze became intense and hinted at disapproval. Jacquin did not react to the man's stare; he maintained a steady posture and carefully studied the man's face. He had a fierce, intimidating look that likely didn't soften even in repose: bull-calf brow, thick lips, a broad nose, and arched, prominent eyebrows that were black and contrasted with the heavy, gray sideburns. Bridget Ellen did not appear to have inherited any of her father's features. In fact, it was difficult to picture them as father and daughter, except maybe in a shared stubborn temperament.

All that Jacquin could correctly conclude was that he should not have come here.

The rancher was known to locals and his workers alike as Rancher Ray, an informality that he accepted good-naturedly, as if he wanted to be regarded as someone of no special importance—just one of the bunch. But beneath that easygoing disposition lurked a man not to be trifled with.

Ray Colson was a wealthy cattle rancher whose success came solely from his own sweat, grit, and plain hard work. In short, he was beholden to no man. Prior to '72 he'd still been struggling, but as it turned out the war was the best thing that could have happened to him commercially. His cattle, which were specially bred but costly for the general consumer market, suddenly became valuable to the armies of the South. Politically he had no sympathies either way—the conflict between the states only represented dollar signs as far as he was concerned—and if he could have sold stock to the North and earned a significant profit, he would just as quickly have signed a contract with the Union army to provide them with prime beef. As it was, however, he could hardly keep up with the demand from the Southern forces. He sold his beef in bulk and soon made a fortune. He continued to profit until it became apparent that the Confederacy was heading into defeat and was so weakened in its economy that rations that had been supplied to soldiers could no longer include the quality meat product that Colson's ranch provided. This was not a concern to Colson. With the war nearing its end, he knew that he could soon expand his market into the North, which inevitably he did, adding an increase in value on each and every head.

That was the background of the man Jacquin now faced. Ray Colson wore a formidable expression once his cold, penetrating stare fell upon the young Indian standing on the far side of his daughter's palomino. As his eyes squinted and his sun-reddened features creased into lines that resembled crevices, his face registered as a deep frown. He said nothing, and, standing his own ground, neither did Jacquin speak. It was a stalemate between the two men of an opposite and perhaps opposing birthright and social standing.

There was a palpable tension in the air before Bridget Ellen fidgeted in her saddle and attempted to break the mood by speaking outright: "He saved my life today, Papa."

The rancher heard her but wasn't ready to release his burrowing stare.

The girl insisted that he listen, utilizing her half-demanding, part-petulant way of addressing her father and, once she had his attention, detailed what had happened earlier that day, speaking in a swift tone of voice, all the while noticing the steady eye contact between the two men. Jacquin's gaze was not meant to be disrespectful or to present a challenge; he just did not want the rancher with his probing eye to think that what his daughter was telling him was not the truth—that their being together suggested something different, even a secret rendezvous, to which the old man surely would have expressed strong disapproval.

After Bridget Ellen was through explaining what had happened that afternoon, there was a silence that carried forth on the still breeze over the grassy rise, a draft that provided a brief if welcome cooling through the valley. And then, while there was no easing of his critical expression, Ray Colson pulled the pipe from his mouth, absently wiped his fingers around the stem, and said in a voice betraying no indication of gratitude, "My daughter ain't no liar so reckon what she's tellin' me is true."

Jacquin said nothing. Now that he'd seen firsthand the man's rigid personality, he didn't expect to be thanked for his effort and was not disappointed.

Ray Colson emitted a guttural sigh, glanced at his daughter, looked back at the young Indian, and shoved his pipe back between his teeth, speaking around the stem. "Our house is yonder. You're welcome to come by—sit for a spell." There was no real genuineness behind his invitation, but the girl understood her father and his often coarse, short manner and realized a brusque invitation was about the best she could expect from him.

"Do come," she urged Jacquin.

Jacquin turned his eyes toward her. She sounded sincere, though he also did not forget her reservations prior to her father showing up.

He remained wary.

"It's a hot day, and we always have a pitcher of cold lemonade on hand," Bridget Ellen further offered.

It *was* a hot day, sweltering, with the moisture of sweat seeping through Jacquin's flannel shirt, hardly giving him either the appearance—or aroma—of a proper guest at such a magnificent residence. Jacquin's throat was parched with a dry thirst, and he would appreciate a liquid refreshment. Replying with only a nod, he accepted her invitation.

Ray Colson scowled at his daughter, a quick yet telling expression that Jacquin did not notice; then, without uttering a word, Colson spurred and wheeled his stallion around and rode off back in the direction from whence he came.

"I do not know what to make of your father," Jacquin admitted quietly, his eyes following the rapid gallop of the stallion. "Nor him of me, I suspect," he then added.

Bridget Ellen spoke earnestly. "My father is not an easy man to understand. He can be difficult, opinionated. But he says what he feels, and, if he didn't want you to be our guest, he would have said so."

Jacquin kept his curious gaze focused on Colson as the burly rancher whipped his horse down the hilly slope back into the valley. Perhaps the girl was right, but trust still did not come easily to Jacquin. He couldn't be sure if it was a failing in his nature or just a form of self–protection, since from as far back as he could remember he'd been taught that among the white man his people were held in low esteem. Jacquin could never quite totally accept that credence, yet neither could he completely reject it. Still and all, there was just one person to whom he gave his trust and that was the man he worked for:

Mr. McNally. He was a simple man, an honest man who was the only one who could look Jacquin directly in the eye and treat him not as a Comanche, but as a person, a fellow human being.

He was a man who had both earned and deserved Jacquin's respect.

Jacquin and Bridget Ellen sat outdoors under the shade of the veranda where they were poured tall glasses of lemonade from a frosty pitcher served by a well-groomed colored man whom Jacquin observed was immaculately attired in a white jacket, black pants, and crisp, white shirt highlighted by a proper bowtie. While the servant tried not to be obvious in his curiosity, he frequently looked askance at Jacquin, frankly puzzled, if not a little concerned, by the presence of the young miss's guest. Jacquin was used to being regarded with subtle or peculiar side looks, which he had learned to tolerate. In this situation, he found those furtive glances not to be annoying or insulting . . . but rather intriguing.

Through his years of self-education, he had learned the history of the Negro people and felt an odd sort of kinship with them: how a long and bloody war had been fought over the right of a white man to lay claim over another human being, a person born with a different skin color and raised in a distant culture, who was considered of little more value than a workhorse plowing a field. The Negros were brought across the sea bound in chains, and those who were sturdy enough to survive the often-turbulent voyages were then sold to wealthy plantation owners in a flesh auction and cast into slavery, where they were taught discipline and to obey the orders of their masters. They weren't looked upon as human beings but as possessions, commodities. Transgressions, however minor, were punished by lashes handed out by an eager overseer and required to be witnessed as a warning to the other slaves. And there had been other brutalities and acts of human degradation committed against these people, be it man, woman, or even child, with death often being the most merciful penalty of all.

Such behavior was deemed acceptable, since the Negro held no claim to American soil. But neither, truly, did the white man. They simply made their way into territories that did not rightly belong to them and, through violence and aggression, attempted to exert dominance not only over the lands but also over the affairs of the native people. And it didn't end there. The Indian who had respected the wildlife that inhabited his territory watched the cruel and needless slaughter of the beasts, particularly the great buffalo, that provided sustenance for their tribe. There were times when food became scarce, and children would go hungry because the precious meat would rot and become a prime breeding ground for maggots or pickings for the scavengers once the animal had been skinned of its hide, the part deemed most valuable to the profiteers.

In moments of such contemplation, it became difficult for Jacquin not to surrender to his centuries-old heritage and want to strike out against these injustices. The Comanche blood would burn hot through his veins, and the calling of his people and forefathers would suddenly try to overwhelm his spirit. It was then that Jacquin had to rely on the sheer power of his will to settle himself and counter his anger by reflecting upon the suffering endured by those whom his people considered their enemy. He regretted and even felt shame at the violent shedding of the blood of those innocent families simply seeking a life of new possibilities with a dream of prosperity for themselves and their children, intending no harm to the Indian in their quest westward. It was a conflict within himself that Jacquin had yet to totally resolve.

For the moment, though, he wouldn't allow himself to

consider such thoughts. Instead he took his leisure, enjoying a tall, cool glass of lemonade with mint leaves floating on top. Still, his mind was not entirely at rest. He wondered about his companion, questioning why she had asked him to come with her to her house. Was her invitation a sincere repayment of kindness—or just an obligation? True, he had saved her from a possible tragedy, but to his way of thinking she owed him nothing. He wanted no one to feel indebted to him. He would not accept gratitude because *he* found it difficult to express appreciation. He could not recall ever saying "thank you" to anyone. He wasn't rude; it just happened not to be in his nature. Yes, he was favored with a job by Mr. McNally, but he didn't consider that as generosity or charity, as Jacquin had proven his value to the man. He was a good worker, and Mr. McNally would occasionally remind him of his worth to the store. That kind of gratitude—a simple acknowledgment of a job well done—was sufficient for him.

He didn't share much talk with the girl that afternoon. Bridget Ellen seemed unsure of what to say now that she was back at home and safe and comfortable in her surroundings. Most of the time they sat in silence, exchanging occasional awkward glances, each—or at least in Bridget Ellen's case—struggling to find something to say, and then what conversation they did have was perfunctory. She asked Jacquin if his unusual name had any particular meaning, and he explained that it meant "fragrant." But as to why he was given that name, he claimed not to know, though suspecting that it might have been a name of one of his ancestors. Bridget Ellen was rather amused by the meaning, since "fragrant" was hardly the way to describe Jacquin at that moment, as he was sweaty and slightly pungent from being out in the oppressive heat for a good part of the day. Perhaps she intended her observation lightly, but she quickly saw that her humor was not shared by her companion. He took pride in his name. Jacquin then countered by making the comment that it was peculiar for Bridget Ellen to have two first names. Was not one name sufficient?

Bridget Ellen didn't have an answer. She'd had no choice in the matter, naturally, and she had no idea why she'd been named what she had. If there was some family connection, she'd never been told. But at his remark she blushed self-consciously.

Jacquin's comment was not offered idly, spoken solely to get back at the girl. There were many in his tribe who had adopted dual names, but they had specific meaning and were representative, honors bestowed because of strengths, features, or characteristics in the individual. Jacquin thought it rather frivolous that someone like Bridget Ellen, simply because she was born into privilege, should be allowed two given names. In fact it seemed not merely frivolous, but also pretentious.

In any event, their time together was not as enjoyable as Jacquin had hoped, and finally he set down his half-empty glass and got up to leave. But first he gazed out into the expanse of the north valley, for those seconds appearing to be deep in contemplation. Whatever his thoughts, he kept them to himself.

"Do you have a far way to go?" Bridget Ellen asked him.

His eyes remained transfixed on the vast, open landscape. "Not very far."

"If you'd like I could probably get one of the men to pull out the buckboard to give you a ride," Bridget Ellen offered. "But I don't even know where you're from."

"The town called Lone Creek. That is where I live . . . and where I work," Jacquin said in reply.

Bridget Ellen was somewhat puzzled to hear this. Perhaps it was simple ignorance or maybe how she was taught through her schooling, but she found it difficult to imagine how a Comanche not only could be permitted to live but also to work among white folk. Lone Creek was not many miles from her father's property, yet she had never been to the town. For reasons that he had never made explicit, Ray Colson forbade her to visit Lone Creek, though he himself made occasional trips to the town, even while the dirt-dry community provided little value to his own professional interests.

And Bridget Ellen most certainly knew that her father had never mentioned anything about an Indian working in the town. But, since their talks were brief at best, there would be little reason for him to do so.

Her voice was reserved when she said to Jacquin, "You have a job in Lone Creek?"

"Yes. I work with a man named Mr. McNally. He owns a store in town." Jacquin paused and looked quizzically at the girl. "Have you never been to Lone Creek?"

Bridget Ellen shook her head. "No."

"I know I have not seen you in the time I have been there. Yet the town is not very far from where you live." Jacquin made an expansive gesture with his hands, as if to embrace the wide holdings of land.

Bridget Ellen knitted her brow and started to say, "My father—" She stopped herself.

"Your father," Jacquin said mutedly. He decided it wise not to say anything more—though with his intuitive nature he had already formed an opinion of this family. And it suddenly troubled him, for reasons he perhaps should have acknowledged before accepting the girl's invitation—before he allowed his personal feelings for Bridget Ellen to interfere with good judgment. Her father only allowed him onto his property because he did not want to upset his daughter, with whom Jacquin determined he held a close bond.

Perhaps too close.

"I must leave," he announced abruptly. "Soon it will be dark."

"But I'm sure I can arrange a—" Bridget Ellen started to say.

There was no need for her to finish. Her offer would only lead to a delay and perhaps even have other consequences. "I will walk. I travel quickly by foot. Like the mountain cat."

Before Bridget Ellen could speak another word, Jacquin turned and started on his way, walking with brisk strides. He would not give in to his urge to run even as the fear came upon him that he could expect trouble unless he got himself far away from the Colson property. He could never explain it so that it would be understood by the girl, but his Comanche instincts had become attuned to a danger—a lurking threat that he could not precisely identify but that had come upon him with a silent, subtle, yet definite forewarning that he would be wise not to ignore.

He never looked back. He cleared the open valley and proceeded up the bluff through the thicket nestled on the southern rise. Here the heat seemed to vanish, and the air was cool and moist. A look at the position of the sun told him that it was approaching dusk. The skies were still clear, but daylight would dim before he could return to Lone Creek and his small room at Mrs. Ellison's boarding house, where he would be safe. His senses remained alert, his ears receptive to any sound that he could not recognize, and as a young man of the land most were noises familiar to him. His eyes were sharp and shifted with the keenness of a night predator foraging for food, ever vigilant for the faintest stirring that did not belong in the surrounding underbrush.

A quick movement in the bushes and he halted, his body reflexively assuming a defensive stance. He held himself still and silent, trying to determine from where the sound came . . . and by what—or whom—it had been made.

All was quiet. But to Jacquin it seemed *too* quiet. The silence was palpably oppressive, as if whatever or whoever was trailing him lurked nearby, an enemy deliberately staying concealed until ready to strike, like the deadly rattlesnake. But this foe would not give warning. Jacquin refused to relax his guard. While he'd never taken part in an outright battle, as a boy he had been trained, as had all youths, in the way of the Comanche, learning how to protect himself by not underestimating the skill, intelligence, or cunning of his attacker. It was ingrained in him from a young age to become the hunter rather than the hunted.

He started to pull up the front of his shirt that was loose over his trousers. A sheath tied by a thin rope around his waist hung underneath the flannel fabric, hidden from view; even the girl Bridget Ellen hadn't noticed. His hand stealthily reached for the knife tucked snugly into its leather pocket. Man or animal . . . if he or it dared to move upon him, Jacquin was equipped to defend himself. He withdrew the knife, and a glimmer of sunlight reflected upon the razor-sharp blade.

He was ready, prepared to protect himself against any act of aggression, an action that he would not initiate, but his response would be at the discretion of his enemy.

The silence, the stillness of where he stood was not disturbed. Whatever was lying in wait was patient, taking every precaution to ensure his presence would not be determined by sight or further sound. Jacquin remained conscious that it was *he* who was at a disadvantage. His enemy was nearby, there was no doubting that, watching from some spot as yet undetected by the senses of the young Indian and protected by the dense brush. Jacquin understood that his tracker would not act in haste, noticing how Jacquin stood armed and aware of his presence. An impulsive charge against a knife-wielding Comanche guaranteed that there would be injuries, perhaps even death.

While uncertain of what might emerge from the scrub he maintained the confidence that, so long as he held his ground and did not surrender to panic, he would be protected.

Yet . . . as time passed and not so much as a crackle of branch or rustle of leaves was heard in the depths of the brush, Jacquin grew curious why his enemy had not made his move. Might it be that he was waiting for the coming of nightfall? To take cowardly advantage when cloaked in the shadows of darkness? No. Jacquin suspected who his pursuer was, and also who was responsible for setting this person—or persons—on his trail, and he doubted that any white man could possess that much patience. But he, Jacquin, did. And, until his enemy dared to show himself, he could wait for as long as was necessary.

Jacquin heard the *whoosh;* it came upon him suddenly. Before he could react he felt a sharp blow against the side of his head that dazed him. His enemy had been lying in wait in close proximity to where he was standing and, instead of attacking him outright, had hurled a blunt object at him, hitting his skull. In the next instant Jacquin was lunged at and wrestled to the ground. While Jacquin still maintained a grip on the knife, his fingers steadily weakened, his body went limp, and that was when he was pounced upon by a second figure, who emerged from the underbrush. The first man who attacked him grabbed Jacquin by the wrists, thrusting both arms behind his back and holding firm, pulling him upright. The second man claimed the knife that had fallen into the dirt.

"You won't be needin' this," he said in a sneer as he positioned himself in back of Jacquin.

Jacquin struggled to regain his senses. He could feel a wet, warm sensation at the side of his head, which he held lowered against the throbbing pain.

"Yep, a stinkin' Comanche," the brute standing before Jacquin said in a rough, raspy voice. "Can smell a murderin' redskin a mile away."

"Set free from the reservation—or maybe yuh just run off.

Ain't that so, *Johnny redskin?*" said the voice from behind.

Thick, grimy fingers dug into Jacquin's cheeks, lifting his face upward to meet the grinning mouth and cruel eyes of a dirty, broad-shouldered cowboy.

"You don't know us, Indian boy," the cowboy said. "But yuh ain't gonna forget us neither."

"I know enough," Jacquin said boldly. His defiance was met by a sharp backhand across the face, intensifying the ache in his head.

"We don't cotton to that kinda talk from no Johnny redskin," the cowboy said, speaking through gritted, yellow teeth.

Jacquin shook his head in a futile effort to clear the clouds that swam in his head, but that movement only increased the pain that wracked his skull.

"If'n it was up to me this knife would find a place in your belly, carve your gut real good," the cowboy said, rubbing his thick thumb along the edge of the blade, creasing the skin but not separating it. "Only t'ain't up to me. I'm here just to give yuh a reminder, somethin' that you won't be forgettin', so you'll keep your redskin ass outta this valley." He lifted the knife and gazed at the shimmering surface with a look of satisfaction. Then he touched the blade against Jacquin's right cheek and smoothly and gently ran it up and down his flesh.

"You Injuns all have tight skin, stretched tight like them drums yuh pow-wow on," the cowboy commented with a snide, lopsided grin.

The man standing behind Jacquin spoke. "Wonder what that tight skin would look like all loosened up."

The cowboy drew in his lips as a crazed glare reflected in his eyes. He rubbed a closed fist across his chin as if in exaggerated contemplation. "Kinda wonder that m'self. How that sound to you, Johnny?"

Jacquin became indignant at the insult to his name, and he

once more spoke in defiance: "I am not called Johnny."

The cowboy snarled "Shaddup!" and struck the boy another sharp, backhanded blow across the face that nearly rendered him senseless.

Jacquin realized he would be tortured before he was killed and in desperation struggled with all of his might to free himself from the powerful grip, even as he knew his efforts would be in vain. He finally surrendered his struggle, but he would not surrender his dignity and held his expression rigid as he locked his gaze deep into the man's eyes.

"I will remember you," he said with intention.

There was something in the way Jacquin spoke those words that momentarily halted the cowboy. But he quickly regained himself.

"Sure, yuh will, Johnny," he said.

The cowboy once more lightly traced the blade along the boy's cheek. And then a rage contorted his features as he drew back the knife. "This'll make sure you keep your dirty Injun face away from any white girl, Johnny redskin," he growled, and in a quick move the tip of the blade was plunged into the flesh just below the boy's right eye. The cowboy grinned savagely as he drew the blade downward, parting the skin like the peeling of an orange. The pain was intense, but Jacquin did not cry out even as his eyes glistened with the tears he could not hold back. The knife continued its slow descent to the corner of the boy's lower lip, then the cowboy twisted the blade into the chin. He finally pulled the knife free in a swift, deliberate movement.

His face now bloody and torn, his expression one of anguish, Jacquin felt his body start to collapse. The man who had been holding him released his gorilla grip, and the young Comanche dropped to his knees, his hand pressed against the side of his face in an effort to staunch the flow of blood, now starting to spot the ground like scarlet raindrops.

The cowboy joked to his companion, "Well, reckon it proves one thing. They bleed red just like us."

"Yeah, an' plenty, too."

The cowboy who'd wielded the knife held back momentarily, then prepared to drive a hard kick into Jacquin's gut as a last reminder. His partner talked him out of it. They'd earned their pay, he said. His companion replied that it wasn't for pay but for pleasure that they'd taken care of the dirty redskin. Nevertheless, he stopped himself from delivering that final, more personal punishment. The point had been made in a way that "Johnny redskin" would never forget. Both men laughed as they walked back off into the bush.

★ ★ ★ ★ ★

PART THREE:
BACK ON THE TRAIL

★ ★ ★ ★ ★

CHAPTER SEVEN

. . . And that was the background to the tragedy as I was able to piece it together. At a later date, I learned other significant facts from stories and truths related to me by others. There was more to come concerning the unfortunate Comanche youth Jacquin, including his transition from a gentle young man of curiosity and ideals into . . .

Well, I'll get to that soon.

For now, I knew that Jacquin never returned to Lone Creek or to his job at the mercantile. People speculated that he might have gone back to be with his tribe. Some even thought that he might have died or been killed—either by accident or murder. But no one was concerned enough to find out. Who really cared about the disappearance of an Indian? One day he had simply up and vanished. And soon the presence as well as the memory of Jacquin was forgotten. The only person who expressed worry about his mysterious absence was Mr. McNally. Yet, even he came to acknowledge that staying in one place for long was not always the way of the Indian and that perhaps Jacquin had simply grown restless.

The months passed, and the town of Lone Creek did pretty well for itself. It survived those early years, hadn't been swept away in a dust storm as some had predicted, and indeed showed signs of prosperity. The population started to grow, and more business enterprises popped up along the dusty main street. And while the town was not that many miles from Chesterfield

City, it didn't invite the lawlessness that had become the dubious reputation of the city where I'd put down roots with my
new family.

But even that started to settle; reckon it was the coming of
progress. Advancement could not be achieved, let alone
maintained, when citizens were afraid to leave their homes on a
Saturday night for fear of being shot down by an outlaw or even
just a mean-tempered and overly-intoxicated cowboy.

I'd been approached a couple more times to consider taking
on the responsibilities of town sheriff, and each time the offer
was made a little more tempting, with a bit more honey added
to the pot, and each time I declined. I was relieved to have that
pressure taken off me when a retired Texas Ranger by the name
of Hastings Caldwell took the post, without the aid of deputies,
since his high pay would not allow for it, and he, alone, did a
fine job dealing with troublemakers and lawless hombres—no
discussion or arguments, just run out of town or straight into
the hoosegow. I was to learn that Caldwell was one of those
who'd set out after Silvano Ramos back in the day, but he met
with little luck in apprehending the outlaw band. But that was
of no matter now. He had a sterling reputation, and that held a
lot of value for a city desperately in need of law and order.

Time passed uneventfully, and I'd taken to growing a full,
thick, and wide mustache. J.C. wasn't particularly fond of my
new facial addition; called it bristly like a push broom and
claimed it scratched her cheek every time I gave her a kiss.
What with her backing away from me whenever I was in the
mood to show a little affection, I finally had to take the scissors
and razor to the hair above my upper lip and try to remove my
little forest without nicking myself under the bush. The truth
was now that I'd given up my work as a witness seeker, I grew
the mustache as a kind of tribute to my mentor, Calvin C. Birk:
Colonel Calvin. I never admitted that to J.C., because I didn't

want her to feel guilty about needling me with how much it annoyed her when it came to my attempts at romance, to say nothing of how it likely made her feel less attracted to me. She even embarrassed me with comments about how it concealed my attractive upper lip. Of course, as far as my appearance was concerned I couldn't give a damn, but . . . Well, hell, I was a married man, and I reckon my wife deserved some consideration.

Anyhow, she was pleased to see my clean-shaven self once more. Suppose I wasn't too disappointed myself. Yet my decision had a more practical side. I'd stubbornly come to see that it was kind of hard to politely eat a meal when you've got to try and maneuver your soup spoon through a bushel of hair drooping over your upper lip and then have your dinner companions watch the broth sluice down the sides of your mouth almost to your chin.

Our newspaper enterprise was still in competition with Theodore Sherwood's *Leader*, and it often was a struggle to keep our printing press operating with production costs running high, but thankfully we did maintain a small but loyal readership, who helped us pay the salaries of our two employees and keep food on our table. And that was necessary, as both of our girls, Lorraine and Bethany, were growing like the proverbial weeds and had developed appetites I'd never thought possible in young ladies of their still-tender years.

We kept going day by day. J.C. was in charge of our finances, since she had the business acumen that I lacked. Hell, back in my day as a witness seeker I'd collect my pay (when I was compensated), head into Mexico, blow the wad on having a good time, then wait for the next assignment so that I could do it all over again. I knew nothing about saving money—and why should I? I worked hard, felt entitled to my pleasures after a successful mission . . . and, most of all, I had absolutely no responsibilities.

Marriage and a family had changed all that, and it troubled me on those nights when I'd awaken to find J.C. not asleep next to me. I'd creep out of bed and see the glow of the table lamp inside her office downstairs. I wouldn't disturb her, not even let her know I was there. But I'd carefully peer through the slight opening of the door and see her at her desk going over paperwork with an expression of despair. Her face would be twisted and tired, and she'd run her fingers through her hair and sometimes clench a fist in frustration. It was money owed to the collectors come a-callin'.

She would never really admit that to me—at least not with too much worry or emphasis—though I suspected why she'd kept these concerns mostly to herself. She didn't want to tell me we were in a financial quagmire, because she knew I'd likely insist on taking over the reins, and there was only one way I could do that—by returning to the only trade I knew.

I remember being told by my pa when I was a lad that you can't keep prodding a dying horse. Seemed a cruel way to express it when you're hearing it through the ears of a boy, but the meaning sure became clear when as a man you accept it figuratively, not literally.

Our "horse" was on its last leg, yet there still might be a chance to save it.

CHAPTER EIGHT

Johnny Scarface.

Jacquin adopted the name himself, based partly on what he was called by those men who had assaulted and mocked him. They'd taunted him by giving him a white man's name, had insulted him and his race before inflicting their primitive, permanent punishment. Very well. Now he would use that insult to his advantage. He'd decided on the path he would now follow. His destiny had been chosen—not by his own desires but by what had been thrust upon him. He wanted a name that people would not only remember, but one that every man, woman, and child would fear. A name that would creep up on them while they slept and haunt their very nightmares. At first repulsed by what greeted him as he gazed into the reflective surface of the creek by which he camped, he gradually came to accept his scarred visage and because of it chose the moniker that would accompany him on his trail of vengeance. His face would also serve as his own reminder that no white man could be trusted. No pale skin was his friend. The men who had attacked him and their kind would pay for the cruel crime that had been inflicted upon him. The blade of the knife had been their weapon, and he, too, would wield its sharp edge against all whom he now deemed were his enemy.

He had been born with a sensitive spirit and did not condone the violence of his people, even though it had been explained to him by the elders that they, too, had suffered mistreatment at the hands of the white man. His questions and occasional criticism of their ways had made the peaceful Jacquin almost an outcast among his tribe. But it was different now—and the white man had made it so. And in an effort to prove to himself and his people that in his heart he was a true Comanche, a warrior, and that he could set out to do what he determined he must without any reservation, he chose as his first kill the one person who had welcomed and befriended him: Daniel McNally, a man to whom he bore no malice. His reasoning was that, if he could kill a man he did not hate, toward whom he felt friendship and even affection, the others against whom he would exact his revenge would be easy.

I later learned that the young Comanche who now rejected his birth name of Jacquin and wanted to be known as "Johnny Scarface" waited until nightfall before coming back into town, emerging from the hilly woodlands where he had lived in solitude, preparing his body, mind, and soul. He'd been gone from Lone Creek for several months, tending to his facial injury while sustaining himself by living off the land, as was taught to him by his Comanche brethren. He ate the vegetation and consumed small animals when he had the need for meat. While his disfigurement was permanent, the wound could also be treated by ways in which Comanche warriors cared for their own battle injuries. The land itself held healing properties. If blessed with gratitude to the higher spirit, the soil would be cleansed of impurities and promote healing. For several days, he made a paste of the earth, which he spread over the flaming tear in his cheek, letting it harden against the sun throughout the day. Come night and he would wash off the mask in the clear waters of the creek, chanting in his native tongue his words of gratitude. The deep, jagged scar would forever course its trek along the side of his face, marking his profile. During his long period of solitude, Johnny Scarface came to embrace his wound, as it was the physical manifestation of who he had become. While his vengeance had a personal stamp, he also knew that his actions would earn him a proud reputation among his people. His inquisitiveness and attempts to understand the ways of the white man had made him a curiosity among his tribe; his condemning of their violence branded him an outsider; yet, he now realized it had all been for a greater purpose. He was meant to go out among those who disrespected the sacredness of the land through their building of towns and cities where drinking and gambling was not only permitted, but encouraged. This included the ranchers who corrupted the ground with the blood and carcasses of animals they slaughtered with no consideration other than the coins that filled their pockets. He'd heard it said that these people were building an empire. But at what cost? "Progress" was being built on the bloodshed of man and beast and the despoilment of nature, to be further propagated with the construction of the railroad. Thousands more would be coming to trespass upon the land, and they would not travel in covered wagons that left them vulnerable to attack; now they would be protected in steel carriages. Jacquin understood *then* . . . and he understood *now* that, despite all resistance, the white man's domination over these territories was inevitable.

Perhaps what had happened to him was of minor importance compared to the greater crimes perpetrated by those motivated—*blinded*—by money and conquest, but it provided him with the impetus to do his part to correct these injustices. It might just entail a small victory, but even a minor triumph could make a difference. He would establish his own place among the great Indian chiefs and warriors in history. The legacy he would carve for himself would not be a blemish upon the nation of his people. The responsibility for what was to come would solely be his—*his alone*—but the guilt for these crimes would be laid elsewhere, even if never properly acknowledged.

The white man had already staked his claim, continued to do so, and was free to pursue whatever means he felt necessary to protect and maintain his property and possessions—including thievery and murder.

If that was how it was to be, it was only right that a man descended from the true heirs of this land should be allowed the same privilege.

Though the young Comanche named Jacquin had once expressed ideals he hoped would lead to a strengthening of the bond between his people and the white man, those principles had died.

With the birth of Johnny Scarface, the killing of all those he had tried to befriend became his new pursuit.

CHAPTER NINE

The scar-faced Comanche waited until the streets were quiet. Lone Creek was not a boisterous town. There was a saloon, but, outside of the occasional Saturday night when citizens felt the need to relax with extra portions of liquor and some loud and lengthy entertainment, the establishment was usually ready to close by eleven o'clock. On this Tuesday night, nearly all of the businesses along the main street had their front windows darkened, and the few scattered houses at the edge of town had their curtains drawn. An eleven-thirty bedtime was generally the routine.

Activity for the day had ceased . . . except at the mercantile Daniel McNally owned, where a faint light glowed through the storefront window. Johnny Scarface knew that at this hour McNally would be alone and likely going over the day's accounts. Mr. McNally was a kind man but a shrewd businessman; he kept a careful eye on each dollar that came into his establishment. While he occasionally grumbled at the amount of credit he extended to the citizens of the town, he also understood that in a growing community cash was short for just about everybody. As he'd expressed to his young employee Jacquin when a ledger was signed but no money exchanged hands: when Lone Creek finally got on its feet, he would be properly compensated for his generosity. Never let greed stand in the way of helping people in need, he said. This was one of many lessons the storekeeper passed on to the young man—lessons that at the time were appreciated by Jacquin.

But that seemed a long time ago. Such words no longer held any significance for Johnny Scarface.

While the street was empty, and it was unlikely his presence would be noticed, Johnny Scarface still moved with the stealth of a night prowler as he slid through the shadows of the town toward the alley that would take him to the mercantile's rear entrance, where at one time he had supervised many deliveries . . . a meaningless memory now.

Despite his determination to carry out that which he felt he must do, he could not forget how kind Mr. McNally had been to him, and it became imperative that he block those memories from his mind. He could not regard the man as a friend . . . but rather as a necessary sacrifice. Mr. McNally's death would enable Johnny Scarface to carry on with his mission. His vengeance; retribution for the violence that had been thrust upon him by the white skins; for the cruelty that had left him embittered and literally made him a marked man. Once this deed was accomplished, others would follow. And they would be carried out without the regret he could not completely deny might penetrate his soul on this night.

Johnny Scarface crept along the back way, his body cloaked in the blackness where the moonlight could not reach, and he cast aside those little stabs of doubt by reminding himself that the man whose blood he would soon shed did not share the same blood as himself.

The back door was secured, but Johnny Scarface easily and quietly broke the lock, opening the door slowly to stifle the creaking of its hinges. He entered the storage room, moving as silently as a desert predator. He inched his way toward the door that opened into the store proper, noticing the thin shaft of light that pooled out from under the door onto the dusty hardwood floor. He held himself steady for several moments, his breathing controlled, his body braced against the door. During his time living in solitude in the wilderness, he'd learned how to focus his concentration toward a single purpose, without the intrusion of conflicting thoughts. Now he put that training to the test. He centered his concentration to erase all hesitation from his mind . . . and then his hand closed around the knob, his fingers slowly twisting it.

McNally stood with his back to the door. He was at the counter busily checking the day's receipts, as Johnny Scarface had assumed. The Comanche was well within the store before McNally felt an additional presence and turned around. It took him a moment to recognize who it was, since what initially greeted his eyes was but a silhouette. His first thought was that he was facing an intruder, come to rob him. But as the figure advanced into the light supplied by the kerosene lamp on the counter, the look of uncertainty vanished from McNally's features, and instead he regarded his visitor with an expression that at first registered astonishment, and then . . . a tentative relief.

"Jacquin," he said. He breathed out and gave his head a brisk shake. "You had me frightened there." He took a few seconds to compose himself. "I wondered where you'd gone."

"You were worried for me?" Johnny Scarface asked impassively.

"Yes. I—I didn't know if something had happened to you. You just . . . left without saying anything."

Johnny Scarface said nothing, his expression set, as he walked farther into the room. When he was close enough to his former employer he twisted his head to the side, giving McNally a full view of his disfigured profile. McNally's features reflected his horror as he gazed at the long ugly scar creasing the side of the young man's face.

His words were spoken in a whisper. "My God. Who did that

to you, son?"

Johnny Scarface abruptly turned his face wholly toward McNally, his eyes boring into the storekeeper with a cold, penetrating stare. His eyes had turned coal black, as if his soul had been possessed by some demonic presence. The fierceness of his expression caused a rise of foreboding in McNally. He'd never seen such a look in the young man before.

"I can fetch you a doctor," he offered, his voice unsteady.

Johnny Scarface slowly shook his head. "I have been my own doctor," he said.

"But . . . your face . . ."

"The scar has healed as well as it will."

"Tell me, Jacquin . . . who did that to you?" McNally said over a lump forming in his throat.

"People," Johnny Scarface answered. "*Your* people."

McNally surrendered to the cold dread that overcame him. "*My* . . ." he barely managed to say.

Johnny Scarface stepped closer toward McNally, who, in reflex, took a slow step backward.

Johnny Scarface regarded him with a quizzical expression. "You are afraid?"

McNally hesitated before nodding his head. "Yes, Jacquin. I . . . I confess I am afraid. You seem different. Not like yourself."

"Why should you be afraid? You treated me well," Johnny Scarface said. His tone was gentle but exuded a subtle menace.

McNally's lips trembled. "What is it that you want?"

Johnny Scarface didn't answer, just continued to lock his stare into McNally's eyes.

McNally spoke more deliberately. "Why have you come back?"

"There is only one thing that you can give me," Johnny Scarface said.

McNally's brow was moist with beads of perspiration. "What

. . . is that . . . ?"

Johnny Scarface's smile was baleful. He was standing next to the counter that displayed various hunting knives under the glass. Back when he was Jacquin he used to admire the display and, in fact, was saving some of his weekly pay to eventually purchase one to replace the old blade that later had been taken from him, after it had been used as a weapon against him. Reflexively Johnny Scarface touched his fingers against his ruined cheek. Then he lifted his fist and slammed it into the countertop, shattering the glass, the shards cutting into his flesh, but he paid them no heed as he reached for the knife he'd most wanted to own, bearing the longest, sharpest blade that curved like a hook. He picked up the weapon and then slowly turned his focus back toward McNally, whose eyes were wide with uncomprehending panic.

"Jacquin," McNally uttered, his mouth gone dry.

"There is no Jacquin," Johnny Scarface announced.

"Please . . . just tell me what it is you want," McNally pleaded.

"Your life," Johnny Scarface told him coldly.

McNally succumbed completely to his terror. He felt his body start to weaken, go limp. He struggled to keep steady on his feet.

For the briefest second a look of sorrow, an expression of regret, showed on the Comanche's face. McNally was quick to notice and saw that as a hopeful sign that his life would be spared . . . that some sense of reason had come to the young man.

But Johnny Scarface's features once more became a mask, expressing no trace of emotion or compassion. He stepped slowly toward the frightened McNally . . . and he thrust the blade forward, deep into McNally's chest.

McNally's eyes and mouth widened in shock and disbelief. Johnny Scarface pulled the knife free before McNally dropped to the floor.

Johnny Scarface watched as the body twitched in a death spasm before becoming still. He'd acted without hesitation, and within seconds it was over.

Johnny Scarface had performed his first kill.

But that was not the end of it. What he did next could not have been performed by the boy Jacquin. But there was no such hesitation for the revenge-driven Johnny Scarface. Because it was part of what he must do. *They* had left their mark on him. Now *he* must leave his mark on them—his brand, so that they would come to know of his vengeance.

He knelt beside the storekeeper and pressed the tip of the blade next to the dead man's right eye, opening a deep cut.

He hesitated only for a moment.

And then he drew the knife downward.

Chapter Ten

I'd heard of the murder of the Lone Creek storekeeper, of course; the town was in the territory and not too far from our vicinity. There wasn't much information provided other than it appeared to be a robbery, since merchandise had been taken from the establishment—yet strangely no cash. We ran the story in the *Chronicle,* but it generated little ongoing interest among our readership. Crimes and outlaw exploits were not that unique and were handled by our paper in a straightforward fashion; for readers seeking sensationalism they could go to our competitor, though even Theodore Sherwood's *Leader*'s reporting of the incident didn't reach the paper's usual heights for explicit detail. Even the strange slashing of the dead man's cheek did not arouse that much curiosity, since most assumed it was a wound sustained during a struggle between the storekeeper and the thief—or thieves. And then the incident was pretty much forgotten. In truth, the robbery and killing of a store owner held little significance when the "legend" of Silvano Ramos still captured the imagination of many people. I reckon the brutality and sheer audacity of the Ramos gang were the crimes others were measured against. Also, the bitter truth was that death came cheaply on the frontier, even as citizens worked together in a dedicated effort to build safe and lawful communities. I saw the inroads of development, but there was still a long way to go when it came to clearing out crime.

On the other hand, I remained contented in my new life. J.C.

was damn near the perfect wife, the perfect partner. She could be tough, even with me when the occasion would arise. After all, I still had a lot to learn about being a husband. But she also was about as loving a woman as any man could hope for, and I couldn't picture a real mother being any more attentive and affectionate to children than J.C. was with our two girls.

I reckon our only real trouble was our ongoing battle to keep the newspaper running. The truth was we had accumulated more creditors than readers, and, as a result, the advertisers who had been our main source of revenue were falling off precipitously. And, naturally, Theodore Sherwood remained a formidable adversary, both in business and, to a point, even in our personal lives. It was hard for a man of my cynical nature to believe Sherwood thought he could sucker me by his attempts at sincerity, which were as clear as the muddy streets of Chesterfield City after a good downpour. Whatever his game was, and that wasn't hard to guess, he was always putting on a charming and even generous front when our paths crossed. If J.C. and the girls and myself took occasion to go out to dinner, and if Sherwood happened to be present, he'd secretly take care of our meal bill, vanishing before we could protest and later feigning ignorance when I'd try to repay him. But he wasn't fooling anybody, and, if I was annoyed, J.C. was downright resentful. It got so that if we wanted a night out we'd first check with our restaurant preference to make sure Sherwood hadn't made his own reservations for the evening.

Yet he'd usually still show up with all of his pretense and in all of his unctuous glory.

I didn't know exactly what strings Sherwood was pulling, but I reckon I wasn't completely surprised the day J.C. and I had a sit-down in her office, and the look on her face was more pained than usual, adding lines to her complexion that I'd never noticed before. I didn't remark on that; neither did I make mention of the strands of gray that were beginning to appear in her hair.

In fact, I didn't need for her to tell me what concerned her and so spared her having to speak the words.

"The *Chronicle*'s finished," I said.

J.C. hesitated before she acknowledged with a slow rocking of her head.

I sighed and sat back in my chair, lowering my eyelids. If it wasn't so damn early in the day I would have poured myself a drink.

"Son of a bitch must have known this was coming for a while," I muttered under my breath.

J.C. nodded again.

I lifted my eyes and looked directly at J.C. "And I reckon we won't be going out with a bang."

"It's my fault," J.C. said reproachfully. "I should have been more attuned to the wiles of Mr. Theodore Sherwood, especially with his expansive displays of generosity."

I shrugged and said, "Hardly expansive. Maybe a few dinners he paid for . . . and a beer or two at the saloon."

J.C. gave me a critical look. "You never mentioned that."

"Never knew 'til later," I explained innocently. "By the time I was ready to pay, Zachery the bartender said it had already been taken care of. If I recollect, he said by a 'friend.' Well, I'd had many a saloon drink paid for by friends since I came back to Chesterfield City. Just never counted Sherwood among them."

J.C. slid her chair closer to her desk and made a tent of her fingers, a gesture I'd become familiar with whenever her mood became contemplative. "What I can't rightly figure was his reason," she said. "Was he doing it to soften the blow or to ease his own conscience?"

"You're giving him too much credit, saying he's got a conscience," I put in, trying to inject a little bitter humor into our situation.

J.C. pulled a deep sigh as her expression became crestfallen. "I loved this business," she said wistfully. "Put everything I could into it, but what chance do you have when someone cuts the cost to an advertiser by ten or even twenty percent?"

"Because he can afford to," I said. "No big favor he's doing anyone, either. Once he takes over he'll recoup those losses and then some."

J.C. gave a nod of her head in agreement.

"Reckon we relied too much on the loyalty of our readership," I remarked.

J.C. smiled faintly but kept whatever thoughts she may have had to herself. She then reached for the bottle of bourbon she kept in the side drawer of her desk. She took two glasses from the bureau shelf and without saying a word poured us both a drink. I confess I was a mite startled, since I'd never seen J.C. take a drink from that bottle, but I also understood. Early in the day or not, the time was right for a stiff one. She raised her glass in what was intended as a grim toast.

"To the memory of the *Chronicle*," she said.

Not exactly something I wanted to drink to. I never much cared for funerals. Yet the sad fact was that it was over. No point in kidding ourselves. As I swallowed my drink my concern was: what to do next?

I guess J.C. might have been reading my thoughts, because as she set down her glass she gave me a rather ironic look and said, "For what it's worth, our Mr. Sherwood isn't leaving us completely stranded. He's made us an offer on some of our equipment."

"The printing press?"

J.C. nodded.

I held back what I was thinking. An offer of sympathy if ever I'd heard one. Our press was almost an antique. It could have been around since the Middle Ages, one of Gutenberg's early designs, constantly breaking down with the repairs cutting into our already meager profits. Fortunately, one of our workers possessed sufficient mechanical aptitude to fix most of the minor foul-ups. But even those often required the replacement of specialty parts that weren't cheap to purchase.

"Is that all?" I said.

Once again J.C. must have guessed where I was heading with my remark. She smiled wanly before saying with a cynicism masking as nonchalance, "Oh, he offered me a job—as copyeditor of the *Leader*. Generous compensation, too."

I didn't have to ask J.C. what her answer to him was. And the somewhat broader smile J.C. gave me told me outright that it wasn't necessary.

But I did say, "Well, for what it's worth he couldn't ask for a better editor."

J.C. smiled meekly, brushing aside my compliment.

"He also wants to put Maxwell and Amos on his payroll," she said, referring to our two men who worked the lettering and operated the press machine.

"I'm sure they didn't stall at the offer," I said with a sardonic smirk.

J.C. frowned. "I can't hold it against them. They have families to support."

"And we don't?" I returned.

I relaxed my attitude and reached across the desk for the bottle of bourbon. What coursed through my mind at that moment was how I might have made a colossal blunder by rejecting that book deal back when I was looked upon as a "celebrity"—or even when I turned down the offer to become town sheriff. Time had passed, and I knew that, even if I were so inclined, I couldn't profit from my one-time reputation. I had become just another average citizen of Chesterfield City, Texas.

"He'll give us three hundred dollars for the press and supplies," J.C. said.

I looked at her over the rim of my glass. "Is that a fair price?"

"Given its age, condition, I didn't see the need to dicker. The other items . . . well, no need in holding on to them."

"You don't look at it as charity?" I then remarked.

J.C. reacted as I should have expected. "That was a practical decision," she said with a snap. "We have no further need for the press." She added with a subtler inflection, "And we'll need the money. And if I could have found another buyer, I would have. Even if it meant taking a loss."

I felt properly chastised. But I also couldn't deny my resentment. I felt an unease as my thoughts started to lead me toward the direction of what my next move might have to be.

And once more J.C. surprised me with her perceptiveness. I didn't know if she was a mind reader or if whatever was showing on my face was a dead giveaway.

"You're not going back," she said firmly.

I looked at her, squinted my eyes, but didn't say anything.

The expression on her face was as dead-set serious as I'd ever seen it.

I played ignorant. "What are you talking about?"

It was a feeble attempt at innocence, and with J.C.'s astuteness I should not even have bothered.

She didn't have to answer. She just bored into me with her eyes. A stern, knowing look.

There was no point in my trying to kid her. I had to speak forthrightly, as difficult as that might be.

"I don't know," I said with a slow, weary wag of my head. "We have two girls to look after. And—Well, you did something you really didn't want to do, selling a piece of you to that buzzard Sherwood. That old printing press that he'll probably take apart and sell for parts, profiting off every nickel."

"That was my decision," J.C. reminded.

"I know," I agreed. "Even if you had asked me I'd have no right to tell you what to do. But sometimes we have to make our own decisions."

I'd made a valid point, and I could tell that J.C. understood what I was saying—even if she couldn't agree with it.

"But you've been away from it for so long," she argued. "And it's . . . dangerous."

"And it's also all that I know," I said back to her.

"If that's the only option I . . . I'll go work for Sherwood," J.C. said flatly.

That was almost comical, but I held back my smile. For one thing, I didn't believe the man's offer was genuine. Secondly, if it *was* a legitimate proposition, he'd do his damnedest to break J.C.'s rigid backbone, using every demeaning and humiliating tactic at his disposal to deflate her spirit, and I couldn't watch that happen to her.

I *wouldn't* let that happen.

CHAPTER ELEVEN

In the meantime, the Comanche named Johnny Scarface had made his second attack, and though it was not known at the time, this kill had a special significance, as it involved a ranch employee of Ray Colson's—an ambush that presumably was meant to demonstrate to Colson that this sudden and unexpected violence was nearing closer to his doorstep.

When the body was found up on a rise where the man had stood his late-afternoon watch over the grazing pasture, there was no question that George Dawkins had been murdered. Knifed in the chest. The grimace that was reported to be on his face reflected both the suddenness and violence of his death. Unlike the killing of store owner Daniel McNally, which appeared to have a robbery motive, this murder seemed senseless, since, to anyone's guess, Dawkins was a likable sort with no known enemies, and, more suspiciously, none of the cattle he'd been guarding had been rustled, nor had any possessions been removed from the man's body. His valuable gold pocket watch and cash were found intact.

There was just one other unusual feature to Dawkins's killing: a deep gash on the side of his face, running from just under his right eye to his lower jaw. It couldn't be determined if that wound had been made before or after he'd been killed.

Unlike the Lone Creek murder, which shared that same similarity, this crime could not be easily explained.

Rancher Ray had lost a man to violence and demanded the

full efforts of the law to apprehend the murderer. County law was represented by Sheriff Hastings Caldwell, and I was frankly both surprised and a mite concerned that early evening when just past suppertime he came by our place to ask me to ride out to Lone Creek with him.

Caldwell was a tall, lean but broad-shouldered man with a square-cut jaw. He had a proud, aquiline nose, shrewd eyes, and a wide, thin-lipped mouth. I reckon he was probably in his early forties, but he had a lot of experience drawn onto his features. Maybe not surprisingly he reminded me of Sheriff Briggs, not so much in appearance but in his straight-shooting attitude. He was carrying two .45s in his gun belt. I hadn't had many dealings with him since he assumed the post of sheriff. I suspect he knew about my experience with Silvano Ramos; he might even have known about my being approached to take on the duties of sheriff. But to his credit he'd never once mentioned either to me when we'd nod greetings to each other when we passed on the street.

That's why I say I was surprised to see him standing in our doorway, his big, broad hat held in both hands that looked as if they belonged to a cattle puncher.

"Hope I ain't disturbin' your supper," he said, looking rather humble at his unannounced visit.

I was a little guarded in my attitude. "No. We've finished eating."

He gestured into the parlor with a lift of his chin. "Mind if I step inside?"

Actually, I did mind. I had no idea why he was calling and didn't know how J.C. would take to a visit from our resident lawman. But I nodded for him to come inside.

"Care to sit down?" I offered.

He gave his head a shake. "No, this is fine."

His refusal to make himself comfortable was all I needed to

know that this was not a social call. I waited for him to speak his business.

"Know it's not in your line anymore," Caldwell started to say—before J.C. entered the room. She had just put the girls to bed. Upon seeing the sheriff standing in the parlor looking stern and official, a quick expression of concern crossed my wife's face. I tried to ignore it since I didn't know what was coming. The sheriff appeared reluctant to speak his piece in front of J.C., but there was nothing I could do about it. I even tried to lighten the mood by joking that there was no point in trying to keep anything from a newspaperwoman, conveniently avoiding the word "former."

He'd turned down my invitation to take a seat but accepted with a polite nod once J.C. made the same offer. Not that J.C. looked any less ambivalent as to why he was here. Once he was settled in the armchair and J.C. and I were seated next to each other on the couch across from him, Sheriff Caldwell spoke to the point. Almost. First, he admitted that he was familiar with my reputation. Before I could argue that my reputation had been highly exaggerated, he put up a hand to halt me and made it clear that it wasn't my so-called "heroics" with Silvano Ramos that were important to him. No, it was what he had learned about my past experience as a witness seeker—the occupation I seriously had been considering a return to, not by preference, but as a way to guarantee at least a basic security for my family.

I could see J.C. start to grow tense. I think Sheriff Caldwell noticed it, too, by the way he cast me a furtive glance, as if to say he'd find it much easier to talk if she weren't present. But she wasn't going to leave the room, so whatever it was that he'd come to tell me he'd have to say in front of my wife. He shuffled his big body in the chair and proceeded to tell me about the murder on Ray Colson's ranch, his eyes fixed and unwavering, directed all the while at me. He presented a graphic description of what had happened—what he'd seen earlier in the day when called out to the ranch—and appeared uncomfortable at having to be so explicit in front of my wife, even though, in credit to her, she had the stomach for it. J.C. had also done much of the reporting for the paper and frequently had to visit places where violence had taken place. She had developed a strong constitution.

I spoke the first thing that entered my mind. "Indian?"

The sheriff shrugged. "Can't say for certain. Only that the killing ain't dissimilar to what happened to that shopkeeper over in Lone Creek."

Yet this murder had occurred miles away from that locale, and the victim wasn't a business owner where the motive appeared to be robbery. Rather, the murdered man in this instance was a simple cowboy who worked on Ray Colson's ranch.

"Any connection between this fella and that storekeeper?" I questioned Caldwell.

He blew a breath out the side of his mouth, then scratched a finger at his temple. "Kinda too early to tell. But at this point doesn't seem to be. What I can tell yuh is that Ray Colson is mighty upset."

I was familiar with Rancher Ray—at least by reputation. While I'd never personally met the man, I'd taken the occasional ride out toward his property on lazy days to admire his spread. Even when he'd make an appearance in Chesterfield City I never bothered to greet him—nor him me . . . that is, if he had ever been informed of who I was. J.C., on the other hand, knew Colson, and he was another individual about whom she'd formed a rather raw opinion. In fact, she held him in equally low standing with Mr. Theodore Sherwood. Because of the way she'd been trampled on, I sometimes got the feeling that she held in low esteem, if not downright contempt, any man who had achieved success—honestly or otherwise. Well, maybe she

had the right to feel embittered. I couldn't pass my own judgment on Ray Colson, since I knew nothing about him outside
of his reputation, which was contradictory to say the least . . .
but I trusted J.C., and, since I sided with her in her strong dislike of Sherwood, I wasn't about to dismiss her similar attitude
when it came to Rancher Ray Colson.

I had to lay it on the line for Caldwell.

"First off, as you yourself said, I've given up my profession,"
I told him. I tossed a quick glance at J.C. and noticed how she
looked pleased, if not entirely convinced, which I reckon was
understandable under the circumstances.

The sheriff edged forward, abruptly, in his chair as if to
emphasize his point. "The thing is, Ray Colson wants reliable
men to track down whoever killed his worker. Men who can
bring in quick results."

"Hell, I don't even know this Rancher Ray," I said with a
grimace. "Never met the man."

Caldwell said briskly, "Maybe not. But he knows you."

I settled back on the couch. I found that curious. If Ray
Colson was familiar with my past, why hadn't he ever come to
introduce himself on those visits into Chesterfield City? Most of
the town—and even people throughout the county, in homes
bordering where Colson owned his spread—had at one time or
another come to meet me or just shake my hand back when I'd
had my . . . notoriety, as it were. But not Rancher Ray Colson. I
hadn't cared enough to consider his absence a slight. Truthfully,
I still didn't.

But *dammit*, I confess my mercenary side became stimulated
by what the sheriff next told me.

"Colson's a rich man," he said. Caldwell wasn't a man to
mince his words. And at hearing that I again shifted my gaze
toward J.C., who turned to face me with a barely concealed
look of displeasure. I ignored her reaction, willing to face the

consequences later. Consequences that were sure to come if I gave the sheriff the answer he wanted to hear.

"So what exactly are you telling me?" I said.

Before Caldwell could say more, the voice of our daughter Bethany called out from the bedroom: "Mommy."

J.C. looked a bit annoyed at being called away at this point in the conversation, but I was glad for it. I wanted to hear more about the possible financial benefit before J.C. could return.

When she was far enough out of earshot, I leaned forward in my seat and said directly but in a conspiratorial tone, "What kind of money am I looking at?"

Caldwell arched an eyebrow. "I can't speak for him. That's something the two of you will have to work out."

That was true enough. I found myself wondering, though, whether there might also be an extra incentive for the sheriff. I don't know what prompted me—maybe my instinctive distrust of Ray Colson—but I went and asked him outright: "And how do you benefit from this?"

Caldwell looked at me sharply, and his tone was harsh. "I strictly represent the law in this matter."

I'd offended the man and the integrity of his badge. I regretted my insinuation and apologized. Caldwell had a good reputation, and he seemed a decent human being. He took his job seriously. But I stated my own position that I was no longer a part of the law, adding that I never really was. I was simply hired for pay. I never was sure if that made me a strictly honorable character. But I also wanted to make it clear to the sheriff that I wasn't in the league of a bounty hunter.

I also had another more practical consideration.

"Don't own a horse," I said.

Caldwell had a quick answer. "Can get yuh one. That ain't a problem."

There followed a lengthy silence between Caldwell and

myself. The sheriff was patient; I suspected he had to be. Rancher Ray had probably instructed him to bring me back—or more likely *demanded* that he do so. By this time, J.C. had come back into the room. Again, she sat next to me, only this time she reached out and took my hand and held it. I didn't know if she'd heard any of what was said, but she was both interested and apprehensive in listening to what was going to come next.

I sat thoughtfully for just a little longer. And then I permitted myself an insolent comment. "I don't know if Mr. Colson would be willing to meet my price."

"Don't sell him short, Gambel," Caldwell responded rather quickly. "When he wants something, money is no object."

J.C. and I looked at each other, her fingers now massaging my hand with a kind of nervous intensity. It actually started to hurt a bit, but I didn't pull away. I knew she didn't approve of any of this, but I wanted her to see that I was bargaining without a base, trying to determine if we really could benefit sufficiently from what might be offered by the wealthy rancher so that we wouldn't have those concerns about our future . . . our children's future.

My boldness went a bit deeper, feeling that I had the right to speak openly if my participation was so valuable. "Just a mite curious. Is Mr. Colson concerned about his own well-being in light of what happened?"

Caldwell gave me a speculative look. "You askin' might someone be gunnin' for *him*?"

"Yeah."

Caldwell's eyes shot daggers at me. "I have no idea." His attitude softened. "But a man like Colson always has enemies. All I know is I gotta head out there, and Mr. Colson asked for me to bring you along."

"And how do *you* feel about that?" I asked straightly.

"Huh?" Caldwell looked puzzled by my question.

"Him asking me along," I explained. "After all, *you're* the lawman."

Caldwell looked to consider his reply. He gave me a peculiar stare. But he understood why I'd posed the question. By Colson asking me to accompany him, was that a reflection on Caldwell's ability? That maybe he didn't feel the sheriff alone could handle the task, which, of course, would be an insult to the man's pride.

In short, might this whole arrangement not be to Caldwell's liking?

Though my mind wasn't made up in this matter, I quickly determined that I would not partner with someone who resented me. Especially on the hunt for a murderer. I'd already traveled with that uncertainty when I rode with Francisco on our hunt for Silvano Ramos.

Caldwell's answer had a blunt edge. "One of his ranch hands was killed on Mr. Colson's property, and I have an obligation to look into it. His reasons for wanting you along . . . Well, those are his own. I didn't question." Caldwell then looked sheepishly at J.C. He turned his eyes back toward me and wore a self-conscious smile. "I apologize for gettin' riled. No call for that. Truth of the matter is, I'd also prefer it if'n you'd come along."

Well, Caldwell had eased himself out of that one pretty well. He spoke his words with a modesty and honesty I could respect. I recognized the situation he was in, and it was clear that Ray Colson could make things a mite rough on the sheriff if I didn't ride out with him; the man carried a lot of weight in the territory—both figuratively and literally. I could go that far at least, I decided. Hear Rancher Ray out. I didn't have any concerns about Colson making my life miserable; other circumstances had taken care of that. But, as I said, I did see a possible opportunity that would help ease my family out of the financial bind we were in. If Colson wanted my help in tracking this killer, it would come at a high cost. As far as I was concerned, that was the only way I'd even consider getting myself involved. If I were to return to my old profession even peripherally . . . those services were for hire. And I wasn't planning to sell myself cheap.

I asked for Caldwell to wait for me downstairs in what used to be our print shop. I wanted to have a word alone with J.C., and I felt that she, too, would have something to say.

"I'm just going to ride out with him to the Colson ranch," I gently told her.

"And then?" she wanted to know.

I answered with a shrug.

J.C. wore a bitter expression. "You know that's another man I have little use for."

I smiled. "Notice how you didn't express that in front of the sheriff."

"Didn't have to."

"Well, haven't met Rancher Ray, but reckon I heard enough," I said. "Might be interesting to meet him face to face."

"I listened to a lot of talk, but I can tell you Ray Colson is not a man I would trust," J.C. remarked.

"From what I just heard from Caldwell, Colson doesn't have much choice in the matter."

J.C. sighed. "It'll be past midnight before you get back. Can't you wait 'til morning?"

"Would make more sense," I agreed. "But the sheriff seems pretty insistent."

J.C. focused a steady gaze on me. "It's Colson who's the one that's insistent."

She had a point. What Rancher Ray wanted, he got. I should have gone along with J.C. and put off until tomorrow the ride out to his ranch—might have strengthened my bargaining position a little more. I didn't want to seem too eager. But then it might have gone the other way. I weighed both options and decided it best to strike while the iron's hot. I didn't want to lose the opportunity to earn some much-needed money, and, if I took a gamble on offending Colson by not riding out with the sheriff this night, that likely could be the result. Or possibly come tomorrow and his eagerness to hire my services might not be so urgent, and he might not feel the need to dig quite so deep into his pocketbook.

"Better if I follow the sheriff," I said.

J.C. looked upset. And then she further added, "I don't like the idea of you joining up with a posse, if that's what Colson has in mind."

"Back in the day I generally worked alone," I said, cushioning my words with a smile.

J.C. gave me a hard stare. "Neither sits well with me."

I didn't feel it necessary to remind her of the monetary consideration. She knew better than I our tenuous financial situation with the *Chronicle* now run out of business. Yet I doubted she would accept even the inducement of payment as a convincing enough reason for me to return to my past, and that likely would lead us to an argument. So instead I tried to smooth it out by saying, "No commitment. Just going to hear what he has to say. Maybe all Colson wants is some advice. After all, I do have some years of experience behind me."

J.C. spoke solidly. "I don't think so." She clarified: "I mean I don't believe that he only wants to *talk* to you."

And frankly, neither did I.

She continued. "For one thing, Colson doesn't operate that way. And when he wants something, he doesn't take 'no' for an answer."

"I'm my own man," I assured her. "Always have been." I paused, then added lightly with a smile, "Well . . . that is 'til I met you."

And before J.C. could respond I pulled her close to me in an embrace. I needed the feel of her soft, warm body next to mine at that moment. More than anything, I wanted to be honest with her, tell her that, if Ray Colson would pay my price, I doubted that I could refuse him. It all boiled down to a practical concern, of course, that even J.C., despite all her doubts and reservations, couldn't deny. My family wasn't destitute—yet. But neither were there any lucrative opportunities on the horizon.

And as tough as J.C. could be—a quality I'd come to admire in her—I had to recognize that I was the man in this relationship, husband and father, and as such the care of my family was *my* responsibility.

The killing of George Dawkins wasn't a random act of violence. Nor did some cowboy with a grudge sneak up on him one night and murder him, maybe in retribution for a drunken insult or unpaid gambling debt. Those matters would have been handled swiftly with a well-aimed bullet. Dawkins's chest had been carved into buzzard meat. As I was later to discover, the "likable" ranch hand did have an enemy. One that Dawkins himself may have forgotten about. But a vengeful enemy who remembered all too well . . .

Even as he was being beaten and abused by his two attackers, Jacquin had used all of his considerable strength of will to try and numb himself to the pain inflicted upon his body in order to instead concentrate on the faces of those men. He committed their faces to memory. Neither could expect retribution from an Indian punk who rumor had it was trying to pass himself off as a white man, and so they never made an effort to conceal their identities.

But they had been wrong not to disguise themselves. Very wrong.

Ray Colson was a worried man. His wealth, holdings, and enormous pride aside, he had started to grow concerned that maybe George Dawkins had paid a price for the task that he, Colson, had set him upon, together with another trusted hand, his foreman, Jim Stokes. Both men thought nothing of abusing a redskin. They were of no account, as far as the men were concerned. Colson, however, though issuing the order that had disfigured the Indian he had seen in the company of his daughter, had a somewhat higher respect for the Comanche. While many had come to regard them as a beaten and defeated people and not likely to cause much trouble other than maybe stirring up a little ruckus that simply was in their wild nature, Colson didn't underestimate their true threat. Or their propensity for brutal violence. A new violence that he just might have initiated.

Colson naturally would never confess his personal responsibility in what had been done to Jacquin to either me or Sheriff Caldwell, but I was to learn of a conversation that did occur before the two of us arrived at his ranch as nightfall descended with darkness and stillness and a silence broken only by the chirruping of hidden creatures who only announced themselves when the skies grew black.

The talk between Colson and his other brutish ranch hand, Jim Stokes, had been overheard by one of Colson's staff and related to me at a later time.

Colson's mood was tense, and he was irritable. "Shoulda had you kill that redskin," he said.

"Woulda been easy," Stokes said. "Just me and Dawkins and the Injun. But we was just followin' your instructions, boss. You said to put the fear of God into him, and that's just what we done. 'Sides, you can't be sure it was him that killed George."

"Can't I?" Colson challenged gruffly. "You saw what was done to Dawkins's face; that wasn't put there just random. And don't you start feelin' too comfortable, Jim. If'n it was him, and he remembered Dawkins, he'll likely remember you, too. But we're gonna find him, and it's gonna be a sad day for that savage when we do."

Jim Stokes spoke with bravado, which was easy for him to do with him safe and comfortable inside his boss's study, his mood mellow as he sipped on Colson's expensive liquor. Beyond that, he wasn't about to reveal any fear or uncertainty that might be troubling him in front of Rancher Ray.

"I sliced up that redskin once. He crosses my path ag'in, and I'll carve him up real good," Stokes boasted.

The irony in Ray Colson's character was that, while he had no problem executing violence when it suited his purpose, if it were to hit too close to home, he'd find a way to avoid direct culpability; sideline it, as it were, to the point where he'd seek any way out of the blame, regardless of whether he himself knew the truth.

"Well . . . reckon there's always the chance it ain't him," he said, though his words held little conviction. "Heard 'bout that storekeeper up in Lone Creek who was killed in a likewise manner, face cut up and all. Could be we're just dealin' with an Injun gone renegade. Some escapee off the reserve that's gone wild."

"Reckon that's possible," Jim Stokes agreed, yet his own attitude was similarly doubtful. He pondered and then said cautiously, "Still, you don't want no crazed redskin no matter who he is stalkin' and roamin' 'bout your property."

Colson thought about that only briefly before he forced himself to face the truth.

"No, it's him," he stated firmly, his left hand clenched in a fist. "He's come back to get even." He turned to Stokes. "And that means none of us is safe until he's caught."

I didn't know about his daughter, Bridget Ellen, at the time.

As with her pa, I'd never met the gal. If she'd ever joined him in his jaunts into Chesterfield City I was never aware of it. Could have passed her right on the street and would never have known she was the daughter of this big-shot cattle rancher. Of course, I later found out that she had played a significant—if presumably innocent—part in this drama. My feelings toward her tended to be sympathetic. It was just her misfortune to be the child of a domineering and prejudiced father with no mother around to temper his aggression.

Adding to his other less than admirable qualities, Rancher Ray was also an embittered man, because Ray Colson had a secret that virtually no one was permitted to know, including his daughter.

His wife, the mother of his only child, Bridget Ellen, had been a half-breed, born of a white woman and fathered by a Comanche in what might have been an act of aggression during a Comanche raid on a wagon train where others had been mercilessly slaughtered. The woman, though she was injured, survived and later gave birth to a child, a child who grew into adulthood and was white-skinned enough so that people never knew of her mixed heritage. And that included Ray Colson when he was still a young man struggling to achieve success, when he first met her and quickly fell in love. It was shortly after he married her following a lengthy courtship that he learned the truth, when she was already pregnant with Colson's child. Only then did she reveal to him her tragic birthright. By this time, Ray Colson had already started to build his reputation as a cattle rancher. He would never have allowed the child to be born had he known the truth about his wife. But there was nothing he could do other than try to kept it a secret, conceal the truth both about his wife and the baby soon to be born. While his love for his wife had not dimmed even with this knowledge, it also brought him shame, because he proved a strange contradiction: married to a woman with half Indian blood and allowing her to bear him a child who carried that same heritage, and yet vocal in his hatred toward the Comanche.

Perhaps that was the reason he'd sent his two ranch hands after Jacquin, intent on halting the prospect of a friendship between his daughter and the boy—or, more specifically, a romance. Ray Colson resented that the woman he loved had been spawned by a savage. And his legacy, his child, likewise had Indian blood flowing through her veins. That shameful heritage could not be permitted to go any further.

His wife died soon after Bridget Ellen was born, apparently as the result of a riding accident. If the facts had been better investigated, suspicion might have fallen on Rancher Ray, though he was nowhere near his wife when the mishap occurred. But one theory might have been that he was finally unable to live with those contradictions tearing at his soul, and the misfortune to his wife was actually deliberate and orchestrated. And perhaps the guilt of this act had become so overwhelming that Ray Colson attempted to diminish his culpability by keeping his daughter protected, no matter what the cost. It all remained speculation, but these were the conclusions I reached as I got to know something about the character of Rancher Ray, a man who, despite his wealth and bravado, was not a particularly difficult individual to figure out. My years as a witness seeker enabled me to delve into various personalities: some were genuine; others were merely masks that hid the truth. What I almost instantly detected about Ray Colson was that he was a man who lived with his own fear . . . his own guilt.

But naturally those were not traits he would exhibit when the sheriff and I were escorted by one of his house servants into the main room, where he was waiting for us, all proper and formal— and downright pretentious. Ray Colson was a man who appreciated his comforts and likely enjoyed showing them off even more. Within moments of being exposed to these displays of his wealth, I was curious to see how I would be greeted.

He was standing in a room that seemed as large as the inside of a barn, positioned next to the wide stone fireplace. There were expensively-framed paintings on the wall, but none had any meaning to me. They could have been worth anywhere from five dollars to a hundred thousand, but to my eye they were just depictions of various scenery and nice to look at. I got the sense that outside of boasting of their value they had little meaning to Colson, either.

Colson had a heavy foot planted on the hearth with his gaze cast into the fireplace, where the flames rose and crackled. He was not aware of our entrance until our presence was announced by his manservant. Colson turned his head slowly, his expression suggesting that he was deep in thought and not quite ready to acknowledge us. He said nothing in greeting, but, after a quick glance at the familiar form of Sheriff Caldwell, he focused intently on me and looked to size me up with a slow and steady raising and lowering of his eyes. He then went directly to business, yet continued to ignore me as he spoke directly to the sheriff.

I took an instant dislike to the man.

"I kept the body out back," Colson said. "Figger yuh might need to take another look."

Caldwell chewed at the inside of his mouth. "No need for that. I'd suggest you just get him ready for buryin'."

Colson gave the sheriff a tight stare. "Think yuh should take another look. Might be somethin' yuh missed the first time." This wasn't presented as a request, but rather a demand.

"Seen all I needed," Caldwell told him.

Colson hooked his heavy head in my direction. "What 'bout him?"

Before Caldwell could speak on my behalf I said, "Don't

have to see him."

"No?" Colson said, a hint of mistrust seeping through in his utterance.

"Was never part of my work to examine a corpse," I said, and I guess my words came out a mite harshly, as Colson regarded me with a glower, as if I'd set off on a bad foot by daring to challenge him with my remark.

More from a sense of courtesy than regret I addressed him in a slightly more respectful tone. "Don't mean for you to take offense, Mr. Colson. But the sheriff here described to me the condition of the body. And, as I say, it's unnecessary for me to take a look-see. Back when I was a witness seeker, by the time my services were needed . . . well, the victim was already dead and buried. About all I was ever told, and even that was mostly of little value, was how the killing had been committed. And that usually was done by a shooting or a stabbing. Didn't help nor hinder my work."

Colson's response was passed through tight lips. "Nothin' that clean in this instance. My man was cut open like a side of beef."

"I heard," I told him. "But my studying the body won't make any difference."

Colson responded with a clever look. "Care maybe to offer an opinion then, give an idea of what type of person might be responsible for this?"

I could tell he was trying to figure out my worth. I decided to play along until I could determine if there might be a payday. "Well, not much to go on at this point. But, if I had to make an early guess, I'd say that someone who killed in such an aggressive manner had a personal score to settle. And a pretty deep score at that."

"From my standpoint it was unprovoked," Colson said, and he spoke his words quickly. Too quickly. "George had no enemies. Wasn't one to start no grudges."

I couldn't know for certain, of course, but rumors had been talked about that, before Colson became wealthy and respectable, he supplemented his own cattle herd with some midnight range rustling. Nothing was ever proven, so no legal action had been taken, but hushed suspicions still persisted. Yet, to my way of thinking, the killing of this Dawkins went beyond the theft of cattle. I told him so.

Colson looked to consider my point of view. I could tell by the troubled expression on his face that he'd reached the same conclusion. He was being targeted out of vengeance of another sort. He walked with slow strides over to the liquor cabinet, where he poured himself a snifter of liqueur from a crystal decanter, a refreshment he offered neither to Caldwell nor myself.

"Witness seeker," Colson then uttered, in a tone so ambiguous I couldn't be sure whether he was complimenting or expressing disapproval at my former trade. But I really didn't care. My motivation for being in his house had nothing to do with his opinion of me personally or professionally. It was his money I was interested in. And there was no question he had plenty of it.

"So, I reckon you're an independent sort," Colson next said, phrasing his words almost as an accusation.

I didn't reply. And, again, was he referring to my attitude or my work as a witness seeker? In any case, I hadn't come all the way out to his ranch at an ungodly hour just to joust with the man's ego.

He smirked. "Don't mean for *you* to take offense," he said, though I understood that in his own abrasive manner that was precisely what he'd intended.

"None taken," I replied. Or rather, *lied.*

It was all fun and games, but the thrust and parry of our

conversation was now beginning to bore me.

Finally, after a good swallow of his liqueur, Rancher Ray Colson decided to get serious. He wiped the brandy or cognac from his thick lips and said, "The man who was killed today was one of my most valued and trusted employees. More than that, he was a friend. Just so you should know, I regard all of my workers as personal friends. His name was George Dawkins. Not that his name would have any meaning to you. But his murder affects me deeply. Now I don't know what all the sheriff told yuh, but George wasn't robbed, none of the cattle he was watching over was stolen, all heads were accounted for, so rustling wasn't the motive. Yet he was killed meanly, and for him to die that way . . . well, you just finished sayin' this scum might have a score to settle. That might well be, but I wracked my brain, and I can't come up with anyone who could have that much hatred for me. Yeah, sure a man in my position is bound to make some enemies. But whatever their feelings toward me and whatever I feel toward them, I can tell you for a certainty that no one's carryin' that much of a grudge to do what was done to George."

"And Dawkins couldn't have brought this on himself?" I questioned. "Got someone mad enough to rip him open like that?"

Sheriff Caldwell spoke up. "Told you on the ride over: Dawkins was a friendly, likable sort . . ."

Colson interrupted. "Now hold on, Caldwell. That's what I told you earlier. Dawkins got along well 'nuff with the fellas who work here. Can't say definite what went on when he rode off with his Saturday pay." Concern crept into his voice. "I've got a daughter, and it's my duty to protect her. And neither me nor her can live in peace knowin' there's someone out there with the possible intention of cold-blooded murder on his mind."

I listened carefully both to his words and how he expressed them. Maybe to someone else he might have come across as convincing in his ignorance. But it didn't work on me. My years of dealing with all types as a witness seeker made me not only skeptical of how some people proclaimed their innocence but also provided me with pretty good insight into what seemed genuine and what seemed doubtful. And if Ray Colson didn't know for certain who this killer was, he had a strong suspicion. On that I was willing to bet whatever pay he might offer me. But, for reasons of his own, that information was something he didn't seem eager to share with me or the sheriff.

And, if that was to be his attitude, I wasn't going to go easy on him, either.

"I don't track down murderers," I told Colson flatly.

Colson got a little heated, made evident by the sudden flush that shadowed his features. The man's temper clearly had a short fuse.

"That ain't what I hear," he blurted. "I had extra people protectin' my property when that bandit Ramos was on the loose. And I know that not even the Rangers could track him, but that three men went after him, and only one returned." He pointed a finger in my direction, an emphatic but unnecessary gesture.

"I told the story," I said, and I wasn't trying to sound modest, just presenting the truth. "The part I played was insignificant. I . . . just happened to be there."

"Along for the ride, I take it?" Colson said sardonically.

He was trying to get a rise out of me again. I didn't want to lower myself to his level and merely lifted a shoulder in response.

"Yeah, I know, the real hero was the Mexican," he said, speaking impatiently and punctuating his words with a swift brush of his beefy hand. "Well, maybe so. But I don't care 'bout that. Hero or not, a dead man is of no use to me." He brandished another finger at me, and his tone was brusque. "You still brought along the experience of what it was you used to do. And, dammit, I need that skill of yours now. I want this varmint brought in to face justice."

For a moment, I almost felt flattered by his confidence in my abilities. But that lasted only for an instant as my objection to this man and his rude, overbearing presence once more took precedence over any boost to my ego. The man grated on me badly. And what I particularly had to wonder was what he meant by justice. Justice decided by the law . . . or his own brand of justice that likely would lead to a quick lynching?

If *that* was what he had in mind, I didn't want to be a party.

But that wasn't my immediate concern. There still remained the question of pay for my participation in this tracking down. Maybe I was eager, my need for cash getting the better of me, but Colson, despite all his ramblings, hadn't yet touched on the subject of payment for my services—which, if anything, would ultimately be the deciding factor for me.

It seemed to me that the mention of money was a last resort on his part. I hadn't given him the slightest indication that I would take part in what he was asking. Hadn't agreed to anything, hadn't yet laid down my cards, though I confess I was prepared to do so. Nor had he asked me to show my hand. I started to wonder whether Rancher Ray thought I would simply volunteer my services out of a sense of duty to see justice served, become part of that posse J.C. had been concerned about. But he couldn't have been more wrong. What's more, he couldn't seem to accept the fact that as a witness seeker I wasn't hired to go in search of murderers. Of course, situations had arisen where violence did occur, such as what I encountered with that killer family in the Bodrie Hills, a bloody shoot-out from which I was the only one to walk away alive.

All that seemed important to Colson was that I'd been involved with ending the reign of the Ramos gang.

I finally took control of the situation. "You've sorta made it clear what you want, Mr. Colson. Now don't you think it's time we pass the hand the other way?"

At first, he seemed unsure at what I was aiming toward. Then sunrise hit the trail. He twisted his heavy face into a mask of frustration before he blurted, "Five hunnerd."

I kept my expression blank, displaying no reaction to his offer.

"Y' hear me? I'm sayin' I'll pay you five hunnerd dollars to ride along with Caldwell," Colson repeated.

Through all of this Sheriff Caldwell didn't have much to say. For a man of his tough reputation he seemed somewhat timid in Colson's presence. My periodic glances at the lawman told me he might be sweating out my decision. The way it still looked to me, he needed me to agree to lend my skills to this manhunt, otherwise it might go bad on him.

Now it was my turn to stall.

"So, what d'yuh say?" Colson asked with impatience.

"A mighty generous sum," I muttered, adding an approving nod for effect.

"I'd say so," Colson said confidently.

I then punctured his smugness.

"But I'd say my reputation calls for a bit more of your generosity," I said, smiling back at him.

Colson's lips tightened. He was silent for a bit, as I expected him to be, before he grumbled, "How much more yuh askin'?"

"Double," I replied without hesitation.

I could feel Sheriff Caldwell's eyes settle heavily on me. I'm sure he felt I'd just closed myself out of the deal. Maybe not so much by doubling the amount, but by my standing up to Rancher Ray. And maybe I did talk myself out of it. But I held firm.

I expected to get a rise out of Rancher Ray. But he just stared at me in silence, no real expression on his face. Of course, he likely was simmering on the inside.

After several moments he attempted a compromise.

"I'll send along as many men as you think necessary," Colson said. He added as if in a boast, "I can spare 'em."

That was hardly an inducement. If I were to go along I'd prefer just to ride with the sheriff and maybe another couple of men—men with good credentials I knew I could trust. Men who had no personal stake in this. It hadn't escaped me that this killer had murdered a fellow ranch worker, and I couldn't guess how deep their loyalty to one another went—or, if once we found this killer, that Colson wouldn't have secretly instructed his men just to string him up from the nearest tree. The sheriff and I alone wouldn't be able to put up much resistance should such a situation occur.

And not knowing Caldwell too well, I couldn't be sure if he'd even have a mind to.

I turned my attention full to the sheriff. We looked at each other without speaking. Our thoughts merged, and then I focused back on Colson.

"Still doesn't give me an answer about my pay," I said.

Colson's jaws clamped tight so that I could see the cords of muscles standing out in his neck.

"Awright," he said, and I noticed how the fingers of one hand drummed against the knuckles of his other hand counting out the sum. "A thousand dollars."

I nodded, even as my brain kept flashing back to J.C., and how she was going to react once I told her of my decision.

"But there's also gotta be some conditions," I then said.

Colson gave a swift jerk of his head to let me know he was listening.

"I won't ride with a posse," I told him outright.

Colson looked about ready to object. Before he could say

anything, I went on. And I spoke pointedly, again chancing to offend him.

"The thing is, Mr. Colson, I don't think you have it in mind to bring this hombre back to face a jury. Your jury would be the men you'd choose to ride along with us. And, as far as you all are concerned, the verdict has already come in as guilty."

The expression that screwed even deeper lines into Rancher Ray's features told me that I'd hit the nail on the head.

"You find the right man, and there'd be no doubt of his guilt," he said.

I nodded. "Yeah. Hope that to be the case. But I won't be party to a lynching."

"You seem to forget I've got a lot at stake."

"The way I see it," I explained, "until a man is judged legally by a court and jury, any punishment against him is murder, plain and simple."

He threw me a clever question. "You feel that way 'bout Ramos?"

"Those were different circumstances," I said.

Colson scratched a finger against a tiny scar over his eyebrow. " 'Course that's assuming he surrenders himself without resistance."

I nodded again. "Got no argument with any man defending himself."

"Fair 'nuff," Colson said. A rather quick agreement, but my stand had been made, and I wouldn't be backing down.

"Anyway, just me and the sheriff . . . and maybe a couple of men that Caldwell can recommend from town to ride along with us. Men with no personal interest in this."

I was still playing a gamble, still chancing to forfeit a nice payday, but I wouldn't waive my demand. While Ray Colson was not a man who appreciated being told how to handle his affairs, I could sense he recognized it was better for him to accept my terms. If we were successful in our search, he'd get the justice he demanded—the killer no doubt would end up dancing on a rope—but at least in that way my conscience wouldn't be blemished by an outright murder.

"Let's agree to one compromise, though," Colson then presented. "Won't force no posse on yuh, no lynch mob, as you seem to see it. But I'd still like for one of my own men to ride along with you. Can't be no argument with that. 'Fact, won't be."

And that wasn't spoken as a request, but a Ray Colson dictate.

Personally, I remained opposed to the idea of a Colson cohort coming with us, yet I could appreciate Colson's reasoning, since he would be financing our search. The way I tried to justify it, Colson likely wanted someone along to see that we were earning our pay—or at least that I was.

"I have a good man," Colson added. "Reliable."

I tried to keep the disapproval I was feeling from registering on my face.

"Yep, he'll do just fine," Colson said with a satisfied grin. He wasn't speaking to Caldwell or me; he was speaking to himself.

What I didn't know at the time was the "good man" Rancher Ray added to our search was his ranch foreman, Jim Stokes, who had a greater stake in this than just keeping tabs on our progress.

It was well past midnight when Sheriff Caldwell and I wearily rode our horses along the moonlight trail back into Chesterfield City. Neither of us spoke a word to each other, and the only sound accompanying us was the gentle and rhythmic beat of our horses' hoofs against the turf and maybe a skittering of a night critter off in the bundles of bush outside the town's limits. We'd be setting off shortly after noon, which gave Caldwell the chance to round up a couple of good men and me the opportunity to try to explain to J.C. what I'd agreed to—and why. I envied Caldwell's task a whole lot more than mine.

I'd be telling a falsehood if I didn't admit that my mind was filled with doubt on the ride back into Chesterfield City. And not just because of what I knew I could expect from J.C. It was the feeling that I was once more venturing into territory where I knew I no longer belonged. Daring to again challenge odds that wisdom told me were growing ever slimmer. I cast the occasional glance toward Sheriff Caldwell and couldn't help but be reminded of the lawman Briggs. And in that search, for whatever it was worth, we had the advantage of at least knowing what we were up against. Specifically, we knew who our enemy was. Neither Caldwell nor myself had so much as a clue as to who our quarry was on this hunt. Was he alone? Was he part of a gang? What were his weapons, his skills? The more I gave thought to this undertaking the more loco I knew I had to be for having agreed to be part of it. And as I tightened my lips and clenched my teeth I kept reminding myself that, if I wasn't so damned desperate, I'd have walked away from Rancher Ray without so much as a look back. The one thing I'd always told myself when I was a witness seeker was that I'd never permit myself to form an attachment to anyone, never forgetting the fate of Colonel Calvin. Had I remained committed to my profession, neither J.C. nor the girls would have become part of my life. I certainly never would have opened the door to romance. But I thought all that was behind me, my future now headed in a different, more settled direction. Yet . . . that was not to be. I'd committed myself to a family, and, with the situation now being what it was—namely that we were broke—I had to provide for them. And an opportunity, such as it was, had been given—yet not in the way I would have chosen. And that was how I would try to justify my decision to J.C.

The doubt she surely would express would match my own.

★ ★ ★ ★ ★

She was waiting up for me, as I'd expected, sitting on the rocker in the parlor, which was only slightly aglow from the flickering flame emanating from the kerosene lamp on the side table. I tried to avoid looking at her when I entered the room. Because I instinctively knew . . . that *she* knew.

I removed my Stetson and placed it on the pegboard next to the door, stalling, taking longer than necessary for such a simple gesture. Even though the night air had been cool I swept telling beads of sweat from my brow. Before I could turn to face her J.C.'s voice rose behind me. There was no inflection in her tone, just a flat: "You're made the decision to go, haven't you?"

I hesitated for as long as I could—which wasn't very long, though in this situation it seemed like an eternity.

But my answer came not in words but as a mere nod.

An uncomfortable quiet filled the parlor. A cannon fired from a distance of fifty miles away could have been heard within the room.

How could I make her understand? I reasoned that she did . . . yet she didn't. I couldn't fault her . . . and yet I could.

She breathed out a long, weary sigh. "I suppose once you establish a reputation it never leaves you."

"Reputation? I'm not a gunslinger," I countered quickly.

She appeared as little more than a shadow in the dark of the room, and I couldn't make out her expression when she said in a critical manner, "Is there really that much difference?"

I kept my temperament composed. "No one's coming gunning for me, 'cause no one's got anything to prove where I'm concerned. You can't go comparing me with John Wesley Hardin. Now there's someone aiming for a bullet from some ambitious young buck."

"That's not what I mean," J.C. said with a gentle determination, and it was the mildness of her tone that I found most

160

troubling. I almost wished she'd bark at me so that we could get this resolved in an all-out, two-fisted argument.

She rose from her chair and stepped toward me.

"But what—*who*—you once were is never going to leave you," she said. "We've already seen that. The adulation of the people in this town—"

"Which is fading," I was quick to interject. But I reckon not too convincingly.

She reminded me: "The book deal; the offer to become sheriff."

"Look, it was different with Ramos," I said.

"Was it? Was it really? How about what Colson wants you to do? No matter how much you've fought to deny it, people still think of you as a hero."

"I know," I finally conceded in a low voice. "Reckon I've always known you can't change people's thinking."

J.C. was standing close enough to me that I could tell she wanted my arms to reach out and pull her close and me to give her some words of reassurance. I determined that, *dammit*, I wasn't going to give her what she wanted to hear. Yet, at the same time, picking away at me like a persistent itch, was the reminder that J.C. had resisted furthering our relationship until I assured her that I'd given up my past life. And here I was, tossing aside that promise I'd made her. It didn't matter *why* I was doing it; it was *how* I intended to do it.

I don't know what prompted me, maybe frustration aimed at both J.C. and myself, but I spoke words I'd never intended to say. "Maybe . . . for now it'd be best if we let this keep us apart, if that'd be easier. Let me just go on and do this thing with Caldwell and provide the money—for you and the girls."

There was no immediate change in J.C.'s expression, but in the next instant, once she'd absorbed what I'd said, she looked as offended as if I'd laid personal insult against the integrity of her character.

She stated her point firmly, without compromise. "Whatever payment you hope to make from this . . . it's nothing the girls and I need from you, thank you very much."

"A thousand dollars?" I told her.

J.C.'s face was blank. Not even the blink of an eye when I mentioned the amount.

"I'm not doing this for myself," I reminded her.

"Aren't you?" she snapped. And then she half closed her eyes, turned her head aside, and calmed herself.

"I know you're not." She spoke more gently but with her jaws slightly taut. "But the girls don't need money from a dead father."

Harsh, stinging words. But how could I argue her point? Or comfort her concern?

I spoke, I hoped, in a rational manner. "You know that's not what I want. But I've got to look at this otherwise—as a chance for us, an opportunity that'll afford us the time to really think about what's best for our future . . . where we want to move forward from here. It's an opportunity we might not get again."

J.C. also looked to soften her attitude. "But does it have to be *this* way?"

I placed my thumb and forefinger under her chin and gently tilted her head so that her eyes met mine; eyes that were sad and distressed. I spoke with as much sincerity as I could muster. "For now . . . yeah."

Her eyes began to grow moist. "And then . . ."

I responded with optimism. "I told you: and then we have to move on. Take the money Colson pays me and find some place to start over. Some place where I won't be hounded by this reputation of mine, and we can just settle down and be like regular folks."

J.C. spoke hopefully, but still not free of that clouding doubt.

"You think that can be?"

Only rarely had I witnessed that dissolving of her tough exterior, and never quite so much as at that moment, with her tender tone, her eyes glistening with just the suggestion of tears about to roll down her cheeks. The former tough-as-leather J. C. Montgomery had become as delicate as a feather.

"We have to make it be."

Truth be told, I believe that J.C. knew from the moment I stepped out the door earlier that evening with Hastings Caldwell that I'd made my choice—only she needed time to accept what even she understood was the most practical decision under the circumstances. Was there a risk? Certainly. But there was always a risk whenever it came to a new endeavor, when one had to venture into unknown territory.

"When would you be leaving?" she asked.

"Sheriff'll be by 'round noon tomorrow."

"Will it be just you and the sheriff?"

"No. He's rounding up a couple of others." I offered an encouraging smile. "Good men, he says. I trust the sheriff. We'll be better equipped than when we went after Ramos."

J.C. tried to work up her own smile but couldn't quite manage it.

"Just some punk with something to prove," I added, trying to downplay the situation we could be facing. "I'll lead 'em to him, and the lawmen will do the rest."

Brave words, but of course I had no idea who I was dealing with. Just because the murder of George Dawkins pointed to someone out for vengeance didn't guarantee we'd be facing a lone gun. It was then that the memories came flooding back: Colonel Calvin, my own close brushes with death in the Bodrie Hills and with the Ramos gang . . .

Each was a reminder that this might be the time luck would finally run out, and I'd be returning to J.C. and my girls draped lifeless over a saddle.

I had to cast those thoughts aside.

The girls were up early, and I was already sitting at the kitchen table sipping my second cup of strongly brewed coffee. I really couldn't sleep the night before, even after J.C. and I tried to share some lovemaking. I sighed a lot, and so did she, before we finally limited our intimacy to lying close in each other's arms. I reckon I dozed a bit, but come sunrise and I was wide awake, not necessarily rested and refreshed, but awake. The little window in our bedroom introduced the daylight. The whitish shaft struggled to get into the room but only succeeded in partly penetrating the fabric of the curtains. I fussed about in bed trying to get comfortable, maneuvering my body about the feather mattress, until I finally surrendered and pulled myself out from under the sheets. I think in my frustration I even uttered an expletive. In any case, J.C. opened her own eyes. I told her to stay in bed, and she did, and I went to make coffee.

Lorraine and little Bethany stood next to me, both wearing inquisitive if somewhat troubled expressions—at least that was how I perceived them. I greeted them with my best attempt at a smile, which neither returned. Those clever little girls suspected something was up. And at once it was difficult for me. We'd been together as a family for a while, and both J.C. and I had provided our adopted daughters with a much-needed stability after what they both had endured those several years back. But it occurred to me as I looked into their faces that neither had forgotten that terrible time, and particularly what they now possibly saw in me had hastened forth a reminder.

"Where are you going, Daddy?" Bethany said to me. She referred to me as her daddy for most of her young life, because she had looked upon with me as her father. As best I could figure, she had no memory of her real pa. It was a little different with Lorraine, who still remembered her parents. She never really called me by anything specific, though she did address J.C. as "Mama."

Anyhow, to be referenced as "Daddy" was still foreign and admittedly a tad uncomfortable for me. It was a term I'd simply never imagined would ever be applied to me.

By the time I could address the girls, J.C. was already out of bed and standing quietly in the threshold of our sleeping quarters. I scooped Bethany into my arms, holding her face just inches from my own. I gave her a comical look to which she didn't respond.

"You're going away, Daddy," she said, eyebrows furrowed and again regarding me with that mysterious and yet unerringly accurate childhood perception.

I didn't answer her directly. I meekly turned my gaze toward Lorraine.

And then J.C. spoke. "Why don't you tell them?" she said. Her suggestion wasn't intended to be cruel or demanding; rather she was speaking matter of factly. Which in a way made it even more difficult for me to say what needed to be told to the children.

"Yes, honey, I'm going away," I said. Before either could react, I quickly added, "But only for a little while."

I turned to look at J.C. and noticed how her body seemed to stiffen in its posture. She was seeking her own reassurance. An assurance that we both understood I could not reasonably give her. But the girls at least could be kept unaware of the real reason I was leaving them.

I'd hoped to at least share breakfast with my family, but before J.C. could begin preparing pancakes, there came a loud knock at the downstairs door. I glanced at my pocket watch. Sheriff Caldwell had made an early arrival was how I saw it. Or maybe he'd stopped by early with the hope of sharing in our morning meal.

I went downstairs to unlock the door. It was with the latter purpose he'd come, as I could instantly tell by the sheepish expression on his face.

"Man livin' alone don't always get a good feed," he said.

"We might as well both start off on a full stomach," I said by way of invitation. Caldwell responded with an appreciative smile.

We ate our breakfast in quiet. Glances were exchanged around the table, but no one said much. I expected that J.C. might have more to say, but I reckon she restrained her concerns out of respect for the children.

Breakfast over and it was time for Sheriff Caldwell and me to start on our way. The two of us ate well, cleaning off our plates, the sheriff finishing his pancakes before me and trying not to appear anxious. Still I felt rushed and gobbled down my last morsels of food more quickly than I would have liked. We both rose from the dining table, and with a nod of my head I instructed J.C. to follow me into our bedroom. I glanced at Caldwell . . . he gave an approving look—as well he might. As I closed the door behind us her first words to me were, "Where are the others?"

"I'm sure they're here, waiting outside probably," I said.

"They were welcome to come inside for breakfast," J.C. said.

I answered with a shrug. "Maybe Caldwell didn't want to impose on our hospitality any more than he had to."

"Maybe," J.C. said with a gentle smile.

What was most important to me now, what I'd deliberately withheld until that moment, was the cash I pulled from my trousers pocket: the five-hundred-dollar advance I'd demanded from Colson. The security he owed my family during my time away and, more importantly, in the event I didn't come back from this search. I also obtained Colson's guarantee that, should something happen to me, the rest would be paid to J.C. immediately.

It wasn't an amount the cattle baron handed over willingly—or an agreement that particularly pleased him. Yet, unlike the sheriff, whom I still wasn't completely sure Colson didn't have on his payroll, my services came at their own cost and with their own specific payment schedule. I wanted a substantial advance with the balance to be paid once our task was completed, or presented to my family if I should be killed.

I recalled how Colson eyed me coldly. "And what if you don't succeed?" he asked. "What if you ride back here empty handed? Then I'm out a grand."

"That's not my problem. My time is still worth something," I replied. He wasn't impressed by my answer, and so, to appease him, I added, "Just know that I'll be putting forward my best effort. And if you know what you do about me, you should also know that's considerable." I gave a sunny smile. "Otherwise you never would have sent for me."

After I reminded him of my qualifications, he finally agreed to my terms: half of my fee in advance and the balance to be paid whatever the results of our search. Colson still had to have the last say, if not in words than by gesture. He thrust those crumpled bills into my hand with haste. I accepted the cash without a thank-you. As far as I was concerned, my family's financial situation notwithstanding, the appreciation only went one way. Colson's payment was really just pieces of paper. My payment to him, my exchange for his money . . . was likely his life.

J.C. looked at the money I held out to her in pressed fingers for a long while, as if debating whether to accept it . . . perhaps because, to her way of thinking, those crumpled bills represented something she was afraid to come to grips with.

"It's only a partial payment," I said. "The rest comes when I come home."

"*When* you come home," J.C. emphasized.

"Yes," I said strongly, leaving no room for doubt.

I reckon the words we spoke behind that closed door were heard in the outer room. Because, after she took the money and we stepped outside, I caught the look the sheriff gave me, and the expression set on his face seemed to suggest there might be a different outcome. I gave the sheriff a sharp, disapproving look. Whatever his feelings were, I didn't want them expressed in any way in front of my wife and kids. But I would have been a damn fool not to recognize that my wife had surely already picked up on what she saw in the sheriff's eyes. Be that as it may, I knew that she harbored her own worries.

"I'll be waitin' for yuh outside, Gambel," Caldwell said, and then he drew in his lips, bowed slightly and politely to my missus, and stepped outside the parlor.

It was a strange and difficult silence that followed. Before saying anything to J.C. I focused my attention on the girls, lowering to my haunches and encouraging them to come to me for a hug. Initially they resisted, and I exaggerated a frown and a bit of a pout to show my disappointment. But then J.C. gave them both a little nudge, and they ran toward me like two eager ponies set free from the corral.

We hugged in a threesome, and I can say that, since I'd been with these girls, it was the first truly genuine show of affection I'd ever gotten from them. It was a warm yet poignant feeling I experienced. If I'd ever had doubts before, I now knew without any question that Lorraine and Bethany were my daughters, and that I could accept them as such.

We stayed in our embrace for a long while. They didn't seem to want to let go, and I wasn't about to rush them away. I glanced up at J.C., who was standing there patiently, and, from what I could tell by the look on her face, she felt those exact same emotions that I was dealing with: the separation, the uncertainty. Of course, that wouldn't make our good-byes any easier.

Finally, it was J.C. who told the girls in a gentle fashion to say good-bye and go to their room so that she could have some time with Daddy, and then it was just the two of us. We stood looking at each other. Words had to be spoken. But what to say at this time? The truth was that it had really all been said. But there had to be more than just a good-bye.

"I know this isn't what you wanted," I said in a mutter. "And I reckon if you knew back when that things would come to this . . ." My words trailed off. It wasn't necessary that I say anything more.

"No, it's not what I want," J.C. said solemnly. "I won't lie to you, to convince myself or even to ease any guilt you might have over the decision you made."

"I can't allow myself to feel guilty," I told her just as earnestly.

She nodded, looked to be struggling with what she was going to say next. "But . . . I also can't be faulting you for wanting to provide for your family. That would be plain selfish."

I appreciated hearing her say that. It wasn't exactly *how* I wanted to hear it expressed, as the doubt and chords of distress were still evident in her voice, but it was enough and, as I saw it, the best I could expect from her. I walked toward the kitchen area and hefted my saddlebag, which I'd packed with supplies the night before. Then I went to the cabinet (which was under lock and key) where I kept my .44-caliber Colt Dragoon revolvers. I hadn't handled those pieces in a long time, and, at first, they felt foreign to me as I hefted both before fitting them into my gun belt. Then I took the box of cartridges and shoved it into the pocket of my duster, which was hanging on a peg by the door. I didn't want to load the revolvers in front of J.C. and purposely kept my eyes averted from her while preparing my firearms. I hastily wrapped the duster around myself so that she wouldn't have to look at my holstered weapons any longer than necessary. Still, it was a futile attempt to relax her apprehensions.

We embraced, and, much to my disappointment, I detected a resistance in her. She was stiff; her body didn't soften into me as it always did whenever there was true passion between us. I released her, pulling away with a gentle maneuver.

"You take care of yourself and the girls until I get back," I said.

J.C. nodded. And then with misty eyes she said, "I could tell you to be careful but seems kind of silly because . . . I know you will."

"You bet." It wasn't hard for me to read her face and determine that she still held onto the hope that I might change my mind.

I smiled, and it was a genuine smile of promise, not one put on for her benefit.

"I've got a lot to come back to," I said.

CHAPTER TWELVE

Loading the supplies and my bedroll onto my horse gave me a queer but not unfamiliar sensation. In a way it felt like a lifetime ago, yet almost as if it were just yesterday, mounting up to pursue a witness to a robbery or a murder, trekking over hills and passing through canyon walls and crossing over valleys or desolate flatlands so expansive one might think there could never be an end in sight. At times, my only companions were the buzzards flying overhead in anticipation of a bone-picking meal. Then there were the venomous critters in hiding, eagerly waiting for our bodies to surrender to weakness or a parching thirst or the unrelenting elements, likewise ready to feast upon our flesh. A dangerous, oftentimes monotonous job you did for pay—to search for and bring back a man or woman whose testimony might condemn the accused to prison or the gallows or, if lucky, set him free.

I often didn't know the outcome of my assignments, but in some of my solitary moments I had to ponder whether the witness I'd brought back had acquitted the accused or helped to place a rope around his neck. What was I achieving through my efforts: a chance at freedom or punishment? In the beginning that sort of troubled me, but in time, and with some of the things I encountered in my journeys, I reckon I became somewhat jaded. Some of that cynicism had fallen by the wayside—or so I thought—now that I'd become a family man. But once I went back to my old ways, I discovered that wasn't necessarily true. Like a flash of lightning streaking through the dry desert air, I'd instantly reverted to the mindset of a witness seeker—cautious, cynical, and keeping my trust in check.

Only this time it wasn't a witness in hiding I was seeking, but a brutal killer who appeared methodical in his method, a man who might be working alone—as I suspected—or could be riding with a pack of like-minded desperados. It was inevitable that memories of Silvano Ramos came back to haunt me; I'd barely escaped that experience alive, likewise, my earlier encounter with that family of locos in the Bodrie Hills. With these memories tumbling through my brain, I had to ask myself flat-out if I was crazy to be embarking on another hunt. But, just as I'd felt an obligation—one borne out of guilt—to accompany my now-dead Mexican friend Francisco on his quest, I had a responsibility to provide for my family. I confess to feeling a deep resentment toward Theodore Sherwood for forcing me into this situation. I suppose J.C. could have gone to work for him at his newspaper, but I would never allow her to compromise her dignity and her professional ethics by working for that rattlesnake.

Sheriff Caldwell and his two men, whom I assumed had been deputized, were waiting for me outside, seated in their saddles and ready to ride. It was the first time I'd met these men, and much to my relief they looked fit and capable. Caldwell introduced me to them: Brad Calhern and Logan Malone. I felt even more confident when I was informed that they, like Caldwell, were former Texas Rangers and also that Malone had performed earlier service as a lieutenant during the bloody four-year War Between the States. I was further to learn that both had become farmers since retiring from law enforcement but had grown bored tending the land and were eager to step back into some action. There was a good chance they would get their wish.

Neither man was married. I discovered later that Malone was a childless widower; his wife had died while giving birth when Malone was on assignment with the Rangers. Tragically his child, a boy, died just hours later. That explained the rather melancholy disposition I detected in the man. Calhern, on the other hand, was a bachelor. What I noticed about him, a peculiarity, if you will, was that even though he had a face that resembled a clenched fist, he was oddly affectionate in the way he cared for the canvas sack he had looped around his shoulder, handling it delicately, taking periodic glances into the slight opening of the sack, his mouth giving way to what seemed a private smile. If he were a prospector, one might have guessed that sack was filled with gold. Well, I didn't know, nor did I question. Whatever he carried was his own business.

As I mounted my horse I said to Sheriff Caldwell, "I think Ray Colson will be pleased."

The sheriff sort of smiled, a sly twisting of his mouth. "Surely. But he ain't gettin' off cheap." Here Caldwell gave me a deserved hard look. "I get paid a wage for my work, so I get the same money regardless of the outcome. But these fellas work for hire, at a separate cost."

I furrowed my brow. "Weren't they deputized?"

Caldwell nodded, still smiling. " 'Course."

I was curious. As sworn deputies these men volunteered out of a sense of duty, without the expectation of compensation. Or so I assumed.

"Well . . . then they're working in an official capacity," I remarked. "Public service."

Caldwell gave me a wink. "That they are."

I asked in a conspiratorial tone, "Is Colson going to be told that?"

Caldwell's smile turned devious. "Not necessarily."

I reckon he wasn't being entirely forthright, but I gained a new admiration for the sheriff. Maybe he wasn't as deep under Rancher Ray's thumbnail as I'd thought, not so easily intimidated as I initially considered him to be. And I reckon I was also wrong in my thinking that he might be on Colson's payroll. I didn't enjoy admitting my mistakes, even to myself, but if truth be known I wasn't above making wrong judgments. Through years of practice I was quick to form conclusions—sometimes *too* quick. Hastings Caldwell was a lawman doing his job. And he'd brought along recruits who would ride alongside us as deputies. Still, Caldwell wasn't opposed to seeking a cash bonus for their service. After all, both were friends and former colleagues of the sheriff. In short, if Colson wanted this killer caught, he'd have to open his pocketbook a little deeper.

Yeah, I was impressed with Sheriff Caldwell.

I wanted to clear the air before we set out. "Should be telling you, Sheriff: I made the mistake of maybe thinking wrongly of you."

Caldwell gave me a look to encourage me to speak up. He didn't say a word, but I think he already caught the drift of what I was going to say.

But I resisted. I felt I'd said enough. I offered the man a respectful nod and tip of the brim of my Stetson and let it go at that.

And to Caldwell's credit he simply rocked his head in return. The important thing was that we were starting out on even footing.

We'd be stopping in at the Colson ranch first. Now that I was officially on this pursuit, I had some questions to ask Rancher Ray before we started on the trail.

As we rode away, I felt my heart sink, because J.C. had not come outside to see me off. While a part of me didn't want to leave town with her watching me go, I held onto the memory of how she'd stood outside her office on the boardwalk that day when Sheriff Briggs, Francisco, and I set out after Silvano Ramos. Seeing her there, on that occasion, gave me the determination to return to her—almost providing a sense of invincibility that neither Ramos nor his bloodthirsty bunch could defeat.

But today . . . Oh, we'd hugged, if stiffly, but our good-bye to each other hadn't expressed much. Maybe it wasn't necessary. Or maybe . . . despite her attempts to understand, she still resented me for jeopardizing the future we were attempting to build together, with the added responsibility of two children who had made progress in overcoming the loss they had suffered. I didn't know. It was all guesswork. What I'd discovered was J.C. was a hard lady to figure out. But even riding away without the memory of her standing outside our home, I made a vow that I'd come back to her—and the girls. And then somehow, some way, we'd really settle down as a family. Maybe I'd use my pay to purchase a fine piece of property in the country on which to homestead, with suitable land where we could harvest healthy crops; maybe eventually even raise some Texas beef cattle. Unlike Calhern and Malone who, Sheriff Caldwell said, grew weary of farming and needed a return to adventure, working the soil was a future I could readily see myself embracing.

I took a last glance over my shoulder as we started down the main street out of town, onward toward the valley and Ray Colson's spread. And that was when I saw J.C. standing out on the boardwalk, as she'd done before. With one difference: my daughters were standing on either side of her, looking tearful as they weakly waved their good-byes at me. It was a heartbreaking picture, yes, but at the same time I couldn't quite keep the smile from my lips.

And I told myself—silently but with conviction—that I'd be back.

The task ahead of us would not be easy. That would soon become evident. The previous night, after Sheriff Caldwell and I had returned to town, the killer had struck again—with his trademark of savage intent. We discovered this when the four of us rode up to Ray Colson's ranch house and saw him pacing on the porch, looking both nervous and impatient. We also noticed a big, brown dog bounding about the property. I didn't know whether the animal was pet or protector, but, if the latter, we would soon find out he'd failed miserably in his duty.

When Colson saw us approaching he appeared irritated rather than relieved. He started down the steps toward us, his strides brisk but somewhat unsteady, as if he'd indulged in a few glasses of his expensive liquor prior to our arrival. If that were so, those drinks were likely intended to steady his nerves.

"Expected yuh all here a few hours ago," he said in a throaty growl. Even at a short distance the smell of alcohol wafted off his breath.

The first thing I noticed was that his heavyset face looked unnaturally drawn, his eyes pouched and slightly sunken, as if he hadn't slept the night before—or was in the throes of a vicious hangover.

On this morning, Sheriff Caldwell demonstrated without question that he had backbone when dealing with this formidable figure.

"Hadda get my men," he said brusquely. He motioned toward me with a jerk of his head. "And Gambel here has a family he had to tend to."

I appreciated his saying those words and responded with a slight nod.

Of course, none of this made a difference to Rancher Ray. He mumbled, "Awright, awright." The reasons for our delay were obviously not worthy of his consideration. And, with what was to come, I reckon I couldn't hold that against him, just as I couldn't fault him for hitting the bottle so early in the day.

"Had 'nother killin' last night," he announced. "Another one of my hands. Name of Jed Yates. Whoever killed Jed looks to have come upon him sudden like, with no chance for Jed to defend himself. And Jed coulda done just that if'n he'd had the chance." His breathing was labored, and he took a moment to steady himself. "One of my men found his body in the north pasture this morning. Like Dawkins, Jed was slaughtered, part of his face ripped apart."

"What was that about his face?" I inquired.

Colson was terse. "Just told yuh—"

Before I dismounted, I pointed a finger to my right cheek and drew a line straight down.

Colson's features tightened into a taut mask. He gave an abrupt nod.

"This isn't just coincidence, two of your men murdered," I said. "There's a purpose behind what's been happening here, and that's why we have to talk."

"We'll talk inside," Colson said. "But first I'd like yuh to come 'round back and take a look at the body. Had it put in the barn, covered it with some burlap. Don't want my daughter to have to see it."

As before, I didn't see the need to examine the dead man. The condition of the body would prove of no value to me. The only injury that interested me was the scarring of his face. But I agreed to view the corpse.

I could plainly see how overwrought Rancher Ray was. He seemed so absorbed in his worry that he never acknowledged the two deputies who were with us. Nevertheless, he would have to evaluate the pair soon enough. When it came down to terms we—or should I say Sheriff Caldwell—sort of had him over a barrel; Colson wouldn't be in a position to argue with paying some additional cash if he wanted good men to assist in this search. Because by now Colson damn well knew this wasn't merely some common outlaw we'd be going after. This killer's actions had proven to be deliberate—and I was willing to wager my own pay that his murderous intentions were directed specifically at Rancher Ray. He was just biding his time . . . making slow inroads as a taunt before making his final strike.

Why, however, remained the foremost question. Based on my own observations during my two visits to the ranch—again a discernment culled over several years' experience as a witness seeker—there existed a bold pride and arrogance in Colson's personality that could possibly provoke such contempt. But a hatred strong enough to lead to murder? Well, that I couldn't know conclusively. But it provided me with something to go on. At the very least it could provide a possible motive.

The body of the young ranch worker was not a pretty sight. If I hadn't been exposed to so much death during my former travels I might have reacted with revulsion. But I regarded the dead man with no expression whatsoever. Yet with all the killings I had witnessed and even participated in, this ranked among the worst when it came to the desecration of a human body. He hadn't merely been stabbed. His body had been ripped open from chest to mid-section. I looked at Sheriff Caldwell to catch a reaction and, outside of a clenching of his jaw, his stiff countenance was also unchanging. But what was obvious to both of us was that the wound disfiguring the face of the corpse had a personal significance. A mark, a stamp of some sort. We had our look; no one said anything; then with a sweep of his arm Colson motioned us toward his big house. As I followed behind him and the others a strange pondering overcame me. Well, maybe not so strange, but intriguing. I thought about Rancher Ray's money and his position, the envy I could have felt for the man; how I was now forced to take his pay to help support my family when we were close to losing everything that we had—which, in comparison to all that Rancher Ray owned, was meager indeed. So, who was better off? I contemplated. It occurred to me that his wealth and possessions could not have held much meaning to him at this time, with a killer on the prowl, stalking his land and attacking his workers with savage intent. In fact, it wouldn't have surprised me to learn that maybe he even harbored some resentment over his holdings, as the money and authority they represented likely had somehow put him in the tenuous position where he now found himself.

Once inside the house Colson ushered us, not into the main room where we'd met the previous night, but into the smaller space of his study. Once we were all inside he shut the door behind him. I looked around the room, impressed by the decor in spite of myself. An expensively designed and comfortably-upholstered couch nestled against the far wall. There was a button-backed leather swivel chair pushed next to a wide walnut desk that boasted an impeccably polished surface, which reflected with almost a mirror-like clarity. Three equally-inviting guest chairs were placed strategically about the room. Books were lined up on shelves inside a wide and expansive glass cabinet set against almost the whole of one wall, giving a visitor the impression that Colson was a man of some refinement and learning, though I suspected it was all just pretense. Rancher Ray struck me as a man without literary interests whose reading didn't extend beyond his financial ledger. Today he was dressed in typical ranch wear, but I took notice of the wide belt he wore, decorated with a large gold buckle shaped like a crest of some sort, with an engraving I could not decipher. Though his belt was wrapped tightly around his ample waist, he managed to hook the thumb of his right hand into the leather next to the buckle, and that remained his stance.

He requested that we not talk too loudly, explaining that he didn't want his daughter to overhear our discussion. Then he said further, "My Bridget Ellen is a gal of strong will. Unless I tell her why I don't want her to leave the house she'll go off and do whatever she has a mind to." Then his father's concern came to the fore, and his voice was gentle yet troubled. Reckon the fella did possess a human side.

"Yet . . . how do I get her to understand without telling her what's been happening?" he breathed.

This was a question that none of us could answer, though I did say, "She doesn't know about the other killing? About what happened to Dawkins?"

Colson gave his head a vigorous shake and seemed annoyed by my question. " 'Course not. I wasn't 'bout to tell her that. She'd either become frightened or try to prove that she's not afraid by defying me and going off with her usual routine, jumping on her horse and ridin' off to wherever it is she goes on her daily jaunts." He shoved a blunt finger in my direction. "And that's the more likely possibility. As I said, she's strong-willed." He paused before adding quietly, reflectively, "Like her late mother."

And likely no different from her father, I thought to myself.

Sheriff Caldwell spoke. "Know you were asked this before, Mr. Colson. But maybe now that you had some time to think it over, is there any reason you can think of why some—"

Colson wouldn't let the sheriff finish. He cut him off and spoke with impatience. "A man like myself has enemies all throughout the county, Caldwell. Every time I spit tobacco juice the wrong way someone's accusin' me of tryin' to work some dirty deal."

"Putting it that way, Mr. Colson, doesn't exactly narrow our list of suspects," I said in a reasonable voice. "But I still say it has to be a pretty specific enemy for him to do what he did to those two men." And then I hit him with a blunt reminder: "And what he might be aiming to do to you."

Colson looked hard at me.

I went on. I wasn't intimidated. Besides, if Rancher Ray wanted our help . . . if he was holding back on anything that might guide us in our search, it was time for him to fess up.

"A typical dispute can usually be handled with a single gunshot, a hide-and-wait ambush from a concealed spot so the killer can scoot away without being identified. The way those bodies were maimed, especially this latest one, carved up like a holiday turkey . . . Well, that was up close and personal. And that kind of killing took some time. Wasn't a rush job, no sir. In his own way that killer wanted you to know who he was. And that's why, Mr. Colson, you have to have a better idea who this person is beyond just someone your business practices might have offended."

I could feel Sheriff Caldwell's eyes fixed on me, even as I kept my own gaze fastened on Colson. What was the old saying: A guilty man can never run from himself? And even though I'd probably insulted Ray Colson's pride with my words, I don't think he could fault my perceptiveness.

But Colson would not give out the information we needed to know to track the killer. And when I learned it later, I understood why. He couldn't say anything that might implicate him in the brutality that had befallen the young Comanche, Jacquin.

"Don't think I haven't given this a lot of thought," he growled. "Kept me up most of the night, in fact. But I can't put a finger on any one man who'd go to such extremes to get at me. If that's even what this is." He wore a deep frown as he looked to contemplate. "I'm thinkin' . . . yeah, that maybe those two boys went out and did somethin' to bring this on themselves."

It was a worthy attempt to extricate himself from any blame, but when it came to separating fact from fiction Rancher Ray wasn't dealing with an amateur.

"That what you think?" I said. My words and my tone were deliberately doubtful.

Colson considered a little further, and then he said with emphasis, "Sure. Has to be. Those boys work hard all week; get their pay and blow off steam on a Saturday night in town. I don't keep tabs on 'em. All liquored up . . . well, there ain't no tellin' what trouble they might get themselves into."

One would have to be a fool not to know that Colson was not only lying . . . but hiding something. Protecting a truth or even a guilt that he was not willing to admit. One that he was trying to cover by seeking any other way out, like distancing his own blame, putting the fault for what was happening not on himself but on the reckless actions of his ranch hands. Reckon neither had anything to lose now that they were dead, but what it told me was that Colson was either too much of a coward or too responsible to want to incriminate himself.

None of us spoke, and the silence went on for a long time, and that seemed to agitate Rancher Ray, which I took as another telling sign. He likely suspected that we had our doubts, even though neither the sheriff nor myself was in a position to contradict him. I didn't know at the time how deep Caldwell's own suspicions went, but, as for myself . . . I hardly had a shadow of doubt that whatever had led to the killing of those two men rode a trail right back to their boss.

There was a knock at the door to the study. Colson went to answer it. We saw a man standing in the threshold. Right away I detected something about the character I didn't like. He eyed each of us speculatively—myself, Caldwell, and the two deputies—before he said curtly, "I'm ready to ride, Mr. Colson."

Caldwell and I glanced at each other. Perhaps anticipating opposition, Colson lifted his hand to forestall the inevitable. "I'm paying you for a service," he said, speaking directly to me and bypassing the sheriff. "And I want Jim Stokes here to ride along—as my representative."

The sheriff spoke before I could.

"Frankly, still don't see the need for another man," Caldwell argued.

"You don't; *I* do," Colson said bluntly.

There was no point in debating. We both knew this was part of the arrangement. And anyhow, there were three of us following the way of the law. If Stokes intended to cause problems—either on his own whim or through Colson's instructions—he would be just one man against us, easy to convince otherwise. And I still tried to be at least a little generous, rationalizing that maybe Colson had a legitimate reason for wanting him to come along.

Rancher Ray turned his attention to Brad Calhern and Logan Malone, as if finally taking notice of them for the first time since our arrival, and said, "Reckon you fellas wanta talk pay."

While they discussed financial arrangements (to which by all rights Calhern and Malone were not entitled, since they'd been officially deputized and not eligible for additional pay), I walked from the room into the entrance hallway. I soon heard rapid footsteps coming from above me on the second floor of the house. I looked up and saw a pretty young girl poised by the banister. Our eyes met; I nodded politely—but she just stood there with a questioning and also somewhat disapproving expression on her face. I reckon I startled her—a stranger standing alone inside her home.

This was my introduction to Rancher Ray Colson's daughter, Bridget Ellen.

I suspected who she was and wanted to talk to her. From the words spoken by Colson, he likely had a difficult relationship with his daughter. Still I pondered whether Bridget Ellen knew something that Colson wouldn't want her to make known to us.

Possibly. But I felt certain that Rancher Ray would never permit me to speak with his daughter. He wanted our help, yet he also kept putting up fence posts to hinder us.

The girl was dressed in casual riding gear, looking quite fetching actually in her light-blue blouse tucked into the waistband of tight-fitting blue jeans, which themselves were tucked into shiny, black riding boots; her strawberry-colored hair was softly tied back in a ponytail. She was clearly preparing to leave the house to take her horse out for some exercise when she spotted me, which, of course, was exactly what her father had emphasized he did not want her to do. It wasn't my place to interfere, and so I stood aside as the girl briskly but silently started down the staircase. Once she reached the floor of the entrance hall she halted to give me a probing look, as if trying to determine whether she'd ever seen me before, perhaps as a casual guest of her father. I answered the question for her when I gave my head a shake. She gazed at me for a few seconds longer before she started for the front door. However, before she could step outside her father thundered into the hallway.

The stern gruffness in his voice stopped her in her tracks. "Where d'yuh think you're going?" Colson demanded from his daughter.

I stepped out of the way to let them deal with this situation themselves.

She regarded him with a puzzled expression. "Out to take Ranger for a ride." She added with a slight emphasis, "Like I do every day."

Rancher Ray waited for a moment before speaking in a less severe tone. "Today I'd be askin' if you might not."

Bridget Ellen's eyes widened slightly, but before she could utter a protest her father said, gently yet with intent, "I'm askin' just for today. Just stay 'round the ranch."

The girl looked about ready to argue. But then she stopped

herself. I found it sort of intriguing. Wordlessly and without expressing the attitude I'd expected from her, Bridget Ellen did as she was told, returning upstairs. After a few moments, Colson exhaled a breath.

He spoke quietly, perhaps more to himself. "First time that girl's ever obeyed me without a fight."

I offered, "Maybe she's not so headstrong as you think."

Colson ignored my comment.

"I've made arrangements for the men's pay," he then said. "I'm true to my word, and whether or not you come through you'll all be compensated."

I nodded. I was pleased to hear him say that, and I would have to trust him. But I was disappointed not to be given the chance to talk to Colson's daughter.

He started back into the study, and I followed, glancing over my shoulder to see if the girl might be standing upstairs, watching. She wasn't. Not that it would make any difference now. My only chance of speaking with her was to somehow get her alone, and then hope she would tell me something of value . . . if she *could*. There was always the chance that Colson was correct, and she was ignorant of all this.

But I couldn't quite accept that.

Caldwell and the two deputies were waiting in the study, as was Jim Stokes, seated off in the far end of the room, looking to deliberately keep his distance. I didn't pay Stokes much mind, but I got the distinct impression that Colson was anxious to see us leave. My feeling was that my running into his daughter had made him uneasy.

I knew I was taking a risk at inflaming his temper, but I also was impatient and wasn't quite ready to let him off the hook.

"Would have liked to have a word with your daughter," I told him straight out.

Colson's eyes shot daggers not only at, but through me. Then he seemed to settle himself. "I told you, my daughter doesn't know anything. And I want to keep it that way." He paused. "At least until after you capture this killer. Might feel different once I know that she's safe."

I tried another angle. "For now. But you know as well as I that outlaws and bandits run rampant throughout the West. Ramos is a prime example."

I was met by an inquisitive stare. "Thought you claimed your involvement with Ramos was . . ." Colson struggled to find the proper phrasing. Finally: ". . . on the outside edge."

"As far as ending his reign of violence, yes. I had nothing to do with his death," I said. "But, as a witness seeker, a lot depends on skill. Then there's other qualities. Like perseverance. And cooperation. Cooperation I often needed to see my work reach a successful completion."

These were words Colson refused to appreciate, and he didn't hesitate to let me know. "It's my daughter's safety—her *life*—that we're talking about! Of course, I want to see her protected. But . . . there's only so much I can give you. And that, my friend, is nothing at all. I'm as much in the dark as you."

I spoke with an edge of defiance. "I wish I could believe that, Mr. Colson. I honestly do."

Once more he presented us with an emphatic denial—that frankly was becoming tiresome. But what I found unfortunate was that he seemed willing to jeopardize the life of his daughter rather than risk revealing his secret, whatever that was. His pride and his position took priority over her welfare. And I wasn't sure that attitude wouldn't eventually cost him.

I didn't know whether to despise Rancher Ray or pity him.

Even though we were starting off rather uncertainly, I had the gut feeling this would be a short adventure. I suspected that, while our quarry was dangerous, he wasn't as cunning as the bandit Silvano Ramos. Ramos was a man who by his very nature had to keep cleverly on the dodge, especially since he was riding with a pack of desperados who relied on his leadership. He was one man responsible for the actions of a cutthroat gang. The man we were after was a killer, but of a different breed. It seemed that he was acting alone and was possessed of a singular purpose, not motivated by money or personal gain. And because of that resolve he might not be so careful—or so precise—to cover his tracks.

CHAPTER THIRTEEN

With no lead provided, we really had no specific direction to follow when we mounted our horses to begin our search. We would be forced to begin trailing the killer with nothing more than practical guesswork. My deduction was that, if our killer kept himself in hiding, he most likely would seek appropriate cover during the daylight hours, since he'd proven himself to be a night predator. If that were so, the most likely hiding place for him would be up in the mountains. But he wouldn't disappear too deep into the rocks, crevices, and canyons. He'd go into hiding someplace where it would not be difficult or risky for him to emerge and make the distance required to continue with whatever compelled him to commit these vicious killings.

Caldwell turned to me on the saddle and said, "Well, Seeker, you've held a pretty good record. Supposin' you tell us where to be headin'."

I held back from offering my theory, deciding instead to give him the option. "At this point, Sheriff, your guess is as good as mine."

"Fair 'nuff." Caldwell glanced about in each direction. Then he stuck his forefinger into his mouth and popped it out in an odd gesture, and with that finger he pointed west—the direction I would have chosen, as I'd figured he would. Fact is, it wasn't a brain-challenging decision: each of the other directions except for the heavily forested southern region were open for miles upon miles, dotted with little towns and communities. True, our killer could sit at his leisure in a room, hotel, or saloon, until he was ready for his next attack, but I wouldn't have laid money on it. While these crimes were personal, they were also primitive. And someone who could murder like that was not a person who would want to be seen around other folks. There would be something about his attitude that likely would arouse suspicion. So, it seemed more probable that our man was hiding somewhere in the mountains . . . in total solitude.

But locating him would still be a daunting task.

At the start of our journey I rode alongside Sheriff Caldwell while his two deputies kept pace not far behind us, trailing us almost like a pair of protective shadows. We'd gotten a later start, and the sun's placement in the clear, cloudless sky told us that this was going to be a hot afternoon, so it was debatable how much progress we'd make today. It was always an advantage to start out before sunup when the air was cool and your energy was high. Come 'round midday, especially if you didn't keep yourself wet on the inside, fatigue was bound to set in. I'd already taken a number of swallows from my canteen and was scouting about the landscape for another source of clean drinking water.

"Thought a fella with your background would know better than to drink too fast," Caldwell said, amused.

"Yeah, but it's been a while since I've had to worry about quenching my thirst," I replied.

Caldwell nudged his head into the distance. "Well, take it easy. There's a clear water stream and some shade a few miles yonder."

That suited me. I fit the strap of my canteen over the saddle horn.

Caldwell then said something that caught me off guard, though it heightened my respect for him as a person and lawman.

"I really hate that son of a bitch Colson."

I was intrigued by his bluntness but didn't urge him on; turns out that wasn't necessary.

"Yeah," he went on, "one of those types who takes advantage of his authority. Has a team of men he can boss 'round, so he thinks that applies to everyone." He scowled, went quiet, and for the next several moments the only sounds heard were the hoofbeats of our horses. Then: "Probably wrong to call it 'authority.' More like his 'privilege.' I don't mind obeying those who've earned the right to give an order; hell, had plenty of that back when I rode with the Rangers. But take away Colson's money and his big house and property, and just tell me who he would be?"

I smiled. "Not much."

"Damn right," Caldwell stated resolutely. "His influence is in what he owns."

I admired Caldwell for his perceptiveness and honesty.

He loosened one of his hands from the reins and jerked a thumb at his sheriff's badge. He said, "This tin star signifies that I'm in service of the county, and because Colson holds so much influence I've sometimes gotta kowtow to him. But I got my own pride, which I've earned. I want to catch this killer, but I ain't doin' it solely on Rancher Ray's behalf."

I couldn't resist adding, "Kinda feels that way, doesn't it? That we're in his employ."

Caldwell resisted giving an answer, even though I'd left myself open to his reminding me that I and the deputies certainly were working for Colson.

Since we'd become rather friendly——or so I assumed with the sheriff speaking frankly to me—I considered telling Caldwell what I'd not bothered to say to him before.

"Appreciate you telling me that, Sheriff," I said. "Feel it's only right that maybe now I speak truthfully."

Caldwell eyed me with a look of wary intent.

"No," I assured him. "Nothing critical—not now anyhow. Like I started telling you before we left Chesterfield City . . . Well, wasn't sure about your association with Colson and—"

Caldwell cut me off completely. "You kinda made that clear. Y'thought I might be on his payroll?"

"Yeah," I confessed. "I did."

"Wouldn't say much for my character, would it?" Caldwell said, turning to me with narrowed eyes that gave off an intimidating glare. And then his features relaxed, and he grinned.

"As I'm learning," I responded, with a smile intended to take the edge off of what I'd wrongly assumed about the man.

To further ease my discomfort at misjudging him and likely to show there were no hard feelings, Caldwell held his grin when he said, "Just say I owe you one, and we'll call it even."

I mused, "Why did he kill this Yates fella?"

Caldwell had an immediate answer. In fact, he spoke the words I'd already been thinking. "No personal grudge ag'in Yates. It's a message intended for Colson. He's lettin' him know that ain't nothin' gonna stand in his way. And he killed him that way, like he did with Dawkins, just to put some extra fear into him. Bad 'nuff to die, but to know you're marked for death in such a manner . . ."

"If that's his intention, he succeeded," I said.

"Yep. A lot of rage and intention there," Caldwell agreed. "And as we both figger, meant directly for Colson."

I considered. "And after Colson, then what?"

Caldwell thought a long while before he sighed a frustrated breath. "That I don't know."

We spoke a little more about his past and my time as a witness seeker, our conversation inevitably getting around to Silvano Ramos and Caldwell's failed attempt to track him during his time with the Texas Rangers, and how they had wanted

Ramos and his bunch captured after the gang massacred two of their men. And while they were glad to learn of the outlaw's death and the disbanding of his outfit, they were also disappointed that they hadn't been the ones to bring the gang to justice, to avenge the death of their fellow officers. It was a good talk.

We rode the flatlands until mid-afternoon. By now the sun was beating down on us hard, and our mounts were tired and thirsty. Once we came to the little oasis Caldwell had mentioned, we rested under the dappling shade of a small gathering of mesquite trees and fed and watered the horses. Given our pace we would reach the foothills come nightfall. Even from our distance we could tell that the terrain leading into the mountains might be tricky to negotiate. It contained steep ledges and rocky pathways—a type of landscape not unfamiliar to me, since I'd traversed many such difficult passages through the years—but I couldn't be sure when it came to my companions, particularly Calhern and Malone, who in one respect looked to be past their prime when it came to superior horsemanship. Yet I also couldn't totally underestimate their riding skills since they were all former Rangers. As for Jim Stokes . . . well, up to that point all I could say was that he rode behind us, and he rode slow and silent, to my thinking, keeping a deliberate distance.

The heat of the day gave way to the cool of the evening, and we decided to set up camp within the border of some high rocks. We debated whether we should start a fire over which to cook our supper and to provide us with some warmth once the chill of night came full upon us. But we didn't want to betray our position and alert our quarry that we were on his trail.

"If he's up there and sees our fire, might just drive him in deeper," Caldwell said, gazing up into the lower grounds of the mountain range. "Maybe give him the advantage if'n he suspects we're on his trail."

I nodded. Those were my exact feelings. Depending on the skill of whoever we were up against, once he spotted us, we, the hunters, might find ourselves the hunted. From the right vantage point it wouldn't be hard for a man with a rifle to start picking us off like chickens in a coop. Thus far he hadn't killed with a gun, but we couldn't know definitely that he didn't carry one.

And then Jim Stokes spoke, and his words were direct and succinct. "I'm bettin' square he's in them mountains."

I focused on Stokes. We all did. He was sitting on a large rock putting great industry into building a cigarette. He struck a match against the side of the rock to light it.

"Maybe you know somethin', Stokes," Caldwell said, hinting at suspicion.

Stokes blew out a fine stream of smoke and gave the sheriff a quizzical look. "Know somethin'? How could I know anything?"

"Just kinda interesting what yuh said, 'bout him bein' in the mountains."

Stokes replied with a shrug, "Well . . . sure. If he is in these parts, where else would he be keepin' himself? Ain't much chance he'd be walkin' 'round in the open air."

Of course, that was probably true, and the sheriff knew it, too. But I understood Caldwell's method. We both had our suspicions about Jim Stokes. He might provide us with the key that his boss refused to offer us. And maybe it was already beginning to have some effect, because after several moments of heavy silence among our group:

"I just work for the man," Stokes said unexpectedly. He repeated: "How could I know anything? I do the work he assigns me, that's all. His affairs are his own."

"No one said anything about Colson," Caldwell said pleasantly. "Why'd you just now bring him up?"

"Well . . . that—that's what this is all about, ain't it?" Stokes shot back.

The sheriff nodded. "Possibly. Still don't know anything for certain."

I had to hand it to Caldwell: he kept his voice calm and even, no hint of accusation. It was as if he were engaging Stokes in a leisurely chat.

The sheriff and I exchanged a glance. I gave him a wink.

Stokes spoke abruptly. "Look, let's open some beans and get ourselves some supper."

"You okay to eat cold from the can, Stokes?" Caldwell asked with a wry smile.

Jim Stokes scowled, gave a hasty nod, and ground his words out through his teeth. "Ain't the first time. Hell, it's all belly wash anyway."

His attitude wasn't fooling any of us. He might have looked big and burly and possessed of a rough, bullying attitude, but he didn't seem so intimidating in presence or manner now having to sit with us, join us in eating our cold meal. I again had to question whether his participation was merely as an observer to see that Colson's investment in our search wasn't being frittered away. His conduct was already showing cracks. Reckon neither he nor his boss thought we would get wise to what Colson's real purpose might be.

We prepared to settle in for the night. No fire. Cold supper. A definite night chill starting to move in, settling in from the mountains. Our sitting arrangements were an individual preference. Caldwell and I both pulled off our saddle rolls to serve as a cushion. Those who had a sturdier bottom chose to seat themselves directly on their saddles. And by those I meant Calhern and Malone. Didn't understand their reason for choosing such discomfort, especially since they'd been riding on tough leather for a good part of the day. Hell, sitting straight on the ground would have been more comfortable. Well, I didn't give it much thought anyway, seeing that they were a couple of hard-asses. Well, laconic was a more accurate description. Neither prone to idle talk, between each other or even with their old *compadre* Caldwell. They preferred to keep to themselves, and that was fine with me. I understood their loner preference; I was pretty much one myself at one time. I still was, with the natural exception of my family, and yet even J.C. could appreciate my occasional need for time alone. Anyway, what mattered most was that Calhern and Malone were men who kept true to their responsibility, and who I felt could be counted on should we run into danger.

Jim Stokes, on the other hand, seemed restless. He found a rock on which to perch his butt, but he didn't stay put for very long. For a moment or two he was seated, then he was up and pacing, acting antsy, peering yonder, into the black shadows of the mountain range, looking to see . . . who knew what he was seeking? My guess was that he was *considering* what might be out there among those rocks.

Caldwell was also watching him. I waited to see if the sheriff might say something, and when he didn't I took it upon myself to prod Stokes into talking.

"Why don't you come clean, Stokes?" I wasn't about to mince words.

He reacted with astonishment to my unexpected comment. "Wha—What're you talkin' 'bout?"

I spoke as easily as I could, no threat, no intimidation. "Make it simpler all around if you'd just tell us what you know."

Stokes turned his face full toward me, his expression, even in the darkness, revealing a building indignation.

"Quit tryin' to box me," he said.

"Could look at it the opposite," I said. " 'Cause from where I sit, you look like a man with something gnawing away at your conscience."

"I got nothin' on my conscience," Stokes protested.

I quickly shifted my eyes toward the sheriff, then turned my attention back to Stokes. "Well, that I can't say. But I'm not gullible. Being a pretty good judge of character and having to sometimes dig a little deeper than what shows on the surface, which by the way isn't too difficult in your case . . . I'm just commenting on how it appears to be."

Stokes spoke with a defensive arrogance. "Nice try. But I had nothin' to do with any of this."

"No one's accusing you," Sheriff Caldwell reassured him.

"No?" Spokes challenged. "Don't seem that way to me." He gazed at the two of us with squinted eyes. "I'm wise to you both."

"We're just lookin' for any help we can get; you can appreciate that," Caldwell explained. "You knew those two men, worked side by side with 'em. If'n there was a reason for them gettin' killed—a reason that you might even have some guess at—might just help us get this over with quick. Ain't no fun sleepin' cold without a fire."

"Mr. Colson asked me to come along; that's all I can tell yuh," Stokes said with what he intended as a finality.

"So, Colson picked you for no other reason than he trusts yuh?" Caldwell said, casually scratching a finger behind his ear.

"Yeah. Yeah, that's 'bout it."

"All right," Caldwell breathed. He slapped the palms of his hands against his knees and spoke to us as a whole. "Well, likely a long day ahead of us. Might as well bundle up and get some shut-eye."

And that was enough for now. No point in trying to push the issue with Stokes being so stubborn. Naturally neither the sheriff nor myself believed him. If Stokes didn't have some direct involvement in this, he at least had to know something of the circumstances that led to these killings. The signs were evident, and I picked up on every twitch in his manner and each halt in his speech. For a man of his imposing physical presence, his nerves were shaky even as he put a deliberate effort into not letting his uneasiness show. His edginess could have been partly from what we might come across in our search, but I suspected he was more fearful that his resistance to our questioning might eventually crack, which was what the sheriff and I were counting on. Tomorrow was another day, and I figured that with each bit of distance we traveled, especially with some continued prodding, Stokes's defiance would weaken a little more. He might not lead us to the man we sought . . . but our hope was that he'd confess to us what he did know, which might include the identity of the killer. On this journey knowing who our enemy was might be every bit as important as finding him.

The morning skies offered a queer hue over the southern horizon, trailing cloudlessly behind the pink- and orange-tinted reminders of a dawn now dissipating in the direction where we'd be traveling, its remnants hidden behind the majestic, purple-peaked mountain range. It was an unusual start to the day with an indefinable peculiarity in the air. I wondered if I was the only one receptive to it.

We brewed some coffee over a small fire that we didn't think would be too noticeable in the early daylight, ate some biscuits and salty bacon, but didn't linger over our breakfast. We cleared camp and started on our way.

It was interesting to watch Stokes as we rode into the foothills through a yawning box canyon known as the Simeon Pass. The hills leading into mountains with rocky outcroppings would prove perfect for an ambush if someone was aware that an enemy was approaching.

"If our man is anywhere up here he's gotta be skilled with a horse," I heard Sheriff Caldwell mutter, most likely to himself. He appeared apprehensive negotiating the steep climb. His deputies rode with extreme caution, as did I. I cast periodic glances over my shoulder at Stokes, who still insisted on pulling up the rear, though in closer proximity than before, keeping a careful eye on our own progress, gently urging his horse to follow our trail as precisely as possible. His unease might not have been solely from navigating our treacherous passageway. He could just as well have been anticipating the sudden report from a rifle—a shot that would echo through the open air before penetrating its target; a bullet discharged from a weapon he'd never see, fired by a faceless enemy.

Or was that enemy "faceless" . . . *to Stokes?*

We successfully steered our mounts through the rocky slope, loose stones being kicked free by the hooves of our horses and plummeting a distance into the lower canyon. Then we were on a wider level surface, a pathway that reflected a brilliant white against the glare of the sun, and I dropped my horse back in its pace until I was alongside Stokes. He was perspiring and regarded me with a look of disdain. Was it embarrassment at me seeing him bathed in nervous sweat—or him expecting to be bombarded with another round of questions that he wasn't prepared to answer? My own demeanor was unruffled—deliberately so. It was a difficult course we'd just traveled, our hearts were beating a little faster than usual, but, while I could maintain the facade of outward calm, the sweat covering Stokes's face gave the impression that he'd just pulled his head fresh from the waters of a creek.

"Thought fellas like you were made of sturdier stuff," I said to him.

"Used to ridin' the flatlands, herdin' the boss's cattle," Stokes replied, trying to deliver his words in an effortless tone that was as see-through as the sweat that glided down his brow. "Don't often have to cross no mountain pass when you're doin' that."

I glanced upward, shading my eyes against the brightness of the sun. "Don't think we'll have to go much farther anyway."

Stokes eyed me curiously.

"No," I said. "Wouldn't be worth the effort. Wouldn't make much sense."

I could see that Stokes wanted me to explain what I was driving at. I held off just a little longer to test his patience.

Finally he said, "You tellin' me this for any particular reason?"

I obliged him with an answer. "Why would he bury himself high in the peaks when he still hasn't finished what he's set out to do? Yeah, I'd say chances are good he's not far from where we are now, maybe even watching us. Hell, might even have a bead on us."

"That's a pleasant thought," Stokes said, trying to make light of the situation even as his expression sobered. Then after a bit: "You still s'pect I got more to say."

Whatever knowledge or guilt Stokes was carrying became increasingly more evident.

I smiled. I never opted out of a potential opening and gave it to him with both barrels. "I don't suspect, Stokes. I *know.*"

His mouth twisted into a grimace. He hesitated before saying, "Well, you're 'bout as wrong as can be."

"Tell you what: let's just argue that you do know more than what you're admitting," I said, speaking in an easygoing fashion. "Let's go a bit further and consider that maybe you're even somehow involved. If that were the case and our killer knows or recognizes you as we're riding along just as we are, supposing if he's perched up among these rocks and has a mind to start shooting, who do you think he'd take first aim at?"

The situation I presented got Stokes to thinking, I could tell. I watched as wary eyes veered upward, then to either side of us. Yet the son of a bitch still insisted on maintaining his innocence.

"If'n it was me and I s'pected I was bein' pursued along the trail, I'd be pointing my gun straight at the man with the badge," Stokes said cleverly.

I pulled the brim of my Stetson up over my brow and gave my head a slight shake. It was a good answer, but it still wasn't going to let him off the hook.

"Mighta been a time I would have believed you," I said. "You know, take a man at his word. But I'm sure your boss told you the line of work I was in. Through practice and experience I had to develop a more cynical attitude. Not that I don't trust people altogether; there are honest folks out there, sure. But for better or for worse I found they're in the minority. Yeah, I got to know people sometimes better than they knew themselves . . . got to thinking as they would. And most of the time that brought me straight through their front door. To where there's that separation between the outright truth and a downright lie, and I'll tell you: that isn't always as wide a gap as you might think. Can't rightly explain how that works, Stokes. Only that I'm hardly ever wrong when I form a judgment about a person."

Stokes seemed to be listening, but he had nothing to offer. At least not openly.

"Not always easy work, as I'm sure you can appreciate," I added. "Needed a fair amount of cooperation from those who knew more than I did. But overall I earned my pay."

Stokes finally made his say. "Heard you hunted down Ramos."

"No secret there," I said.

Stokes gave me a purposely perplexed look as we rode up along a wide ridge. "How is it you was the only one who came back?"

"I wasn't the only one."

"Yeah. Sure, there were a coupla children," Stokes said dismissively. "But what part did they play?"

"Their folks were killed," I reminded, speaking deliberately.

"What part could you expect them to play?"

In his brutish way, Stokes shrugged my question aside.

"I read what was wrote in the paper," he resumed, rubbing the knuckles of his free hand along the coarse stubble peppering his chin in an obvious gesture. "Sure didn't give yourself a whole lotta credit. Me and the boys back at the ranch kinda wondered 'bout that."

I said, "Told it as it happened. What more was I gonna say? Make myself out to be the hero I wasn't? I might be a lot of things, but I'm no liar. Bent the truth only when I felt it necessary, back in the day."

"When you was a seeker?"

I answered with a shrug.

Of a sudden Stokes's words sounded mighty peculiar, as if he were gunning toward something we both knew I wasn't going to like.

"Yeah, you sure was one lucky sonofabitch. Three men ride in, only one comes out alive. And ag'in the whole of that Ramos bunch. How many was in that gang? Tell me, how is it that you got away from them others?"

I kept myself composed, focusing my eyes and my attention straight ahead. I hate to admit it, but if I'd met Stokes's gaze at that moment chances were I would have knocked his ass right off the saddle. I relieved this urge by reminding myself that Stokes was just trying to turn the tables on me, get me riled as I'd likely riled him with my own suspicions about his pretended ignorance.

Stokes twisted the features of his grimy face while he nodded his head in thought. "Yeah, now I recollect. You said those *banditos* let you go . . . after you killed their leader."

Yep, he was really trying to get my goat, and, dammit, getting mighty close to succeeding.

Stokes then said briskly, "But then it wasn't you that killed

Ramos. It was the Mexican. Used some sorta slingshot from what I hear. Hit him squarely and killed him right dead. Like that Bible story, huh?"

"Might call it that way," I said.

Stokes came across as befuddled. "Still mighty odd that his *banditos* would just let you go free like that. Killer bunch like that. No percentage in keepin' yuh alive, the way I see it."

"Wondered that myself," I said neutrally. "But I'm here now, and I don't question whatever their motives."

"Reckon not." Stokes again scratched at the stubble on his chin. " 'Less maybe they wanted someone left alive to tell the story of Silvano Ramos's last stand."

"Could be," I said without inflection.

"Yep, mighty strange set of events," Stokes said. He exhaled. "But you was there."

"I was," I said. I turned my face toward him. "But this talk isn't getting us anywhere. Be more to our benefit if you'd just speak your piece. Ramos was then. This is now. And keep in mind that rifle I warned you about might still be aimed in your direction."

Stokes looked darkly at me. "It ain't."

"Glad to know you're so certain," I said cheerily.

"You can pry at me all that you want—you and the sheriff. There just ain't nothin' to tell."

I played along. "Like you say, you're simply riding with us on Colson's orders?"

I noticed how Stokes seemed to stiffen in the saddle.

"Weren't no orders; was a 'request,' " he corrected. "Mr. Colson's a good man. Treats me and the others fair. Pays well. He asks me a favor, I'm gonna oblige him."

"Even if it's something you don't have a particular fancy for?" I questioned.

Stokes lifted both shoulders in a deliberate gesture, the

muscles he liked to display bulging prominently under the fabric of his plaid shirt. I got his unspoken message, but I'd come across tougher hombres in my time, so I wasn't intimidated.

"Unlike you, ain't in my background to be chasin' after murderers," he said. "I'm a ranch hand, no lawman . . . or a pay-for-hire bounty hunter."

Understanding he'd intended that last description as a dig toward me, I corrected: "Witness seeker."

"Whatever you wanta call yourself. You're still huntin' people. And gettin' paid for it."

"Seeking," I again clarified. "I brought 'em back riding alongside me, not stretched over a saddle."

Stokes eyed me conspicuously. "Never had to kill no one?"

I spoke truthfully, not that Stokes was deserving of my honesty. "On occasion. But never anyone I was sent to bring back as a trial witness."

"That so?" Stokes said dubiously.

I thought back to Ed Chaney. But his death was not at my hand, and I wasn't about to elaborate on that situation. That was a long-ago memory. But then I was struck with another blow when I remembered the tragedy that had befallen my late *compañero* Francisco's sister. A girl named Felicia whom I had searched for and brought back as a witness to testify against her husband: Silvano Ramos, a brutal man but not yet the outlaw scourge he was later to become. The girl refused to speak against her husband in court, but later he still tortured and murdered her. It was the one guilt connected with my profession that could still haunt me.

"Sometimes things happen that you have no control over," I said, my cadence reflective.

I don't think Stokes accepted my vagueness as an answer. But, in a way, it served its purpose: it seemed to have put an end to his questioning. The air between us became silent. To my relief our conversation had reached an impasse.

I'd have more to talk with him about later, as would Sheriff Caldwell. For now, I was tired of his company and urged my horse forward to rejoin Caldwell.

Despite my theoretical threat to Stokes, spoken in the hope of loosening his tongue, I knew there was a possible truth to my words. If our quarry had been hiding somewhere in the foothills or perhaps deeper into the rocky borders or crevices of the lower mountains, we had to keep ourselves alert. We knew nothing about this man we sought. We did not even know how he had been traveling, how he was threading through the protection of darkness to reach his prey. That, of course, entailed some good distance and, certainly, a stealth of movement, but if he was driven by the committed purpose I suspected, he'd carry through no matter how he had to reach his destination.

And it was precisely that thinking that helped me to identify our killer: not the person as such, but his heritage. No white man in my experience would travel like that. Only the Indian possessed that kind of physical endurance and, more importantly, determined spirit. Only an Indian would best know how to traverse the land to his best advantage. They were a proud people and had proven their dedication to right the wrongs as they saw them through countless acts of aggression that only they could justify.

No, if the enemy stalking Colson's ranch were a white man, he would not be so cunning or so ruthless in his kills.

Was he watching us, following us, suspecting our purpose, and perhaps preparing an attack when the moment was right? I hadn't greatly feared the possibility of tracking a white man. But the Indian was a far more formidable adversary. They could move like shadows and attack swiftly before one could move to defend himself. And I knew the Indians in this region were mainly of the Comanche tribe, which made that threat far more dangerous.

I'd experienced trepidation many times in the past but had learned how to manage my fears. Making my journeys alone, I'd had no choice but to bolster my patience and keep tight rein on my fears. But this had suddenly become a different situation. Our enemy was skilled, both in the hunt and the kill. The Comanche had been taught, and his way of the hunt honed and practiced, through many generations. Even with us having the advantage of our number, we could not guarantee our safety from the Comanche. Further, we were on this trail with a man who knew more than he was letting on. And it was this knowledge that began to gnaw at me as we continued along our journey. I felt myself start to grow resentful of this secret that he and Rancher Ray seemed to share.

As I rode up alongside Sheriff Caldwell I muttered a single word: "Comanche."

He looked at me with an expression that went from curious to knowing.

I told him, "Our killer is a Comanche; I'm pretty damn sure of it."

Caldwell's reply surprised me. "I suspected that from the outset."

"Well, fine thing you never said anything," I said miserably.

Caldwell shrugged. "Coulda. Shoulda. But . . . well, if I said what I was thinkin' it mighta set off a whole bunch of fireworks with Colson. In fact, he would have insisted that we bring along half of his ranch on this search."

"Afraid that it might be the start of a Comanche uprising," I presumed.

"Precisely."

I couldn't argue with Caldwell's reasoning. If left to his own devices, Colson, if he even suspected an Indian was involved in whatever was stalking his ranch, might not be opposed to instigating a small-scale war to protect himself and his property. With the cowardice I'd detected protected under his outward bravado, Colson likely would be prepared not only to sacrifice me and the sheriff but maybe his whole stable of ranch hands if need be. Kind of gave me a chill to consider this possibility. Yet it also strengthened my suspicion that Rancher Ray might not just be a fearful man, but also maybe a little tetched in the head.

I mentioned my concern to the sheriff. He neither agreed or disagreed in word or expression. All he said was, "Well, at the least, Colson would have a lot to lose."

"He does now anyway . . . because, if we're right, he's got himself one hell of an enemy."

Up until that point I couldn't know that Ray Colson already suspected who that enemy was. Or that he understood why he and his ranch had been targeted for a personal attack.

What he possibly might not yet comprehend was that he could not be facing a more threatening foe.

CHAPTER FOURTEEN

We couldn't know that, while we had come to an important if not completely decisive conclusion concerning the man we were tracking, Johnny Scarface had once more embarked on his own specific course. This time his intention wasn't murder. He had something else in mind, but it was still part of the vengeance that had corrupted his soul and poisoned his mind.

He'd made his way back toward the Colson ranch, kept himself in hiding until the skies were pitch black, and then using both his sharp senses and the moonlight as his guide he emerged like a nocturnal predator from the thick brush that provided a natural southern border to Rancher Ray's spread and stealthily crept toward the main house. Since the house was so large he couldn't be sure which of the rooms was the one he was seeking, but he determined it must be upstairs. He searched about the property to ensure that he wouldn't be seen. His main focus was on the bunkhouse. There was a light emanating from the windows, and he heard laughter and loud talk coming from within. He thought it curious that the men were laughing and enjoying a good time when two of their own had not merely been killed but slaughtered and that even now the murderer might be stalking them.

Unlike the Comanche, the white man sought courage in the company of others. Alone and especially without the protection of his pistol or rifle, he was a coward and no match for an enemy born of the land and nurtured by the survival instincts of nature.

Only briefly did Johnny Scarface allow himself to recall how not so very long ago a boy named Jacquin had ventured forth from his village in an attempt to find respect both for and from the white man. But now Jacquin existed no more, and Johnny Scarface regarded each of the pale skins as an adversary, a proven enemy to him and to his people. His sympathies and understandings no longer existed.

Yet . . . as he gazed up at the second-floor windows of the rancher's house, darkened except for a single faint, flickering light that he could see behind one of the glass panes, there still remained in him compassion and a trace of humanity—if only for one. Perhaps she would not reject him. Perhaps even she might restore in him what he had hoped to establish upon entering the territory of civilization and progress. But should that fail, he would insist that she help him fulfill the final stage of his new destiny: the proud return to his bloodline.

Johnny Scarface made sure he couldn't be seen; then he dashed across the yard. He moved like a sudden blast of wind and crossed the wide expanse of property in mere seconds, stopping to brace himself against the side of the house, keeping himself secluded in the shadows. He was barely out of breath as he skillfully climbed up the sturdy, diamond-faced lattice to just above the sloping overhang and from there crawled toward the window where he had noticed the single light emanating. He peered inside. He gently tried to open the window, but it was fastened from the inside. He was not deterred. He pulled out his knife from the sheath attached to the sash he wore around his waist and carefully slid the blade under the lower frame, fiddling with the handle until he managed to snap open the latch. He pressed both palms against the glass and slowly pushed up the window, then climbed inside. He entered a long hallway, dimly lit by a kerosene lamp that rested on a wide table against the wall not far from the window. He wore no footwear, and so he made no sound as he padded across the thick carpeting, though maintaining an aggressive posture with his weapon at the ready should his presence suddenly be discovered. There were three closed doors along his way. He paused at the first door, holding his ear against the wood. His hearing was acute, as were all of his senses, and he detected breathing, a faint snoring coming from within. He determined the sound was from a man fast asleep. He allowed himself the slight tilt of a smile before moving on to the next door. Again, he listened carefully but could not hear any sound from this room. Yet he somehow, instinctively, knew this was the room he sought. He closed his fingers around the door knob and tested the door. No resistance. It was unlocked. He slowly opened the door and peered inside. The room was dark with only the flame from the hall corridor lamp casting a dull pattern of light against the inner wall, and he could not make out precisely who was inside. But there was someone lying in the big four-poster bed, a blanketed shape lifting and lowering gently and rhythmically with each inhale and exhale of breath. He took special notice of the bed. It was draped with a pink canopy with frills. There was the faint scent of perfume lingering in the air. Whoever was asleep in this room was a female. Johnny Scarface knew he had found the room he sought. He gently closed the door behind him and stepped over to the side of the bed. Now that he was close to her he recognized her, as the light of the moon filtered through the window into the room, spilling its glow over her sleeping, serene features. He took only a moment to admire her before quietly speaking her name:

"Bridget Ellen."

There was no response, and so Johnny Scarface repeated the name a little louder, to gently alert her to his presence: "Bridget Ellen."

She stirred. Her eyes fluttered; then they snapped open. She

209

was not fully awake and was startled to find an intruder in her room. Not just an intruder—but an Indian! Johnny Scarface quickly leaned over and clasped his hand over her mouth. He shushed her and spoke soothingly to calm her; to let her know she had nothing to fear from him.

"You must stay silent," he said. "I've not come to harm you."

After several moments, he could feel her body start to relax and saw the fear drain from her features, and it was then that he tentatively lifted his hand from her mouth. He took the chance that she would not scream or try to resist him.

She whispered, almost in disbelief, "Jacquin?"

She remembered, and the man who now called himself Johnny Scarface was pleased that she had not forgotten him over this passage of time. But he could no longer accept being called by *that* name, not even by the girl. Jacquin belonged to another time, long ago. Jacquin was dead.

Bridget Ellen's eyes grew wide as her gaze fell upon his scarred features, made more pronounced by the night shadows that played and shifted across his face. She wanted to turn from the disturbing sight but found that she could not look away.

"Yes," Johnny Scarface said. "My face is not how you remember it."

Bridget Ellen suddenly could not suppress a gasp.

"You look at me with revulsion," Johnny Scarface snapped.

Bridget Ellen started to maneuver her body into a sitting position, though holding the sheets tight against herself, as if for protection. There was a faint trembling in her voice when she said, "Who . . . did this to you?"

Johnny Scarface spoke forthrightly. "Men . . . who work for your father. He set them after me."

Bridget Ellen gave her head a determined shake. "No." She could not accept that her father was capable of doing such a terrible thing.

Johnny Scarface looked straight into her eyes. He understood her unwillingness to believe him, but it was imperative that she know the truth.

"Yes. It is so," he said solidly. "That day when I met you. After I left your house, I was attacked by two men who came with a warning. But a warning where mere words were not enough. They had to prove their intent by doing this." He clenched his fingers and thrust a fist against the damaged side of his face. "This is the result of your father's wrath."

"My father would never—" Bridget Ellen began to protest.

"He *did*," Johnny Scarface said sharply.

Bridget Ellen swallowed a breath and spoke in an apprehensive whisper. "Is . . . that why you came back? Is that why you're in my father's house?"

Johnny Scarface spoke to ease her alarm. "Not to hurt you."

"My father . . . ?" she said tremulously.

Johnny Scarface didn't answer. Instead he lowered his head, his body becoming unnaturally still. His reluctance to answer her question concerned the girl. While he promised her that her own life would not be threatened Bridget Ellen feared for her father, the man Jacquin blamed for his disfigurement. She had no idea what the Comanche was capable of if his blood ran so cold.

"You must not be afraid, Bridget Ellen," Johnny Scarface said to reassure her. "All I ask is for you to come with me. If you agree . . . that will be vengeance enough against your father, the uncertainty of what became of his daughter."

Bridget Ellen spoke haltingly. "Are you telling me that if I go with you my father won't be harmed?"

Johnny Scarface spoke solemnly. "That is what I'm saying."

"But . . . you can't be sure those men were sent by my father," Bridget Ellen argued in an attempt to reason with him. "Anyone on the ranch could have seen you leave that day. Because you're an Indian they—"

Johnny Scarface's mood suddenly erupted. "Foolish girl. How can you be so blind? You were there. You saw the way your father regarded me. Yes, he offered me his hospitality, but only so he could keep me in his sight while he made his plans to ensure that a Comanche would not keep company with his daughter again. I will say this: your father has a very keen eye."

Bridget Ellen cocked her head. "Keen eye?"

"Yes. The way he saw how you were with me."

Bridget Ellen considered. And then she fixed her eyes on him, her mouth agape. "I never looked at you in any such way."

Johnny Scarface was adamant. "If I did not believe that was so, I would not have risked coming here now."

Bridget Ellen shook her head determinedly. "No . . . you're wrong."

"No."

"I . . . I was just grateful to you. For what you did."

"Then if only in gratitude I ask you to come with me," Johnny Scarface urged her.

A hint of fear now crept into the girl's voice. "No. No, I . . . I can't."

Johnny Scarface's voice darkened. "Not even to prevent my revenge against your father? A man deserving of my hatred."

"You wouldn't." A slow defiance accompanied Bridget Ellen's words. Even in her uncertainty it showed that the blood of her father also flowed through her veins. "And how could you think I could go with someone who would threaten the life of my father?"

"I offer you only this one chance. You must accept, or else the consequences will be upon you."

The girl's face tightened in anger, and she spat out her words: "Get out."

Johnny Scarface looked at her with a sad, regretful expression.

"Get out!" Bridget Ellen then shouted, and she started to scream.

Johnny Scarface stood there only for a moment, unsure of what to do. With the little humanity still existing in him he did not want to harm the girl. But his options were few—and slim. Should he rush from the room before he could be discovered by whoever else was in the household—including the girl's father? But he knew it was probably too late. And suddenly he felt overcome by a rage. He had given this girl the opportunity to spare her father, and she denied him. He now knew that he had been wrong to think that the girl cared for him. His emotions had allowed him to be perceived as a fool in her eyes. Emotions he instantly declared would no longer blind him to the truth of his spirit—of who he was.

He was no longer in possession of himself, and, with the screams of Bridget Ellen ringing in his ears and surely echoing throughout the house, he reacted instinctively. With only moments remaining before the door to the bedroom would burst open, he flung himself atop the girl and with all of his strength clasped his hand over her mouth and nose and pressed hard, holding firm while he felt her writhe and struggle beneath him. Her fight against him didn't take long. Her body convulsed in a final spasm, then her eyes fluttered, widened, casting their final vision upon the face of Johnny Scarface before the light was extinguished forever.

Footsteps hurried down the hallway. There was only the one way out for him, and that was the window in her room through which the soft glow of moonlight spread a peaceful radiance over a tragic scene.

He thrust himself from the bed and threw his body whole and hard through the glass, hearing and feeling the window shatter while he rolled down the sloping overhang, plummeting the lengthy distance to the ground below, his body landing with a dull thud against the earth. He'd tried to protect his fall by forcing most of the impact upon his shoulder but was still struck by a lightning bolt of pain throughout his upper body. He rolled over several times and managed to pull himself to his feet and break into a swift run, even as he heard voices shout at him through the broken window, ordering him to stop.

He later claimed that far into the distance he heard the haunting wail of Ray Colson as he discovered the dead body of his daughter.

While Johnny Scarface might have believed himself to be unharmed while making his escape, he had sustained injuries. Shattering shards of glass had left gashes and piercings in his flesh, along with less obvious wounds caused by the crushing force of his fall. Once more he must have gone off to his private and perhaps sacred location, where he could summon the spiritual ways of the Comanche to cleanse as well as recover from his wounds.

What we as his trackers didn't know was that it was miles away from where we'd been searching for him.

CHAPTER FIFTEEN

We were making no progress in our search. Hours of monotonous travel were beginning to wear on the nerves of Jim Stokes. Neither the sheriff nor myself let up on him much. The more we badgered him, the more we could see his resistance start to crumble. He was a stubborn cuss, though, whether that was out of some loyalty to Ray Colson or something he was sheltering for his own well-being. My guess was it was a little of both. When we'd camp out for the night he'd quickly wolf down his supper, then go off by himself. We wouldn't see him again 'til sunup. As difficult as he was making it on us, keeping his jaws locked must have been doubly hard on him. A man's conscience is a tricky thing, whether he's protecting himself or trying to shield someone else. As a witness seeker, often my most effective weapon in getting someone to ride back with me was to put a little nudge on one's conscience. This was particularly effective when it was a murder case, and just a few words in front of a judge and jury could free someone who otherwise was headed for a slow walk to the gallows. And it worked the other way when a murderer stood the chance of walking clean away with the opportunity to kill again, and the conscience of a witness had to be prodded to ensure that situation would never happen. Either way, most people didn't welcome the stain of blood on their souls.

But trying to penetrate the conscience of Jim Stokes was proving to be a difficult task. There were moments when I got the feeling he wanted to free himself of this burden he was carrying, but rather than surrender his secret he'd revert to his rough-hewn personality and propose that we might do better just to head back, try to pick up a new trailhead. And while his suggestion had less to do with practicality than his wanting just to be rid of Caldwell and myself, that was becoming the most reasonable decision, since it was evident the man we sought had *not* taken refuge in the mountains.

Sheriff Caldwell stepped over to me as I was going through the routine of unpacking gear from my horse for our nightly campout. He looked about as frustrated as I felt and as bone-tired as the rest of us. I could predict by the expression on his face what he was going to say.

"We're wastin' time and wastin' Ray Colson's money," he said in a mutter.

"Last thing that concerns me is his money," I said in return. I added in a sigh, "But I agree this time could be better spent."

"Ain't ready to give up," Caldwell then announced with a fiery determination that was downright admirable. "Failed once in my duty—when we went after Ramos. As long as I'm wearin' this badge, that ain't gonna happen ag'in."

"Well, don't be blaming yourself for this run, Sheriff," I told him encouragingly. "If we'd gotten a little cooperation, we mighta found ourselves moving in the right direction."

I peered over at Jim Stokes, hurrying to finish his canned supper and soon to walk off for his nightly departure. "Reckon we could beat it out of him," I said, my words along with my intention spoken only half-seriously.

Caldwell smiled. "Idea's crossed my mind more'n once." He drew a breath. "But since that ain't gonna happen so long as I'm legally bound by this tin star, I say we turn in and come morning start back."

It was the sensible thing to do under the circumstances. But I still couldn't hide my discouragement. I wasn't doubting my own abilities as a seeker, though admittedly they had long been dormant. I'd just been working with a handicap—two men who were holding back information, neither of whom would offer up what he knew for fear of incriminating himself in some incident that still remained a mystery.

Sheriff Caldwell could read into my disappointment, and now he took it upon himself to make *me* feel better. "Don't care how good you might be as a seeker, Gambel. Can't find a man who's not there. 'Sides, we just took a shot in the dark that he'd head into these hills. We didn't choose bad, just chose wrong."

I knew that Stokes would not be upset with our decision to head back. Before chowing down my own grub, I sought him out before he could do his vanishing act into the night. It was actually a quite pleasant evening. I'd watched the moon rise over the mountains, appearing as a bright silvery crescent, and the air had the soft, cool caress of velvet. Yeah, I thought almost wistfully, if this were just a plain campout, resting by a warm fire, eating and just enjoying the open and the quiet, it would be a mighty fine night.

I told Stokes what we were planning, and sure enough whatever tension he'd been carrying seemed to evaporate like sweat under the desert sun.

Still, I made one last effort to reason with him. "Think you know your boss is going to be disappointed we're coming back empty-handed."

He maintained his know-nothing attitude. "I was asked just to ride along and keep watch. Finding this fella was your job."

"Which you mighta made a whole lot easier."

Stokes lowered his head and gave it a wag. Then he reached into his shirt pocket for his tobacco pouch and papers and began building himself a cigarette.

I tried another angle. "Reckon it wouldn't do much good if I gave you my word that whatever you'd tell me would stay between us."

Stokes looked at me askance, his mouth twisted in a snide smile. Then he matched and lighted his cigarette, taking a slow, contented drag and blowing out a smooth stream of smoke, watching intently as it dissipated into the night. The son of a bitch was letting me know that, despite my "friendly" efforts to coax the truth from him, I hadn't accomplished spit. But I wasn't ready to surrender. In fact, I was more determined than ever to find some way to puncture that smarmy arrogance. In a way, this had become personal. I discovered I was still a poor loser when it came to accepting defeat of my professional skills, which, like it or not, were still a part of who I was. And I was sure that, short of either of us beating the bejesus out of Stokes, I could count on the sheriff's assistance on this last call. But there was no point in trying to coax anything out of Stokes now.

I'd have to reload and ready myself for a second course of action. In the meantime, we'd head back to the Colson ranch come morning and work a new strategy. This time we'd start our trail by attempting to enforce more effective persuasion. And on this ride Rancher Ray wouldn't have to persuade us to take Jim Stokes along. We would welcome his joining us.

CHAPTER SIXTEEN

The news that greeted us once we rode onto Rancher Ray's property was grim and unexpected. We weren't met by Colson but one of his ranch hands, a fellow named Joshua, who halted our progress into his yard with a raised hand. The look on his face was grave, and he chose to speak not to the sheriff or myself but directly to Jim Stokes. Stokes leaned forward in the saddle.

"What's up, Josh?" he asked his fellow worker.

"Bad news."

I braced myself in preparation for learning that another killing had been committed. Another of Colson's ranch workers had been murdered.

But it was worse than that.

The victim was Ray Colson's daughter, Bridget Ellen. My first reaction, though I struggled to hold it in check, was anger. I could have succumbed to a feeling of guilt, as well, but I knew that the girl's death wasn't my responsibility any more than it belonged to Sheriff Caldwell or the two deputies. While we'd been scouting useless territory with a man who obviously knew more than he was willing to reveal, stalling what otherwise could have been a productive search, a young girl had been murdered—a killing that might have been prevented had Colson or Stokes been up-front with us. Letting loose of their secret might have assisted us and just maybe could have saved the life of Colson's daughter. It might have led us in a direction we could have more profitably followed—to a better identification of the man we were tracking; something that was more substantial than just chasing a shadow.

What happened was a tragedy, true, but the guilt of it had to lie squarely on the conscience of the girl's father.

The man named Joshua glanced at all of us and offered an obvious comment. "Reckon you didn't have much luck."

The sheriff met him with a penetrating stare. It was a remark Caldwell would not expend the energy to respond to. All he said, gruffly, was, "Let us ride through."

Joshua stepped away so that we could pass. Five of us—a solemn procession.

Ray Colson was waiting for us in the main room. We found him sitting in the big, overstuffed armchair that was moved close to the fireplace. The deputies stayed by the door while Stokes, the sheriff, and I stood around Colson in a semi-circle, none of us speaking. Colson seemed to be absorbing the warmth emanating from the fire, even though the air outside was neither cold nor chilly. He was holding a snifter of brandy that looked as if it hadn't been touched. He just sat with his hand slowly swirling the amber liquid in a languid, empty gesture. There was a numb, vacant look in his eyes. He was grieving, but while I felt for his daughter, where Colson was concerned, I could feel little compassion. His pride, arrogance, and stubbornness had brought this misfortune onto himself. I was disgusted, but I was not defeated. I wasn't going to walk away from the man. I'd committed myself to a professional obligation. But if he wanted my help he now had to lay it on the line. I assumed the same condition applied to Sheriff Caldwell.

Colson's faraway mood suggested that he hardly even knew we were in the room with him. It was the sheriff who finally spoke to bring attention to us, but his words were less heartfelt than dutiful.

"Sorry to learn 'bout your daughter," he said, his voice toneless.

It was then that Colson responded in a way no one could have expected.

Without lifting his eyes, he muttered, "She brought it on herself."

Caldwell and I looked at each other, our gazes meeting almost spontaneously. Our expressions reflected our bewilderment. A quick glance at Jim Stokes relayed to me that he might be the only one who understood what Colson meant by his insensitive statement.

Insensitive. Maybe even cruel . . . but looking beyond, I saw that his words perhaps might provide a needed clue.

Caldwell erased any last fragment of doubt I might have had regarding his association with Rancher Ray when he blasted the man straight on. "Your daughter's dead, Colson. Don't that matter a damn to you?"

"What more do you want from me?" Colson said, squeezing out his words. Despite his harsh tone his anguish seemed genuine. But the sheriff, to his credit, was relentless.

"He just killed your daughter, just as he murdered your two ranch hands. And who's gonna be next? You likely. Or maybe he has more surprises in mind and might be savin' you for last. Sure, the main course. There's a reason why he's come after you, and you damn well know what it is."

As frustrating as it was for us, you almost had to admire Ray Colson for his tenacity. I'd met a lot of hard cases in my travels but never one so damn mule stubborn as this man. He either wasn't listening or simply chose to shut out all that the sheriff was thrusting at him. In either case, he steadfastly refused to acknowledge what he knew was the truth. Or, maybe now that his daughter was dead, he simply ceased to care. The man looked about as beaten as I'd ever seen any human being. Yet, his comment regarding Bridget Ellen continued to pull at my curiosity.

I looked over again at Jim Stokes. It was hard to tell by his expression what he was feeling. He wasn't a man too quick to open his emotions (unless you started to corner him, when he'd reveal a cantankerous side), but I sensed that he had some sense of compassion for his boss. But just as it was for Colson, it was a little late for sympathy or regret, though maybe this killing of Bridget Ellen might encourage Stokes to climb over to our side of the fence. The look I gave Stokes urged him to come clean and give us what we needed to know to halt this killing spree. For a moment, I felt optimistic. He met my stare, and I noticed that he seemed to be in a struggle with himself . . .

And then he swiftly turned his face away. It was hard not to grow discouraged. Nothing mattered to these men. Neither Colson nor Stokes seemed to care enough for what might be a threat to their lives. Bridget Ellen's murder likewise made no difference. Her death was acknowledged only in a father's grief, nothing more. All that seemed important was that they keep their damn secret.

If they didn't care, why should I? Frankly, pride in my profession or not, I was fed up. Let them deal with the consequences of their actions.

I turned and said to Sheriff Caldwell, "No point in my staying here. I've got a family to get back to." But I had to get in a final dig, which I directed at Colson: "A family I care about."

Caldwell looked at me, his expression vacant, and then he nodded under his wide Stetson.

"Probably for the best," he said.

Ray Colson finally appeared to reclaim some of his wits and spoke as he lifted himself from the chair. "Wait a minute." It was a typical command, though his voice had lost much of its authoritative timbre.

I obliged him. Colson seemed winded, his breath coming in spurts. He plunked his snifter down on the table next to his chair and exhaled a number of times. His attitude suggested that he was engaged in a conflict with himself, as if wanting to come forward yet still resisting that urge to do what was right. And then I saw him lift his face and turn his heavy-browed eyes toward Jim Stokes. The quick look the two men exchanged was significant. There could be no more pretending.

With a tired wave of his hand Colson gestured for the four of us to take a seat, the first time he had ever invited us to do so inside his fancy home. Caldwell and I sat next to each other on the couch. Brad Calhern and Logan Malone remained standing against the far wall, with Calhern once more paying particular attention to whatever was inside his shoulder sack. I admit I was starting to get a mite curious about its contents, as it seemed that whatever was in there held more interest for him than what really should have been his focus.

Colson went to pour himself a fresh drink—a half tumbler of rye whiskey, a beverage more appropriate to his temperament—which he did not offer to any of us, including his man Stokes. He downed the whiskey in one swift swallow. He seemed to debate pouring himself another glass but instead pushed the tumbler aside.

"You suspected from the beginning that I mighta known what's been behind all this," he said, avoiding meeting any of us directly in the eye. "Since it don't matter no more, I'll be up-front with yuh." His expression went fierce, yet it appeared as if that sudden intensity was intended for himself. " 'Cause no worse can be done to me than what's already been done."

In the next instant, he appeared almost to collapse in on himself. The big bear-like man with the brusque, intimidating manner gave the appearance of someone willing to walk into a bullet to end his pain.

Before he could say more, Stokes spoke up. His eyes twitched in the sallow complexion of his face, and his voice sounded reedy and anxious. "Make sure it's somethin' you wanta be tellin' 'em, Mr. Colson."

Colson smiled bleakly. "You don't gotta be worryin' none, Jim," he assured his man. That statement immediately aroused my interest, because what I determined with a practiced ear adept at picking up subtleties was that, while Stokes surely had an involvement in whatever had provoked these killings, his participation would not be divulged—at least not by Rancher Ray. In short, his boss would protect him.

Stokes still looked uncertain. The tip of his tongue traced across his upper lip in a quick, nervous gesture.

"Maybe he's done all that he's gonna do . . . now that he . . . well, with my daughter . . ." Colson said, his words failing him.

"Who's this 'he' you're talkin' 'bout?" Sheriff Caldwell asked. His words came impatiently. As a lawman, he understood that the longer Colson stalled the more difficult it would be for us to get back on the trail—the correct trail. With the girl's murder happening the night just prior, her killer might still be nearby. Therefore, time was of the essence.

"An Indian," Colson blurted, his rheumy eyes suddenly wide with emotion. "I'm sure it's gotta be him. No one else would have reason to—"

Stokes jumped in before the man could finish. "Mr. Colson, I'm tellin' yuh it's better if'n you—"

"Now you shut up, Jim," Colson thundered, looking mean-eyed at his ranch hand. "You're outta this now."

The sheriff stood up quickly. "What do you mean by 'out of it,' Colson?"

"Mr. Colson—" Stokes started to object.

But Rancher Ray appeared to have made his decision. He regarded Stokes with a regretful look, then said, "Jim, it ain't no use. We both gotta answer for this 'fore anyone else gets hurt."

I readied myself for a long overdue admission and noticed how the sheriff kept a careful eye on Stokes. The atmosphere in the room was tense, and the way Stokes was behaving it seemed that at any moment he might try to prevent his boss from saying whatever he was about to. Even from where I was sitting I could see an angry vein standing out on Stokes's forehead. I couldn't be sure, but it almost seemed as if it were throbbing.

Stokes had started to fidget, at first attempting to steady himself by building a cigarette, but his precision was off, and he finally flung the paper and loose tobacco aside. He then started to pace. I kept my eyes fastened on how his left hand kept dropping toward his waist, the fingers dancing around his holster. I didn't like what I felt was coming and decided it best to prevent what could turn into a desperate if not deadly maneuver on his part. I waited until Stokes walked over near to where I was sitting—then I made my move. I leaped up from the couch and tackled him sideways, both of us falling to the floor. Almost at once his hand tried to make a grab for his .44, but I twisted his arm with my own arm while the fingers of my free hand closed around the revolver and pulled it loose from the holster. Gun in hand, I scrambled to my feet and took a few steps back, dropping the weapon to my side.

Colson looked at Stokes in astonishment. "Jim, you damn fool . . ."

Stokes's eyes glinted coldly. His breathing was heavy, not from exhaustion but emanating from a tightening rage. "Awright, so you got my piece, witness seeker." He twisted his face toward Colson and spoke with vehemence, making it clear that all bets were off. If Colson wanted to come clean, fine. It was every man for himself.

He spat saliva as he spoke. While his eyes were fixed on Colson, the intention of his words was aimed at Caldwell and myself. "All I'm gonna say is I ain't goin' down for this. I was just followin' Colson's orders. He didn't want that Indian makin' time with his precious daughter, so's he told me and Dawkins to make sure he'd never show his face around here ag'in. And, sure 'nuff, that's just what we did. Was just followin' orders."

The sheriff and I turned our gaze toward Colson. He just stood there, no protest, no denial, but the truth came through loud and clear in his long silence.

"Ain't that so, Rancher Ray?" Stokes shouted mockingly at Colson.

A deep sadness looked to come over Colson.

"Whyn't yuh tell 'em what me and Dawkins did to that Injun?" Stokes prodded. "No? Well, I'll tell 'em. You say they got a right to know, so I'll be the one to tell 'em." He started to pick himself off the floor. I tossed his gun to the sheriff, who deftly caught it in mid-air and laid it on a side table.

"We carved him up," Stokes confessed, at first expressing himself with a sort of sadistic glee, and then, once reason overcame him and he studied the cold stares of the sheriff and myself and even the deputies, his attitude became slightly less aggressive. But it didn't matter; he'd spoken his piece, and the truth had been addressed.

Caldwell said to Stokes, "And this Indian is the one you think has been responsible for what's happened here?"

"Likely 'nuff candidate, wouldn't yuh think?" Stokes answered.

CHAPTER SEVENTEEN

Stokes's confession confirmed for us that our killer was a Comanche, one who had been beaten and disfigured by Stokes and George Dawkins on orders given by Ray Colson. Now we just had to determine who he was.

Colson offered nothing more. Jim Stokes was talking for him, and doing a fair job even if all we could solidly get from him was that the Comanche was not a man, but a boy. And for once I believed Stokes really didn't know anything more.

Still, it didn't answer the question why this Comanche had entered the house to murder the girl. If he was seeking revenge, why didn't he attack Colson, the man directly responsible for his blood rage? From what I understood about the Comanche, it was not in his nature to seek vengeance by harming someone close to the person who had wronged him. According to their culture, the carrier of the spear would also be the one to suffer the penalty. Yet that didn't explain why the Comanche had killed the second ranch hand, who seemed to have had no connection to the assault against him.

But the terrible deeds had been committed, and two innocent people were dead—three, as I was later to find out, for I did not know at the time the details behind the murder of the Lone Creek storekeeper. I felt particularly distressed that Bridget Ellen had paid for her father's crime. I felt no pity toward Ray Colson, just disgust. His violent prejudice had turned a boy into a killer. I'd learned enough to recognize these disturbing qualities in the man. Even with what I perceived to be his genuine sorrow, I had to contain myself from throwing a punch at him.

But I felt no such restraint with Jim Stokes, his henchman.

I spoke solidly to the sheriff while my eyes burned holes into Stokes. "You'd best put the cuffs on me, Sheriff. Because whether Stokes here tells us anything or not, I'm about ready to send him to Boot Hill."

Caldwell simply shrugged, much to my appreciation.

"A man's gotta do what he feels he has to," he said, sucking a tooth.

I started to unbuckle my gun belt.

Stokes turned to the sheriff with panicked eyes. Physically he could have pounded me into the dirt on any given day. But today he knew I had the upper hand. He saw that I had let loose the reins on my temper, and when a man is pumped that full of anger, he becomes a formidable adversary regardless of the size and strength of his opponent.

Knowing he wouldn't get any support from the sheriff, Stokes looked desperately at the two deputies, Calhern and Malone, who paid him not the slightest mind. Ray Colson likewise wasn't about to involve himself.

I walked with deliberate steps toward Stokes. Then, allowing him just a moment to prepare himself, I lunged into him, the impact thrusting him backward, his big body crashing against the wall, rattling the paintings hanging above. His head lolled, and he sagged, and I grabbed his shoulders with both hands and pulled him upright. He was dazed, but that didn't stop me. If I gave him the chance to defend himself, the tables might have turned. I had to maintain my advantage by holding onto pure fury. I grasped him by the hair with one hand and tossed several hard blows into his belly with my fist, each punch blasting the air out of him. I don't know how many times I hit him, only that I felt a satisfaction each time my fist connected with his gut. It was a release of the rage I felt upon learning of the death of the girl along with the lies and resistance I had endured from Stokes during our wasted journey into the mountains. While I understood there could be no guarantees, if Stokes had fessed up once we started our ride, things could have turned out differently. We might not have captured the killer, but there was a chance the girl might still be alive.

I heard Caldwell say, "All right Gambel, think you've taken it far 'nuff."

One last solid punch to Stokes's gut, and then I released my grip, and he slid to the floor, holding his belly and writhing in agony.

Caldwell walked over next to me, observed the groaning and moaning Stokes, and nodded approvingly. "Reckon I could arrest you for this, if'n I had a mind to," he said rather leisurely.

I was a little winded from my effort and waited to catch my breath. Then I said, "Reckon you could."

"Yep, officially it's my duty," Caldwell added with an exaggerated sigh. He patted my shoulder and said, "We'll discuss it later."

I gave a slight smile.

But we'd wasted enough time. It was time for us to start back on the search.

Before we left the room, Colson spoke. All he said was, "He was headed south."

The sheriff and I halted, turned to him.

"After he killed my Bridget Ellen . . . I looked through the window and saw that he was running south. Likely up into the brush."

"That means he may be traveling on foot," Caldwell said to me.

I nodded. "That would be a break."

"That's where Dawson and me left him," Stokes finally

admitted, hitching his breath.

"Where he was meant to lay down and die," I said with a glower to Stokes.

"No, we never meant to kill him," Stokes said in protest. "That wasn't what—"

"Maybe not, but if you had, I doubt it would have weighed too heavily on your conscience," I remarked.

"You're a son of a bitch," Caldwell sneered. "You coulda told us this at the start. Instead you led us on a wild goose chase—killing time that just mighta saved that girl."

Stokes cast a glance at Ray Colson, who just stood there with his jaws clamped tight. "It . . . it just came to me now," Stokes said miserably.

But by now we'd all stopped listening to him.

"Sure, makes sense, him hiding in the wilds. Yet close 'nuff for him to keep watch on the grounds," Caldwell said in consideration. "Still a lot of area where he could protect himself."

"And maybe in a defensive position where he could watch us coming for him," I added. "Crossing all the open ground between us and that brush, he could start picking us off before we got even a hundred yards from those woods."

Caldwell furrowed his brow. "Which might also mean he's seen us come out here to the ranch. If so, he likely suspects our purpose. Yeah, Gambel, that's a worry. Lot of brush cover south of here. Could be anywhere, in hiding but watching. Redskins are cagey. He sees us start in his direction, and it'll be either fight or flight. And if it's fight, we're gonna be the ones at a disadvantage."

I nodded grimly.

"There's one more thing you gotta think 'bout," Stokes said. "That brush is thick, oftentimes hard to make passage even by foot. You do make it in there without first gettin' picked off, ain't gonna be easy trackin' him on horseback."

Caldwell ambled over to Stokes and smiled crookedly. "You mean *we*, don't yuh, Stokes?"

Stokes's lower jaw unhinged. He looked desperately at Colson for some sort of support, but Rancher Ray had a desolate air about him, lost in his own little corner of hell.

"You ain't done with this yet," Caldwell informed Stokes. "I got it in my power to arrest you on a whole number of charges. Colson, too. Ain't decided 'bout him yet. But you, Stokes—you confessed to a crime . . . and what if this Indian *is* dead? I don't care if he's a Comanche. Still murder in my eyes. 'Course, since it was a Comanche, I don't have to do a thing to you. Go to trial, and it'd be just your account for the court to hear. He coulda attacked yuh without provocation, and you were just defending yourself. But we know that ain't what happened. So me and Gambel and my two deputies here would have to tell what we know." He paused to take a breath. I was enjoying watching the sweat bead up on Stokes's greasy forehead.

"Yeah, you're comin' along," Caldwell said, his words final.

Stokes swallowed, looked about the room into a bunch of stern faces. "Reckon . . . reckon I am," he said weakly.

Caldwell gave him a deliberately sunny smile. "Knew you'd see it my way. Now you can get your butt on the saddle and take us straight to where this little incident happened."

We were set to go. We left Colson alone in the house to deal with his guilt, and we started toward our horses. It wouldn't be easy because, as Stokes explained it, once we reached the woodlands we'd have to negotiate a narrow, wooded trail, which meant slow and careful riding and where, at some point, we would probably be forced off our mounts and have to carry on by foot. If the Indian had indeed taken refuge in the woods, it was surely to discourage pursuit.

As we were readying our mounts I heard what sounded like a

faint, muted cry. It came from where Brad Calhern was standing. At first I thought it must have been some small yard critter belonging to Rancher Ray. But no. My attention was drawn toward the shoulder sack that Calhern always kept close to him. I noticed that there seemed to be movement coming from within the canvas.

There was something alive inside that sack.

Caldwell muttered, "What the hell you got in there, Brad?"

Calhern didn't answer; he was too busy trying to calm and control whatever it was that looked to be struggling to get out.

The sheriff and I already suspected. We shared an amused glance.

"Angel, *shhhh*," Calhern was saying in a soothing tone.

And then a furry little gray head popped out of the opening. A kitten. Now that his secret was revealed, Calhern looked a little embarrassed.

The sheriff turned to Logan Malone. "Malone, did you know 'bout this?"

Malone just shrugged and gave a slow wag of his massive head.

Well, now I'd seen just about everything. A big, tough, two-fisted Texas Ranger caring for a kitten he called Angel.

"Don't like to leave her behind," Calhern explained, rather meekly. He pulled the tiny hairball out of the sack and nuzzled her furry body against his cheek. It was a rather odd if touching scene.

"Well . . . that's your choice, I reckon," Caldwell said, drawing his Stetson up over his brow. "Just don't forget to keep your mind on your duty."

We had enjoyed our moment of levity, but now it was time for us to get back to work. I gazed as deeply as I could into the proliferation of trees and vegetation to our south and blew out a breath that attracted the sheriff. Caldwell stepped over, his left fist pressed against his hip in a determined stance.

"Ain't gonna be no easier than huntin' for him in those mountains," he observed. Then he let out a sigh. "Probably a whole lot tougher."

I didn't reply. With the exception of Jim Stokes, we had a good team, but, as I'd expressed, we'd be meeting our quarry on *his* ground, where *his* blood had been spilled. It was an area familiar to him, where he had allowed his hatred to fester. I knew with a certainty that a Comanche who had committed murder against a white man would never be taken alive. He would sooner fight to the death than be taken in shackles to face our justice.

But as I secured the cinch of my saddle I contemplated another justice. I had turned to the sheriff to ask him if he intended to later arrest Ray Colson when my question was answered not by Caldwell . . . but by Colson himself.

The report of a gunshot came from inside the house.

CHAPTER EIGHTEEN

Ray Colson was dead. He'd put a pistol to the side of his head and pulled the trigger. I reckon his sorrow—or maybe his guilt—had been too much to bear. Still, I wouldn't have considered Rancher Ray the type of man to take his own life. His death had no personal meaning to me, but it did carry its own significance. He set himself free from whatever torment he was carrying. Yet I was left with a more practical consideration. How would I now be paid the balance owed me? I then learned something even more distressing from Caldwell who, I reckon in fairness, approached me, pulled me aside, and spoke with a deliberate attempt at discretion. He told me that, before I agreed to go any further on this manhunt, I needed to know that Calhern and Malone were set for the same fee as myself—with one major difference. They both had insisted not on partial payment, as had I, but that the whole amount—one thousand dollars—be paid up front. And Colson had agreed.

I couldn't have been slapped any harder with a bullwhip. While I tried not to show any reaction, that effort lasted maybe five seconds. I had sold my services for five hundred dollars. Oh, I understood that every penny was necessary for my family . . . but the tragic truth was that, with Colson dead, *I had been paid in full.* Caldwell just kept looking at me, saying nothing, trying to determine by his probing expression what my next decision would be. He knew I had no further obligation to Colson. He was dead, and I'd been cheated. As far as I was concerned, I'd already earned my five hundred dollars. The sheriff had his own obligation to go on with the search, courtesy of his tin star; the two deputies who thus far really had contributed little still could earn their pay by continuing on with Caldwell, and deal with whatever the consequences. But if I chose I could return home to J.C. and my daughters with a clean conscience. I'd done my part.

Only it wasn't quite that simple . . .

The sheriff put it to me point-blank. "You callin' it quits, Gambel?"

I didn't answer, though what he likely perceived as my answer had to be evident by my expression.

Caldwell lowered his head and spoke just as lowly. "Given these circumstances no one could rightly blame yuh."

"Never wanted to come back to this, you know that," I said.

The sheriff nodded and spoke with self blame. "Well, guess now I regret ever goin' along with Colson, talkin' you into comin' along. No, it ain't fair."

I nudged my head toward Brad Calhern, open in his affection with his kitten now that his furry friend had been exposed to all of us. Then I turned to Jim Stokes, as always standing at a distance from us, looking miserable and more than a little uncertain. I figured I could understand that. He owed nothing more to his boss. But Sheriff Caldwell made it plain that he still had use for him, and Stokes had no choice but to comply unless he wanted to spend a long time inside a jail cell.

Caldwell gave a slight lift of his shoulder and offered an understanding smile. "You got a family to be gettin' back to. Of all of us . . . well, Gambel, you're a lucky man."

"Not married?" I asked him, absently.

"Was," Caldwell said.

He spoke his single word abruptly, tightly, indicating that he didn't want to discuss the subject. That was his privilege, and I wasn't about to pry.

"Well, no point in stallin', Gambel," Caldwell said.

"Yeah." But before I could take my leave my eyes were drawn to that distant wooded ridge that sat upon the bluff, a barricade of tall trees . . . and I ruminated on what menace might be lurking deep within that brush.

"Gambel?" Caldwell said again.

I turned to look at him. I was quiet for what seemed a long while but was probably just several seconds. Then I squared my shoulders and said, "My mistake, Sheriff, was ever agreeing to this in the first place. I'm not a witness seeker anymore. Gave that up after . . . well, after Ramos. But it all kinda came back to me on this business with Colson." I drew a breath. "Can't say I held a perfect record as a witness seeker . . . sometimes came back empty handed. Situations that I couldn't change for whatever reason, people being what they are. But dammit, I never turned back from a job that I didn't at least try to finish."

The sheriff seemed pleased—even as he tried not to show it.

"Might still be able to work out the money that's owin' to yuh," he said.

"Money would be good," I said back to him. "But as a man who's done what he's done for a lotta years, hanging on to a pretty damn fine record of accomplishment means just about as much as what you pack in your pay pouch."

"Can't quite let go of it, can yuh?" Caldwell said.

I replied with a smile. I wasn't about to answer him outright.

"So?" Caldwell prodded gently.

And that was the question. Sure, I was torn in my decision. How much easier it would be for me just to hop onto my horse and ride back into Chesterfield City. I knew we could somehow make do with the five hundred I'd handed J.C. It would require some careful bookkeeping, but my wife was adept at handling finances. Her skill at managing dollars and cents was admirable and had kept us afloat longer than should have been possible. The irony was there was a time I could spend five hundred dollars on one of my post-assignment excursions into Mexico and think nothing of it. Liquor, whores . . . Whittle down the money with little recollection of doing so, outside of the occasional hangover.

But now I had responsibilities, and that money seemed like a pauper's fortune. So, do I chance risking my life and my family's welfare by continuing on to satisfy my pride—for no extra pay?

These thoughts kept twisting and spinning around in my brain as if I were caught up in a whirlwind.

The damn funny part was that, struggle as I might, I'd already made my decision.

CHAPTER NINETEEN

"Tough, ain't it?" came the voice of Jim Stokes, recovered sufficiently from his beating to start riling me again to restore whatever remained of his questionable dignity. "As I told yuh before, huntin' humans for pay . . . Pay which you ain't gonna get now."

Caldwell spoke directly to me, halting me before I could respond in whatever fashion I had a mind to.

"Let it go," he advised. He turned to Stokes and spoke on my behalf. "Don't know what it is you got ag'in Gambel, but count yourself damn lucky he ain't backed outta this, even though it's his right to do so, 'specially now." It was here that he kind of exaggerated the facts. " 'Cause I don't know if any of us would be following this trail without him. And if that were so, Stokes, just 'bout now, I'd be cartin' your ass off to jail."

"Yeah, well I still figger you ain't got nothin' ag'in me but what I told yuh," Stokes said smugly. "And, for all you know, I might just have been sayin' that. Heck, Colson sure as hell can't say nothin' now."

Caldwell drew a weary breath. "The thing 'bout you, Stokes, is that you twist 'round like a wrangler's lasso. But in any case, I got 'nuff corroboration to your confession to lock you up for a mite pretty while."

That shut the big mouth up pretty fast. Only my fist addressing his jaw would have brought a quicker result.

I took another gander up into the density of the woods nesting atop the bluff through which we'd soon be traveling—any part of which could prove a perfect spot for a Comanche ambush.

"Let's see this through," I said with finality.

There were two corpses inside that big house that were shrouded in bed sheets and taken to rest inside the parlor. Caldwell instructed one of the servants to load both bodies onto the back of a buckboard and transport them to the undertaker in Chesterfield City, who would prepare the bodies for burial. We'd likely be deep into our search by that time, so whatever funeral arrangements would be made were of no concern to us. My worry was that J.C. would certainly learn of these deaths, and, not knowing any other details, this might send her thoughts off in a worrisome direction. To prevent that I told the servant entrusted with this task to drop in at the old newspaper office and let J.C. know that I was fine.

"We got a good piece of ground to cover," Caldwell announced as he gazed out toward the southern rim.

It was interesting to study the faces of these men. Caldwell was confident; Malone, sturdy and prepared to face whatever awaited him; likewise, Calhern, once he calmed his gray kitten and got her snuggled back inside his shoulder sack. Jim Stokes looked tense and embittered. For myself . . . well, I'd been given the opportunity to say *adios* to this venture yet decided to carry on. I hoped for a positive outcome. But if worse came to worst, I had only myself to blame for the consequences.

The woods and whatever they held beckoned. Without further delay we urged our horses into step and started off on what each of us hoped would lead to a successful outcome.

It certainly would not result in a particularly profitable financial outcome—at least where I was concerned.

Stokes was right. The brush was thick, the pathways narrow and tight, littered with thick patches of weeds and fallen branches most likely broken off by the windstorms frequent to these parts, and difficult to navigate our horses through. Trees were plentiful, and both the bare branches and the foliage were tough to avoid; even on foot we frequently had to keep our heads bent and lowered to maneuver through what seemed like a forest maze. Our trek was doubly difficult with our heights raised on the saddles, and none of us could be called a small man.

We were following Stokes, who was leading us in a single-file formation toward where he and his cohort had ambushed the Indian named Jacquin. Or so he told us. Frankly, I didn't much trust anything that came out of his mouth. We really had no way of knowing for certain where he was taking us, and I even had the feeling he might be waiting until we were far enough in and maybe the skies would be growing dark, and then he'd attempt to make a break. Hell, with Rancher Ray dead he had no reason to stay with us, except the promise of a jail cell if he failed to follow through with the bargain he'd made with Sheriff Caldwell. Or, more precisely, the strict condition Caldwell had made.

I'd never let go of the harshness I held toward Stokes; in fact, it seemed that as we proceeded deeper into this wilderness the negative feelings I had for him continued to fester. As much as I wanted to throw another fist into him, there would be no advantage to doing so except to satisfy my own hostility. As our horses tramped through the dense underbrush, I paced my mount until we entered a clearing wide enough for our two animals to ride a distance alongside each other. As I expected, Stokes regarded me with distaste.

For several moments I said nothing. It was quiet except for the twigs and branches cracking under the hooves of our horses.

"Y'sure you remember where it all happened, Jim?" I then said to him.

He gave me a searching look, suspicious of my friendly familiarity, calling him by his given name.

He hissed his words so that only I would hear them. "Don't start rilin' me ag'in. I'm warnin' yuh. I'm ready for yuh this time, Gambel."

I ignored his attempt at a threat. "Just gotta be hard knowing what you did cost all these people their lives," I said, speaking easily.

I could feel the tension flowing from Stokes. A quick glance at him, and I saw how his jaws had locked, his lips tightened.

"Wanta take a swing at me, Stokes?" I said in a mocking challenge.

No answer.

"Reckon your boss, Rancher Ray, got what he deserved," I continued. "Now he's gotta face another kind of judgment. Same goes for your friend . . . what was his name? Dawkins? Just too bad that other fella who worked the ranch and Colson's daughter had to pay for what you all did."

Stokes pulled rein, and his horse halted abruptly, its big head lifting. I did likewise, though I brought my mount to a slower stop. Stokes looked at me, and he wore a challenging expression. I was ready. Sheriff Caldwell and the deputies were only several yards behind us. Caldwell drew his horse to a stop, and Calhern and Malone followed suit.

Caldwell swung himself from his mount and started on foot toward us. He didn't appear too pleased and directed that look of displeasure at me.

"Let him be, Gambel," was all he said, his words stern, official.

I just leveled my eyes at Stokes and kept my focus on the man. It was gratifying in its own way that Stokes couldn't meet, let alone hold, my stare. His eyes kept shifting, finally settling on Caldwell.

"All right, Sheriff," I conceded.

"We both got the feelings we have," Caldwell went on, now the voice of diplomacy. "But 'til this is through, would be best if'n we all work together." He paused. "Start dividin', and we'll really give that Comanche the edge."

I had just one more thing to say to Stokes, and I wanted the sheriff to hear it, too.

"Tell me this, though, Stokes. If your boss had asked, would you have gone after that Indian alone?"

Stokes looked rightly stunned by my question. I expected Caldwell to again tell me just to leave it be. But as I'd hoped, he also seemed interested in hearing the man's answer, as was plain from his expression.

But Stokes didn't give us a reply. And that was answer enough for me.

"Thought so," I said with a smirk.

"Okay, let's move on," Caldwell ordered. "Got a lot of ground to cover and nowhere sure where we're headed."

That was true enough. Our only lead was to have Stokes take us to the spot where he and his accomplice had attacked the Indian named Jacquin. But what, if anything, we'd find there I couldn't be sure. We might again just be chasing the wind.

A short while later I discovered I was mistaken, once I heard Stokes call out: "He's been here!"

We'd come to the entrance of a wider clearing. Stokes had brought his horse to such a sudden halt that his animal bellowed and started to rear up on its hind legs before Stokes could settle it. I caught sight of the color draining from Stokes's complexion.

"This the spot, Stokes?" I asked him.

He replied with a hurried nod.

What I was looking at was a curious formation. A pile of rocks laid out in a small circle. Put there not by nature but by the hand of someone with a deliberate if curious purpose. But that wasn't all. The smell of smoke still lingered in the air. A fire had been lit at some point during the night. A small fire, but representative of something that I could not understand. Nor apparently could anyone else in our group. I climbed off my horse, hunkered down, and swept my hand through the burnt pieces of wood, not sure what I was searching for. But soon my fingers brushed against something that seemed out of place. I pulled my hand free and what I was holding was a scorched piece of fabric, with a design I was not able to distinguish. I shared this discovery with my companions, who were equally as puzzled. It was Stokes who took the material from my hand and examined it.

He frowned. "I . . . I can't be sure, but . . ."

"What is it, man?" Caldwell urged him.

"I don't know what it means," Stokes muttered. "Only that . . . yeah, I'm sure it's part of the scarf that Colson's daughter used to wear 'round her neck."

Caldwell regarded him with a hard look. "Y'mean a kerchief," he corrected.

Stokes brushed aside the sheriff's deliberate accuracy. "Well, whatever yuh wanta call it, I'm sure it's what I seen her wearin'. It was a birthday gift or somethin'. From her pa. Uh, Mr. Colson."

I rubbed a firm hand along my jaw. "A souvenir?" I contemplated aloud.

"I don't know much 'bout the way of the Comanche," Caldwell stated. "But are we suggestin' that he murdered the girl and then took this along with him as some sort of prize?"

No one answered. As for myself: possibly. The way I had it figured was that Jacquin, for whatever reason, had killed the girl, taken a small piece of her clothing, then burned it in some sort of ceremony understood only to himself. I reckon at that point it didn't matter why he had done it. Its main relevance was it indicated to our party that he hadn't strayed too far from where we now stood. And if that were so, he might even now be watching us.

"He's here; I know it," Caldwell said with strong certainty.

I think each of us felt that Indian presence lurking nearby. It was tangible.

"We gotta stay together as a group and keep careful watch," Caldwell instructed us. "The way he's made his kills points to him maybe not carrying a firearm. 'Course we can't be certain of that but, in any case, doesn't make him any less dangerous. He's proven he's skilled with a knife, and he probably moves like a shadow. He hits fast and sure. He's a hunter. Still, doubt even a Comanche would dare to strike us together as a group, lessen he simply doesn't care and chooses to die while taking as many of us with him as he can 'fore he goes down. Well, can't start to guess what his thinkin' is now." Here he turned to look directly at Stokes with a cold stare. "But leastwise we don't have to guess 'bout his motive."

I nodded my head solemnly. "Knowing he's a wanted man, he likely will choose to die with honor."

Caldwell nodded back to me. "That's what I figger. And goin' up ag'in a man with nothin' to lose doesn't bode well for any of us. And we have to assume that's how it's gonna be. So that's how we gotta proceed."

Whatever any of us were feeling, none of us expressed it openly, with the exception of Stokes—and with good reason. If Jacquin truly was responsible for these killings—and that pretty much had now been established—and if he were prepared to die rather than face arrest for his crimes, there was one man he surely would want to take with him, a man not destined to accompany Jacquin to the Happy Hunting Grounds.

"It . . . ain't right that I go any farther," Stokes said, his voice high as he stressed his objection.

I couldn't fault him for not wanting to go on with us. Unless Jacquin could be stopped beforehand, Stokes sure enough was a dead man. The features of his face had to be etched like a stone carving into the brain of the vengeful Indian.

But Caldwell had about as little sympathy for Stokes as I did. His answer was a blunt: "Not a chance, cowboy. You're seein' this through with the rest of us."

"But . . ."

Caldwell dramatically straightened his posture to emphasize his authority. He fixed Stokes with a cold fish eye and said, "There's a chance none of us might get outta this alive. But I'll be damned if I plan to give up my life while a cowardly coyote like you rides free."

Very well spoken. Deserving of applause, even.

Our next decision was the direction we should take. The ground was too patched with high grass and weeds to determine any tracks that might give us a lead. We looked to have three choices, each of which would take us deeper into the woodlands: south, east, or west. It was pretty much a coin toss. I was a seeker; Caldwell and his deputies were former Rangers, meaning they relied more on their tracking skills. I left the decision which way to proceed up to them.

Caldwell looked at me; I gave a slight nudge of my head to let him know he was in charge.

He scouted each direction, not that it made any difference, for each direction except north from where we'd come was thick with trees and underbrush. Wherever we headed, we'd not only be riding into unknown but also foreboding territory.

"South," Caldwell then said, decisively. "My hunch is that he'll bury himself in as deep as he can go, and heading south is likely the best way he can do that. And if he knows we're trailin' him, he'll find himself a safe spot to give himself the advantage."

More words not intended to comfort Jim Stokes, who said, "Yeah, to ambush us."

Gazing at the man, I began to question if it was wise that we bring him along. Not that I particularly cared if our Comanche carved him up like his partner in crime—but because he might prove a nuisance, a burden, even a downright hindrance, in our search.

But I could tell Caldwell was not going to budge. He was a man of purpose, and when he made a decision, by God, he stuck with it.

"How far can we go? We only got food 'nuff for a coupla days, maybe three if'n we ration," Stokes complained.

"Yeah, I'd say 'bout that," Caldwell said in a matter-of-fact manner.

"Then what?"

Caldwell shrugged. "We ain't got him by then I reckon we'll have to find ourselves some critters to et. Sure won't be turnin' back."

Stokes looked disgusted at the thought.

Caldwell eyed him critically. "Yeah, none of that fine ranch-house grub you're used to when that supper bell starts a-clangin'. For myself, as a Ranger . . . sometimes hadda go days on end scroungin' up my own meals." He turned to me. "Reckon that was the same for you on some of your travels. Ain't that right, Chance?"

Not really. I usually carried with me a substantial supply of food—maybe not beefsteak but better than prairie dog cooked over a campfire. But Stokes didn't have to know that.

"That's a fact," I said readily, keeping a straight face.

"We coulda brought some grub from the house, carried along an extra sack," Stokes argued. "Plenty of food there."

"Yeah, we coulda," Caldwell said with a lift of the shoulder. "But don't wanta carry any more than we have to. Trail's tough enough on our ponies. 'Sides, if'n you wanta know the truth, Stokes, I don't think any of us are gonna go hungry. My lawman instincts tell me this whole ordeal's gonna be over 'fore our food runs out."

"Over *how*?" Stokes asked cautiously.

"Can't rightly say for certain," Caldwell answered.

Ominous words, but I shared what the sheriff was thinking. If Jacquin knew we were on his trail, his most advantageous move would be to draw us into the woods just deep enough where he could prepare an attack. The question was: how would he come at us?

Caldwell sidled over to me. He lifted the brim of his wide-brimmed Stetson and brushed some sweat from his brow. The air was hot and damp, the sweat pasting our clothes to our bodies, the leafy overhangs of the trees providing little relief. The sheriff spoke quietly. "Hope I'm right, Gambel, 'bout gettin' this done with quick."

"I thought you might be speaking of a different outcome," I said.

"For Stokes's benefit?" Caldwell said with a half grin.

"Might be worth it to ease up on him a bit," I suggested. "Get him too panicked and no telling what he might do."

Caldwell considered, answered with a nod. Then he said, "Think it wise if during our campouts I keep two men on watch."

That was a smart decision. Against the skilled, stealthy approach of a murderous Comanche, a man taking watch alone would hardly stand a chance. But with two sitting guard, each man could keep watch on the other as well as on the camp.

I only hoped that we were dealing with just the one Comanche. That fact had yet to be established.

I'd trekked through rough terrain in the past, but that had been some time ago—a different time—and in some regards I was a different man, sturdier and more resilient. I'd gotten more settled into a sedentary life, the results of which I was discovering as we guided our horses through the woods, wondering how much farther we could lead them until the terrain dictated that we carry forward on foot. I wasn't the only one of our small group seeming to struggle with maintaining my energy; Calhern and Malone were doing their fair share of labored breathing. Calhern, of course, was more concerned for the comfort of his kitten, which he now allowed into the fresh air through the opening in his shoulder sack, her contented purring heard even from the distance I was behind him. Stokes had to be as winded as any of us but managed to cover his discomfort with his endless grumbling. It appeared only Sheriff Caldwell was maintaining his endurance. I don't know if I admired as much as envied the tough old bird.

We'd filled our canteens and water horns from Ray Colson's well, but the heat was relentless, and we had to keep prudent in our drinking, taking sips, not swallows, as needed. I didn't know this region at all but assumed that, because it was heavily forested, we'd likely come upon a source of water, a stream or a creek. But so far, the land was green but dry. It wasn't until later that first day that I saw the approach of a welcome cloud cover, perhaps bringing with it the promise of rain.

By around six o'clock we all were exhausted, and we searched about for a comfortable but sensible place to rest ourselves and our horses and set up camp for the night. By this time, the skies had started to darken, and soon we felt the first drops of rain. The rain made it possible for each of us to drink heartily from our canteens as we set out pans to catch the rainfall. We finally settled in amongst a thick gathering of trees where the heavy overhang of leafy branches would provide adequate shelter should we find ourselves in a sudden downpour. Not to mention that our setting offered us protection should our enemy decide to launch a surprise attack.

We opened our cans of beans for supper. Caldwell passed along biscuits. We ate in silence, entertaining our own thoughts while periodically gazing up at the clouds as they passed overhead toward the east. The rain that the skies promised didn't amount to anything significant, though it satisfied us and our horses. Also, it brought a comfortable, cool reprieve from the searing heat of the day, though we'd likely have to endure another hot, sweaty one come tomorrow.

Calhern and Malone would keep first watch, to be followed by Caldwell and myself. Calhern then volunteered to take the third watch with Stokes. That was a wise decision. Two- to three-hour shifts. We'd get an early start in the morning to take advantage of the cool before the heat settled in.

After supper Logan Malone pulled out a pouch of tobacco and some papers and rolled himself a cigarette. Caldwell withdrew a couple of cigars from his pocket, offering one to me. I accepted with thanks. Caldwell struck a match against his boot heel and lighted his cigar, then mine, but when he leaned forward to light Malone's cigarette, the former Ranger waved aside the offer and lighted his smoke with his own match.

I heard Jim Stokes chuckle. "Didn't think you Rangers was the superstitious type."

Malone smiled grimly. "Not necessarily. But why risk providence?"

Stokes shrugged and began building his own cigarette. "Yeah, reckon we all got our little quirks."

The sheriff glared at Stokes; I could tell he wanted to say something to him but held himself in check.

As the night wore on I was overcome with an odd feeling that lent itself to moments of apprehension. At first, I'd appreciated the security of our setting, but either because I'd opened myself to too much thought or I was beginning to feel a sense of confinement nestled within these trees with the closing in of darkness, I considered how Jacquin had shown himself to be a creature of the night. All of his kills had been after dark—and, with the exception of the girl, committed against powerful men who, physically, if given the chance, probably could have defeated him.

But neither had been given the opportunity.

Jacquin obviously knew how to stalk his prey. And he knew how to strike suddenly. That told me that, even within what we thought was our protected encampment, a skilled Comanche could noiselessly creep through the underbrush, strike swiftly, and disappear back into the safety of the bush without being noticed.

I reckon we each dealt with our own trepidations as the darkness slowly overcame then overwhelmed our little camp. I confessed my own unease—if only to myself. Jim Stokes had to be dealing with his own fears. Hard to tell with Calhern and Malone; outside of Calhern's fondness for his kitten, I'd learned nothing else about him or his fellow former Ranger, since they weren't apt to say much. Maybe it was wrong of me, but it was hard not to feel resentful that, if they were to survive this hunt, they'd come out as richer men than I would. What made that all the more difficult to accept was that neither man had the responsibilities that I had, namely a family waiting for my safe return. What money Calhern and Malone earned was pure profit, for drinking, gambling, whatever else their pleasure, though that might have been an unfair judgment, since neither of the ex-Rangers seemed the type to participate in rowdy entertainment. Still, I couldn't help but dwell on their good fortune as opposed to mine. But I'd been given the chance to walk away from any further obligation and decided not to. I had to let that decision keep content with my stubborn pride.

Because the night skies were so oppressively black, we'd built ourselves a small campfire. Caldwell's reasoning was a sensible, if troubling concern. The way he figured it, if the Comanche was around these parts he likely already knew where we were. It was best to keep ourselves secure in the light of a fire, where we would have a better chance of seeing him should he approach our camp. Because, as Caldwell reiterated what I'd been thinking, chances were we'd never *hear* him coming. He wouldn't tramp through the brush like a bear. He'd emerge as silently as a shadow to cut our throats. While my own experience with the Indian was limited, I had learned through my various travels in lands occupied by native tribes that it was never wise to underestimate their instincts and their knowledge. As once had been pointed out to me, the white man merely scouted the land; the Indian *knew* the land.

Out of spite I was momentarily tempted to remind Jim Stokes that we could all be sitting ducks this night but refrained. As I'd told the sheriff, if we put the fear into him too much he might suddenly turn loco. Until this experience was over, we needed him on our side. I only hoped that, if the situation did turn ugly, he had the balls to redeem himself with courage.

The crackle of the campfire did provide a comforting sound. For the longest time, we all seemed to absorb it without speaking, our eyes almost hypnotically drawn to the shifting orange flames.

After a while Sheriff Caldwell said to me, "You ever get a feelin', Gambel . . . ?" Then he halted and answered his own question. "Sure. In your line of work, you had to."

I turned to him for an explanation.

Caldwell seemed a mite reluctant to say anything more. He fidgeted a bit before looking up into the impenetrable black canvas of night, where there was no moon and not even the faintest twinkling of stars.

He spoke quietly, distantly. "Reckon we all suspect he's

watchin'—or at least knows 'bout us. But I got this sorta ache in my belly tellin' me that come daybreak we're gonna know that he was here."

My gut knotted at what he was saying, but I tried to speak without concern. "Well, it was you who said we weren't going to have a long wait."

Caldwell nodded. "I know. Just ain't sure at which end it's gonna come. Ours . . . or his."

"Sorta what you said to Stokes," I said.

"I know," Caldwell said with a sigh. "Just feels kinda different now."

Caldwell was right. It did feel different.

It was a quiet night and while I managed to get some shut-eye before I took my watch with Sheriff Caldwell, I pretty much slept with one eye open and both ears alert. I heard a bit of mumbled conversation between Calhern and Malone during their guard, but mostly they were quiet, befitting their personalities.

Then it was Calhern and Stokes's turn to sit up. I confess I was slightly uncomfortable giving in to sleep with Stokes keeping watch. But soon it would be dawn, and, besides, I had full trust in Calhern—provided he didn't compromise attention to his duty by focusing too much on his kitten.

CHAPTER TWENTY

It was just around dawn when I awoke to an excited, panicked voice. I shook the sleep from my head and lifted myself on an elbow. It was Jim Stokes who was waking everyone from their slumber. Sheriff Caldwell was already on his feet.

"What the hell is it, Stokes?" he grumbled.

I pulled myself to my feet to join him. I didn't like what we both were witnessing: Stokes was in distress. I noticed Logan Malone awake and looking concerned. But as I cast my eyes about the site, I saw that Calhern was missing.

Caldwell was impatient and demanded to know what was going on. He grabbed Stokes by the collar and held firm with both hands.

"Where's Calhern, you son of a bitch?" he said with suppressed rage.

"He . . . he went off," Stokes stammered. "Been gone for over a half hour. He . . . he ain't come back."

Caldwell held his composure even as it looked like he was readying to slam a fist into Stokes. He refrained from any physical violence, but his features were taut. He drew a deep breath and spoke through clenched teeth. "Why didn't you wake us? Why'd yuh wait 'til now to let us know?"

Stokes spoke in a nervous, rapid voice. "Thought he'd be back. Told me he'd just be away for a few minutes. Didn't think nothin' of it. A man goes off to do his business. So I thought:

hell, I ain't gonna trail him. But then when I did go to find him . . ."

"Which way'd he go?" Caldwell said, releasing his grip on Stokes, who turned himself around and pointed a finger to the south.

Caldwell bowed and slowly shook his head. He didn't have to say anything. We—Malone and myself—shared what he was thinking. For whatever reason, Calhern had ventured into the one region where he never should have gone alone. Because he hadn't returned, that told us he'd either gotten himself lost in the denseness of the brush . . . or, what we feared, that he'd run into the Comanche.

"Just what he mighta been waitin' for," Caldwell mused. "Hope to get each of us alone. Whittle us down one by one."

I tried to speak positively, but I don't think my tone was encouraging. "We don't know that for certain."

Caldwell pivoted his head toward me. "I told you last night what was gnawin' at me."

"You did."

"All right. Let's clear camp. All we can do is follow his trail," Caldwell said. "See what we find. Best we keep the horses tethered and make our way on foot." He looked at Malone, who responded with a solemn nod. Then he shifted his gaze to Stokes, who appeared as doubtful as ever. He fixed Stokes with a withering look. "No one was supposed to be alone on his watch, Stokes. And no man shoulda gone off on his own. You shoulda woken one of us."

Stokes swallowed heavily and appeared properly chastised. I reckon there was nothing he could say. The simple truth was he'd made a bad decision, and because of that we might have lost one of our team—a man we damn well couldn't afford to lose.

With the light of the breaking dawn to guide us, we left the campsite and our horses and walked briskly but with careful steps into the depths of the forest, each of us watchful—both for our missing comrade and for any signs of the Indian we sought, who may already have made his first score against our group. We walked in a deliberate single-file formation: Caldwell at the lead with Stokes behind him, followed by me and then Malone. Stokes was nervous; he took periodic glances over his shoulder, maybe to see how close I was to him in case he decided to try and make a break. I figured that might be exactly what he'd attempt, especially if we should find Calhern dead. But each time our eyes met I responded with a look to let him know that if he dared such a move I'd have no reservation about shooting him down in his tracks, which would be a more merciful end than if the Comanche caught up with him.

About ten minutes into our walk I heard Sheriff Caldwell yell, "Halt!"

He stood motionless, and we all moved over next to him. What we feared was spread out before us, half buried in the tall grass. Brad Calhern had been murdered, lying on his back, arms and legs splayed. His chest had been sliced open, but there was one distinct difference from the other kills: Calhern's face was unmarked; no knife wound had slashed open the side of his face. But he had still died violently, reflected in eyes that were open wide, glassy, staring sightlessly. None of us spoke, though a sound of some sort escaped Stokes's lips. And then . . . there was a movement and a soft meowing coming from inside the canvas sack still wrapped around Calhern's shoulder. Caldwell knelt down and reached inside the sack, gently withdrawing the kitten called Angel. He turned to look at each of us, wordlessly, his expression solemn.

"I'll care for him," Logan Malone offered. Caldwell nodded, stood up, and handed him the kitten. Then he bent down to slide the sack from Calhern's body, which he also gave to

Malone. Almost immediately the frightened little animal buried itself back inside the protection of the canvas.

"Reckon there ain't no point in buryin' him," Stokes muttered.

Caldwell gave him a sharp look. "Shut up, Stokes," he snapped.

"Didn't mean no disrespect, Sheriff," Stokes said. "Only ain't no decent place to lay him, and we sure 'nuff didn't bring along no proper tools to do the job."

This was true. The ground was hard and solid and difficult to break through without the right implements. Well, I'd had to leave many a dead man lying where they'd fallen on my past trails, such as that family in the Bodrie Hills, along with the party I did not bring back, Ed Chaney. But Brad Calhern died bravely and deserved something better than just to lay exposed to the heat and the critters that inhabited the land. That alone was an unpleasant consideration.

Caldwell looked troubled in deciding what to do. Calhern was a former comrade of the sheriff's back when both were Rangers, and the men in that outfit formed a brotherhood. It had to be difficult for him.

Finally, speaking in frustration, he said, "We ain't equipped for this. Just let's gather up some leaves and branches."

"Makes no matter," Malone said. "Calhern was a man of the land. Where he's at now, he ain't got no concerns 'bout where his body rests. We'll cover him here."

Which we did. We covered Calhern's body as best we could. I barely knew the man, and so Stokes and I stepped aside while Caldwell and Malone had their final moments with their fallen comrade.

Of course, Stokes could not keep his mouth shut. He whispered to me, "Wonder if a leafy grave'll be our reward."

"Just keep in mind that's one of three choices you've got," I said back to him.

We returned to where we'd left our horses and started on again, hoping to find some sign we were heading in the right direction. That was well-nigh impossible given the unpredictability of the movements of the Comanche and terrain that made it much too difficult to locate clues. Once again there was something I found myself itching to ask Stokes.

"Tell me, Stokes. Any regrets over what you done?" I said.

Stokes pretended either not to hear or understand my question. I presented it a mite differently, and with a bit more emphasis in my delivery.

"Lotta people are dead because of what you did," I said. "Coupla innocent people, too."

"How was I to know this was gonna come back at 'em?" Stokes responded defensively. Then he said, "At *me*?"

I pretended to consider before firing my second round. "Reckon you wouldn't even be asking that if you were a man feeling repentant."

"You ain't got no guess what I'm feelin'," Stokes said with a sneer.

"Well, I've learnt a few things over the years," I said. "Took me a while to realize that every man's wrongdoing comes with a consequence. Might not always be directed straight at him, but, in some way, he's still gotta carry that burden."

"Well, for what it's worth I ain't proud of what I done," Stokes said with a lowering of his head.

I nodded absently.

"That's what yuh wanta hear, ain't it?" he demanded.

He wasn't going to get an answer from me. But I figured that was about the best he would offer. Strange directions your thoughts sometimes take. I'd had enough of those over the years. I didn't rightly know if some supreme judgment might one day await this Jim Stokes, but if he survived this journey and went on to live a good long life, at some point in his later years he'd likely remember what he'd done and what the cost had been, and I didn't envy him those memories as he waited for that final sunset.

The eyes of the woodlands are deep and penetrating. While they're not visible, you can *feel* them watching you, keeping step with you along the trail. Jacquin had killed one of our group; that was his warning to us that, if we carried on with our search, none of us would be immune to the blade of his knife. I didn't think he'd be that foolhardy to attack us as a whole: he might get one or even two of us, but he'd be shot down almost immediately, and, for someone who through his killings had displayed such relentless determination, that could not be seen as a rewarding end. His strategy was to stalk and kill us individually. As Caldwell had said: to whittle us down. We still had the advantage by numbers, but if we faced even a couple more losses we'd truly be playing in the Comanche's camp. We were halfway there already, progressing ever more steadily into his territory. One couldn't help but feel like Daniel entering the lions' den. I only hoped that God recognized my newfound faith. It had been a long time in coming.

We each were pretty numb with our thoughts after discovering Calhern. I don't know how far we traveled that day, only that the trees and brush seemed to get even denser. Finally, a bit of a relief came when we arrived at a narrow but swift-running creek that intersected the landscape with the current running in a westerly direction. We stopped to savor this refreshing site. Rather than crossing the waters, we decided to set up camp on the north bank. It was late afternoon, and we took out our vittles for supper. I figured we had enough rations for another couple of days, but then we'd still have that ride back. I considered with distaste that we might actually find ourselves roasting some unlucky night critter for our supper.

As we dismounted and led our horses to the water to enjoy a cool drink before giving them their supper of grain feed, I watched big Logan Malone gently pan some water for the kitten, who eagerly lapped it up. I couldn't resist shaking my head in wonderment; the fellow looked to have the size and strength to clear out a barroom full of drunken rowdies yet had the same sensitive nature as his late *compadre*. It wasn't much in light of our earlier discovery but watching him tend to the kitten sort of provided a brief reprieve from the anxiety each of us faced.

"Rough and ready Rangers," I joked to Caldwell, though speaking in a low voice for risk of offending Malone.

The sheriff smiled and gave a nod. "Not so strange, Gambel. Not if you know the history."

"Care to share it?"

"Malone and Calhern were close comrades. During one skirmish Calhern took a bullet intended for Malone; nearly left him a cripple. Took him a long time to recover. You mighta not noticed, but he walks with a bit of a limp. Permanent. The way I see it, Malone might be repayin' the favor, adoptin' that cat."

"Still and all, a coupla strange fellas," I said. "Caring for a kitten."

Caldwell sighed. "Yep. But you couldn't ask for two better men."

That was a fine tribute the sheriff shared with me, yet at the same time it reignited the disturbing question: if a man of Calhern's qualifications could be come upon and murdered with such savagery, how did that place any of our chances? The longer I thought about it, the more I felt that, if Caldwell were to suggest we give up this hunt and turn back, I wouldn't object. Especially since within the next few hours the skies would again turn dark, and those Comanche eyes might once more be watching.

But, until then, we did our damnedest to try and relax. Gray cloud smudges passed overhead in prelude to nightfall. We ate, drank some coffee, and Caldwell and I finished by smoking a couple of his fine cigars. Malone continued to care for the kitten, seeming to joyfully lose himself in the task, while Stokes kept himself busy by rolling and smoking cigarette after cigarette.

Most of all we listened.

The night sounds seemed magnified. Innocent, even gentle, noises seemed to harbor their own subtle malevolence. At least that was how it felt to me. Once again, I was reminded of how far I'd separated myself from being a witness seeker. I'd never before felt the need to pay particular notice to sounds when I halted my day's ride and set up camp. That had always been a welcome time, and whatever surrounded me—from wide night skies to prairie or rocky environment—I'd always regarded with . . . almost a sort of kinship. On those nights, I'd never felt the unease I was experiencing now. Even when trailing Ramos and his gang, I seemed to recall traveling with more confidence. I told myself with a forced humor that either I was getting older or smarter.

But it was on this night I made myself the promise that, once this was over, nothing would ever again convince me to leave the new life I'd chosen for myself.

I hoped that whatever higher power existed was listening . . .

"What if one of us has to relieve himself?" Stokes asked suddenly.

"Do it where we can keep an eye on yuh. Take a leak in the creek," Caldwell suggested humorlessly.

"To hell with modesty," I put in.

"Well, think I'll just hold it for as long as I can," Stokes mumbled.

"Do whatever suits yuh," Caldwell said without interest.

Arrangements were made for our watch. Malone and I offered to take the first guard, then Caldwell and Stokes, and Malone and myself would then make do till daybreak. The watch schedule would likely lead to a tiring ride tomorrow, but what choice did we have? I just wondered if we'd ever clear these woodlands . . . and what we'd find once we did.

The night came and went quietly, without incident. Dawn opened a new day, and we prepared to carry on with our journey. I wondered if the peaceful night we'd enjoyed was intentional: the Comanche holding back, trying to lull us into a false sense of security; hoping to get us to weaken our guard. The other possibility I considered was that maybe it was Jacquin's plan to lure us into a trap. Get us lost in these woods, and then strike when our defenses were down and our exhaustion was high. For all of us this was unexplored territory. Even ex-Rangers Caldwell and Malone had never entered these woods. All sorts of contemplations traveled through my brain as we packed up. And none produced a pleasant outcome.

Sheriff Caldwell walked over to me. "Nice night," he said.

I gave a half-hearted nod. Then I started over toward the creek to wash up and splash some cold water on my face. I hoped that might stimulate me along with a good strong cup of coffee. I could still make do with limited sleep, but when my shut-eye was interrupted as it had been by being pulled awake to stand watch twice during the night, I could feel the residue of fatigue throughout my body. We ate a light breakfast of biscuits and jerky, brewed coffee over a small fire, then climbed up onto our mounts and started across the creek. The water had a pretty strong current, but the creek wasn't deep, and so we made the crossing without much difficulty.

Once on the other side Caldwell halted; then he climbed off his horse. There was a bank of moist sand leading back into the trees in a slight slope, and the sheriff appeared to be checking for tracks. He shook his head and looked to either side of him, lifting the brim of his Stetson and scratching his forehead. Yards away on both sides were grassy and weed-infested knolls. If the Comanche had crossed the creek, he had cleverly taken the path protected by inland vegetation that would prevent him from leaving noticeable and trackable footprints.

Caldwell started back onto his horse. "Reckon we'll just have to carry on," he said. He'd just slipped a foot into the stirrup when a strange, sudden sound pushed out of his mouth, and he looked to jerk forward. I watched as his body stiffened and a look of distress came over his features. He stood upright only for a moment, his hand grasping the saddle horn . . . before his fingers relaxed, and he slowly slid backwards, dropping to the ground behind a large fallen log that rested atop a sandy rise.

None of us could immediately comprehend what had happened. But in a reflexive move I flung myself from the saddle and rushed over. Sheriff Caldwell was alive but gurgling blood. Malone was soon kneeling beside me. We gently rolled the sheriff onto his side . . . and saw a makeshift arrow plunged deep into his upper back, likely penetrating a lung.

"Jesus," I muttered helplessly.

"Son of a bitch got me good," Caldwell gasped, trying to be brave with a weak smile. And then he almost seemed to yip a laugh.

Malone started to rise from his crouch as his eyes darted about.

"Get down," I urged him, gesturing to the log. "We gotta stay down for cover."

"Damn little cover," Malone gritted. His face looked enraged as he withdrew his .44 revolver from the holster and held it at the ready.

At almost the same moment I heard a loud *"Yeyah!"* and the splashing of water. I turned my head to see Jim Stokes spurring his horse back in the direction whence we'd come. The coward was running out on us.

"Malone," I said, and I jerked my head to the side. Malone turned, and then I saw him raise his pistol, aim the barrel . . . and fire.

The shot echoed through the clean morning air as Stokes caught the bullet in the back and toppled sideways from his horse into the creek. I watched as he struggled to get to his feet. He managed to stagger forward a couple of steps before collapsing face first into the water. Lying limp, his body was gently swept away by the current. I lifted my head to look at Malone. I wasn't sure if I should condemn or congratulate his action. But in one regard it made little difference. Stokes would have been of no use to us.

"Lousy yellow belly," Malone muttered miserably as he twirled his six-shooter. He kept the gun in his hand as he lowered to his haunches, next to me behind the log, his eyes continuing to scout the trees and bushes, eagerly seeking any movement. We knew the Comanche was somewhere in there, but where and how far hidden we couldn't know.

We also had a dying man to contend with.

Caldwell was trying to talk, but his words were barely coherent. For a man who had shown strength, determination, and courage from the outset of our journey, it was troubling to see him suddenly look so pained and helpless in what would be his final moments.

"We can't do nothin' for him," Malone said, jaws taut but his voice matter of fact.

That was the sorry truth. Malone and I now had to worry about keeping ourselves alive. But if either of us pulled ourselves upright and attempted to move, there was a good chance we'd also be met by an arrow. I pictured our enemy waiting with his weapon at the ready.

Caldwell found the strength to lift himself slightly on his

shoulder, and he looked solidly at both Malone and myself and sputtered out words neither of us expected to hear him say.

"Let it go, boys. We . . . had no business comin' here." He smiled. "Not on Colson's behalf."

I frowned. Yet even though I couldn't immediately grasp what he was telling us, there was a reverence that I recognized in those final utterances.

"No more killing," he said. "Colson, the others . . . th—they paid the price for what they did. It's over. L—let it be. Just . . . let it . . ." His words faded. And then Caldwell stiffened, exhaled a last breath, and fell dead.

I turned to Malone. He looked flabbergasted.

"That don't sound like Caldwell," he remarked. "Tellin' us to let a murderer go free."

I myself wasn't sure what to make of the sheriff's dying words.

Malone then turned his attention back to our present situation.

"Too quiet," he said. "Them Indians is too damn quiet." He held back whatever emotion he was feeling at the death of his old comrade. But he wasn't fooling me; he had a hurt.

We held our positions, our bodies stretched out on the slope of the rise, protected by the old log, and we waited. Nothing further happened. Caldwell's last words were an urging for Malone and I to call off the search, and as I pondered all that had happened—and why—I realized his reasoning was sound. But it wasn't that easy. We couldn't chance exposing ourselves and risk getting hit by an arrow. So, we had to wait, and that was not an enviable position to be in. Both Malone and myself were aware of the patience of the Indian. They had many qualities the white man simply did not possess—and endurance was one. Jacquin could stay wherever he was for however long necessary, just waiting for one or both of us to get itchy and attempt a move.

Malone started to talk. Maybe it helped him cope with the uncertainty of our waiting. In any case, I didn't object. I didn't much care for that lingering sound of silence.

"Caldwell was a good man," he said. "The three of us shared some good times back in the day."

"When you were Rangers?" I asked.

Malone nodded. "Thing is, when he retired I thought sure he was through with workin' for the law. Was damn well surprised to learn he became sheriff."

"He was good at what he knew," I offered. "Didn't know him well, but he built himself a fine reputation in the short time he was in Chesterfield City."

"Damn right," Malone said, and I detected the slightest choke in his voice.

And time continued to pass . . .

Finally, I had an idea. Maybe a million-to-one shot, but as things stood we had nothing to lose.

I pulled myself up on an elbow, cupped a hand to my mouth and yelled into the bush: "Jacquin."

Malone pulled heavily at my shoulder, his strength almost throwing me backwards.

"What the hell are you—"

I gave him a serious look. "The only chance as I see it is to try to talk to him. Maybe . . . maybe reason with him."

"You can't talk no sense to a Comanche," Malone snorted.

"Maybe, maybe not. But we can't even know for sure where he is, protected in all that cover. Or he could have hightailed it after shooting that arrow into Caldwell, keeping us waiting here while he runs deeper into the woods."

Malone let my words sink in, and then he gave a grudging nod of his head.

I said further, "If he is still there, keeping us in his sights . . . well, like I said, maybe there's a way to reason with him—if we let him know we don't have any fight with him."

Malone appeared incredulous at what I was suggesting. "No fight? He just killed two good men. Friends of mine." He shook his head. "No sir," he said firmly. "Don't care what you think, but I owe these men an obligation."

"You won't owe them anything if you're lying dead with a Comanche arrow sticking out of you," I said. My next words were a little less blunt. "And . . . maybe we should give some consideration to what Caldwell told us."

Malone regarded me with a critical look. "You sayin' we should turn back?"

"I just want to get out of this alive," I told him without embarrassment.

Malone still wasn't convinced of that decision. "Think we might convince him to give himself up?" he offered in exchange.

"Doubt it."

Malone dug his fingers into the moist sand and began scraping at it to create a small mound. I took it as a contemplative gesture.

"My thinkin' is that if we turn our backs on him we'll end up like Caldwell," he said.

That was my concern as well, which was why it was imperative that I try to communicate with Jacquin. I drew in a breath and spoke with utter honesty. "I've got something to go home to."

Malone didn't acknowledge my statement, and maybe with good cause. My reasoning wasn't the same as his, with him being a widower. Instead, he regarded the canvas bag where the kitten was kept, shuffling about inside. "Should let her go," he mused. "Probably stand a better chance stayin' alive out here than either of us."

I knew our situation didn't look too promising, with Jacquin likely waiting for us to show ourselves so that he could end the pursuit in his favor. But I was a bit taken aback to hear those defeatist words coming from a former Confederate officer and Texas Ranger who must have found himself in similar rough spots during his time.

"Awright," he conceded. "You do what you have to."

And so once more I cupped my hand against the side of my mouth and called out, "Jacquin."

Quiet. Stillness. No movement. No sound. We waited.

"Maybe he *did* skedaddle," Malone said, speaking close to my ear.

Possibly. And with the position we were in, I certainly didn't consider that the worst outcome.

"Jacquin," I called again. "If you can hear me, understand me, it's important that we talk. I promise no one will hurt you."

"*He's* the one with the advantage," Malone reminded.

And then a voice reached us from somewhere in the brush: it was a voice that carried with it a tone of indignation.

"More white man lies."

Even discerning the hostility, I felt a relief. We had made contact. Now if only he would agree to speak with me and be reasoned with.

I looked at Malone; he still wore a doubtful expression. I confess I was a little worried about him, especially as I noticed how his fingers fidgeted with his revolver. The uncertainty of such a wait as we were undertaking could make a man edgy. And quick to react.

I yelled out, "Come into the open, Jacquin, so that we can talk face to face. I'll put aside my weapons. No one needs to get hurt."

There was a long wait before he responded, "There can be no trust. I have killed your people. You will not hesitate to do the same to me."

I spoke with as much sincerity as I could muster. "I give you my word."

Another lengthy silence.

"Figger he's thinkin' it's him or us," Malone surmised.

"Gotta convince him it's not," I said. "He has to know we're on equal ground."

"And then what?"

I looked at Malone, waiting to hear what—if any—suggestion he might offer.

"You don't want to hear it," he said with a narrowing of his eyes.

My distrust of Malone seemed to be taking shape. What he was telling me was that he was ready to shoot the Comanche the moment he showed himself—if Jacquin dared to enter our sight. I understood his resentment but still hoped to establish a less treacherous way to deal with the Indian.

I started to rise to my feet, slowly, emerging full from behind the rotted old log. I stood directly in front of what would have been Malone's line of fire—and presented a clear target if Jacquin chose to shoot an arrow into me. Most of all, I wasn't going to give Malone the chance to ambush the Indian.

"You damn fool," Malone sputtered.

I started to unbuckle my gun belt, again, moving slowly, my actions deliberate, hoping that Jacquin could see that I was sincere. I let it drop to the ground.

"If you can see me, Jacquin, I've unarmed myself. I have no weapons on my person. But if you will allow it, I would like to come to *you*."

"You're gonna get yourself killed," Malone said through clenched teeth.

I knew there was every chance of that happening. Yet I felt in my gut that if Jacquin permitted me to come speak with him, it would prove to be an honorable gesture.

I half turned my head toward Malone and made a gentle comment that he might not have appreciated, but neither was it meant to insult the man's courage.

"Just take good care of Calhern's kitten."

"I hear truth in your voice, white man," Jacquin then called out. "I will trust you at your word. But I have watched and know there are two of you. Only you alone must come. I must see you walk alone."

"I can't be watchin' your back," Malone cautioned me.

I understood that. And with the decision I'd made that wasn't a concern. I knew that once I disappeared into the trees and overgrowth I would be on my own. Alone and unarmed. But I had to carry through. What the outcome would be I couldn't say. I didn't even know what I would say to Jacquin once I met him, only that I would need to call upon those resources I had learned and developed as a witness seeker to see this reach a peaceable resolution. I turned back one final time to Malone and gave him a nod.

And then I ventured forward into the brush.

Chapter Twenty-One

He stood bolt upright and was as still and sturdy and, yes, impressive as any of the tall trees that surrounded him, trees that framed his stoic self in their majesty. He exuded a presence that belied what I was seeing with my eyes. He held in his right hand a makeshift bow that he looked to have crafted himself out of the raw materials available to him. In his left hand, he held three stone-tipped arrows, their wedge-shaped tips sharp and hewn by hand. He had used one of those arrows to kill Sheriff Caldwell. It was obvious the three he brandished were meant for myself, Malone, and Stokes—one well-aimed arrow for each of us. He likely had not reckoned on getting as lucky with us as he had with Calhern and prepared to kill us from a distance. I noticed he carried his knife with him, tucked into a knitted sheath tied to a sash looped around his waist.

I examined him. He was a young man—barely beyond the age of a boy—but his face, although youthful, was a mask marked with cruel resentment, made more so by the terrible scar that ran deep and mean from under his eye down his cheek to his lower lip and curving under his strong chin. He was thin, of average height, bare-chested, not particularly muscular but well-built, and he looked capable of defending himself in any physical confrontation.

We stared at each other for many long moments, our eyes searching, to determine the strengths and perhaps the weaknesses we might find in the other. Neither of us was ready to speak. I found it hard not to focus directly on his disfigurement. The side of his face had been ravaged, and despite all that had happened I felt pity for Jacquin. Comanche or not, no man deserved to suffer the torture that had been inflicted upon him. He once had been a fine-looking boy; now his face was scarred, and his eye had a slight droop, looked almost immobile, and seemed to be layered with a film. I kept my arms held at a wide distance from my body to let him know I was not about to attempt some sudden move. Yet it was equally important for him to understand that I had not come to surrender.

In spite of all the violence that had occurred I needed him to accept that he could trust me.

It was up to me to break the silence. "I've been told your name is Jacquin."

"Jacquin no longer exists," he replied sharply.

"By what name do I call you?"

A slightly sinister smile snaked across his lips. "Do you seek permission, white man?"

I remained firm. "No. I ask what you prefer to be called only out of respect."

When he answered, he emphasized his words by thrusting a finger against the side of his face and drawing it swiftly down the long, deep scar.

"The name your people have given me: Johnny. Johnny Scarface," he declared. "It is a name I have come to accept with pride."

At hearing these words a shiver of dread shot through me. Whatever the boy Jacquin had been before his misfortune, he was now announcing himself as a warrior. A hater of my race.

But I determined I would not display any apprehension, as that would be the weakness he surely was seeking, and through which he would gain the upper hand. I kept both my posture and my voice steady.

"My name is Gambel," I told him.

He made no comment to my introduction, just probed me with his dark eyes.

"I know what happened to you," I went on. "And you should know that the men responsible are dead."

"As are others," Johnny Scarface responded quickly.

"Yes," I said slowly. "I cannot undo what was done to you."

"Is that what you have come to say?" Johnny Scarface said, speaking in a tone of repressed bitterness.

"No. That is not all."

Johnny Scarface breathed in deeply so that his chest rose, the sweat on his brown flesh catching the sun that filtered through the leafy trees, glistening like tiny beads in its morning reflection.

"I killed to avenge what was done to me," he stated. He paused before continuing. "And I killed the men you were with only to protect myself. Because I will not answer to your laws."

I nodded without any sense of conviction, simply to let him know I'd heard his words, his reasoning. I could not condone his justifying murder.

"It is unfortunate that men have to be killed," he said. "That was never my intention when I came among your people."

I believed him, even as I dared to ask, "What about the girl?"

Johnny Scarface's features went tense—but only for a moment before his face relaxed, and he looked forlorn. It was a sign of vulnerability that I had hoped for.

"That was never meant to happen. It is the one killing for which I am sorry." After a few moments, he spoke with genuine regret. "The girl screamed. I panicked. I only wanted to quiet her."

"You cared for this girl?" I ventured to say.

Once more Jacquin's features turned stone hard. He refused to answer.

"I'm sorry," I said to him. "But I must ask you, Jacquin, now that we stand face to face: what happens now?"

"You know that I do not answer by that name," he said in an unyielding tone.

I repeated, sternly, "I ask . . . what happens now?"

"To return with you would mean my death," he replied. "Justice from your people would be swift and harsh. As with all my Comanche brothers I do not fear death. But I will not accept my death by injustice."

"It *is* an injustice, what happened to you," I said emphatically. "But many people besides yourself have paid a penalty for that wrong."

"Yes," he said. "And as you have asked, what is to happen now?"

"That will have to be your decision," I said.

Johnny Scarface spoke in a strong, decisive voice. "Now that I understand your purpose, white man, there can be only one resolution."

I nodded my understanding of what that resolution was to be—and how it must be handled.

Johnny Scarface still spoke the answer. "You and I must do battle. A fight to the death?"

"Yes," I agreed. "But I have no weapon."

Johnny Scarface tossed aside his bow and fistful of arrows with a flourish. Then he pulled his knife from its sheath and brandished it in my direction. I felt my body stiffen as I stared at that silver blade, the surface of which appeared dull, as if stained with the blood of those men Johnny Scarface had killed.

Johnny Scarface noticed my reaction and responded. "Yes," he said. "The blood of those responsible blemishes the blade of this knife."

"There is one man whose blood is *not* on that blade," I said.

Johnny Scarface did not hasten my reply. Instead he waited

for me to tell him who I was speaking of.

"The man most responsible," I said. "Ray Colson, the man who . . ."

Johnny Scarface cut off my words instantly. "I know who he is," he said with ire. "My revenge against him is to be different. He saw what I am capable of. Those deaths will be considered merciful compared to what will be his fate."

"There won't be any vengeance against him," I said solemnly. "I told you, the men responsible are dead. *All* of the men."

Johnny Scarface again was patient as he waited to hear me out.

"He took your vengeance out on himself," I told him.

"Explain to me your words."

I told him outright. "He put a gun to his head. He pulled the trigger."

After several moments, dark lines framed his features, and Johnny Scarface spoke with bitterness and bile. "He cheated me."

"He did it after he discovered the body of his daughter," I explained. "So, no, he didn't cheat you."

Johnny Scarface spoke with sudden anger. "I do not agree."

"What greater punishment could there be for a man than to lose his only child because of an act he himself was responsible for?"

I could not read what thoughts were going on inside the head of the stoic Comanche. But he looked to be in contemplation. Perhaps now, learning there was no further need for bloodshed, he would leave, return to his people. He had nothing else to prove. His fight was over.

Or so I thought.

He surprised me when he fixed me with a calculated stare and said, "We will fight fairly." He threw the blade not too far into the distance, then looked steadily toward the area where it had fallen. "Whichever of us first reaches the knife will use it for the kill on the other."

While this was not what I had hoped for I understood that no talk would dissuade him. He was committed to our fighting. Perhaps he regarded me as his last conquest, since I represented, to his way of thinking, the final link to Rancher Ray, as I had been sent out by him.

I had never fought an Indian in hand-to-hand combat and confess I wasn't eager to engage in battle with this Comanche who with a perverse pride called himself Johnny Scarface, a man whose heart was consumed with hatred. And hatred was a powerful source of strength. My strength would come from defending my life. The uncertainty I felt was partly due to not knowing his power and his cunning—and also simply because I had no desire to kill him. I didn't see him as my enemy; I didn't feel the hate that he did. He was as much a victim as any of those he had killed. The true perpetrators were dead: Ray Colson, George Dawkins, and Jim Stokes. Yet, I understood his pride, his unwillingness to surrender under our terms. Only one of us could walk away from this encounter. And if it should be him who would die, it would be a death with honor.

Despite my apprehension, I nodded to let him know that I was prepared to fight him. Johnny Scarface did not need to acknowledge his readiness, though he looked pleased that I had accepted his challenge. I briefly pondered what his response would have been if I'd chosen not to fight.

I had just one final thing to say to him, for whatever it was worth. "It didn't have to come to this."

His reply was abrupt. "Just prepare to die, white man."

He positioned himself in an aggressive stance, his arms bent at the elbow and raised in front, the fingers of both hands dancing, urging me forward. The look in his eyes resembled that of a predatory animal about to pounce on its prey. I assumed a similar pose, and we both moved, slowly at first, shifting ourselves between the aggressive and defensive. Once our arms locked there would be no surrender until one of us was dead. But who would be the first to make that dictating move? Johnny Scarface would kill me if he had the chance, and so my eyes shifted to where he had thrown the knife. I needed the advantage in reaching the weapon, and, when I was in the proper position, I made the first move and lunged at the Comanche.

He was fast, and he was ready. Before I could tackle him, he grabbed both of my wrists and locked them tight, secure as if they were in shackles. He had a strength behind his grip that I had not expected. I used all of my might to break free, and once I did I ducked to a crouch and threw my shoulder heavily into his torso, throwing him off balance. But he was supremely agile and recovered swiftly and was on me before I could turn to lunge for the knife. He was a savage and determined fighter, pinning me to the ground with his forearm heavy against my spine and driving my face into the ground with a free hand that cupped and put pressure against my skull. He was trying to suffocate me, and I struggled to turn my head to either side so that I wouldn't swallow and choke on the grit that was being forced into my mouth.

He was relentless in his determination to defeat me. My energy was ebbing fast, and I momentarily gave up the struggle, hoping that he might likewise relax his hold. If he didn't, if he kept pressing my face into the dirt, I knew I was a goner. Yet, I also realized he wasn't going to kill me by physical force. If I were to die it must be by the knife, as he himself had dictated. And for that to happen he would have to release me from his grip to go for the weapon—and that's when I would have to break free and attempt my own move to secure the knife. After seconds of putting up no further resistance, leading him to believe that perhaps I had lost consciousness, I could feel Johnny Scarface gradually loosen his grip.

And then I pushed upward with all of my strength, thrusting him off me and heaving him onto his side. I scrambled to my feet and threw myself toward the knife, stretching out my arm and tightly closing my fist around the handle. But, before I could draw my hand in and twist myself around to regain my advantage, Johnny Scarface once more was on me, wrapping his arms around my waist, holding me firm against the ground, again trying to force me to choke on the sandy soil. He freed one of his arms, and I felt him trying to reach for the knife that I kept as far a distance away as possible in my outstretched hand. If he got control of the knife, he would kill me instantly. As a Comanche, he was skilled with the blade—and, as he'd proven, knew precisely how to use it against an enemy.

I tried to kick him off of me, thrashing my legs about, but he angled and maneuvered his body so that no blows connected. Finally, in a desperate attempt to lunge his body forward for the knife, he moved so abruptly that he was careless, and I felt my boot heel strike him in the face. Momentarily stunned, he went limp, which allowed me to pull myself free and forward and scramble to my feet. Johnny Scarface crawled awkwardly to his knees, shaking his head against the impact of my blow. I stood just feet from him. I had won this round of the battle and stood breathlessly, with the blade of the knife thrust forward as if it were a prize.

But I didn't look at it that way. In fact, I was disgusted because of what was expected to come next.

When his senses fully returned, Johnny Scarface lifted his head and looked up at me. He was breathing heavily but with a steady, measured rhythm. What I instantly noticed was that the fierceness, the determination of the victory he had seen for himself, had vanished from his expression. Now there was only a look of resignation on his face.

"Finish, white man," he told me.

He conceded and accepted defeat and was prepared to receive death. A battle fought in fairness had been lost.

I held steady, even as I knew that, if it had been him holding the knife, he would not have hesitated to plunge it into me to claim his own victory.

After many seconds I said, "To kill you now would be murder."

Johnny Scarface eyed me directly; there was no compromise in his stare. "We fought fairly; you won honorably."

I frowned as I questioned him. "If I were now to hand you this knife, what would you do?"

He smiled wanly. "Your question has no merit. That is not how it is."

"If you had won . . . ?"

"You would be lying dead," he said without hesitation.

I knew that to be true. Perhaps that was one of the distinctions between our people: pride versus compassion. Of course, I also recognized that was never an absolute, as had been proven in this history of a boy turned savage, where there had been no demonstration of understanding or compassion from those who condemned the ways of the Indian and wanted to expand what they considered civilization across these Western territories, regardless of the cost in human lives.

The crimes committed against and by the Comanche now known as Johnny Scarface were the brutal result of one man's fear and prejudice. And he was just one of many who'd held firm to this primitive view.

"There's an acceptance of mercy," I said. "One that could be a benefit to both our peoples."

"No, white man." Johnny Scarface spoke adamantly. "If I were now to return to my people, it would be in disgrace."

"Why?" I wanted to know. "We fought fairly. You lost, yes. But not with disgrace."

"That is how you see it."

I stared hard at the blemished blade of the knife held tight in my grip. "Yet you would return in triumph with my blood mingled here with the blood of the others?" I said.

Johnny Scarface didn't answer. I suppose to his mind, why waste words on what was not to be?

"Yet you cannot force me to kill you," I told him.

Johnny Scarface smiled shrewdly. "Yes. I can."

And I understood. He could provoke me into defending myself by attempting a sudden act of aggression, where I would have no choice but to use the knife against him. I hoped that wouldn't be. Yet I remained aware that I would never bring him back to stand trial for the crimes he'd committed. If I attempted to do so, he would make a move against me that *would* force me to kill him. As he had stated, he had been thrust into violence by the white man. He would not accept the judgment of our laws.

I faced a dilemma.

"I choose to die with dignity," he said with an inflation of pride.

I again regarded the knife held in my grip. The wood handle felt moist from the sweat of my palms.

"You said that one of us must die by *this* knife," I said, fixing my eyes on him.

Johnny Scarface regarded me with a tight expression, then he nodded his head once, with emphasis.

I nodded back to him, glanced once more at the knife, then in a swift action twirled myself around and threw the knife as far as I could deep into the brush. It landed soundlessly, someplace where it could not easily be retrieved, as I'd intended.

Johnny Scarface gazed at me with dark, uncomprehending eyes.

"Search for the weapon if you must," I told him, gesturing blindly into the heavily wooded landscape surrounding us. "And if you find it, you can come for me."

The last expression I saw on Johnny Scarface's disfigured features was one I could not describe, since it seemed to be a blend of assorted emotions. But it was an image that was never to leave me.

I walked away from him, my back turned . . . yet I felt no threat. Not any longer. To kill me now, at this time, would disrespect his honor. Even if he retrieved the knife he would not thrust it into my back, as we had fought fairly, and I believe he knew that if he were to attempt a final charge, I would not turn to face him.

Still, would Johnny Scarface hunt for the knife? Would he find it and, at some time in the future, come searching for me to finish our fight to preserve his honor?

I would not know, but, over time, a legend grew about Johnny Scarface, and it was then that I learned much of his story. I met with Indians when peace was established between our cultures, and often they would come to me directly and openly share many of the facts. I was told about the gentle boy named Jacquin, whom many in the tribe had regarded with curiosity, while some looked upon him with resentment because of his thirst for a broader knowledge, not content to merely accept his people's prejudices. I learned more about of the tragic change that came over him, why and how he became a warrior, including the reason he had killed the shopkeeper who had befriended him. Much of what was imparted to me did not allow me to pardon some of his actions, but it was difficult for me not to retain a sympathy for the boy when he had been known simply as Jacquin.

Of course, I had no way of knowing if these stories were the truth or maybe fabricated—or if they had simply expanded into legend over time. But of one thing I could feel certain: these incidents were first related to the Comanche tribe by Johnny Scarface himself. I learned that he had spoken of our own encounter and, to his credit, perhaps in trying to improve relations between his people and my own, told of how I refused to kill him when I had the opportunity. Whether this was met with shame or disgrace as he had feared, I don't know. That was never told to me, and I had never asked. Yet, despite all that had happened to him and the violence perpetrated upon him and later committed by him, it seemed hopeful that the quest for a better understanding and the belief in a united brotherhood sought by the idealistic Jacquin still existed in some way in the man now remembered only as Johnny Scarface.

That would be the ending I would have preferred. But I also could not forget that he had returned to his people not as an innocent, inquisitive youth but as a seasoned warrior; had through his deeds earned a badge of honor among those who embraced the idea of an ongoing war against the white man. The troubles with the Comanche had not yet been resolved at that time; there would be further skirmishes, especially among renegade bands that could not accept surrender to the conditions presented by government treaties, and I could not know whether or not Johnny Scarface participated in those attacks. If he had, I was never to learn of his fate.

After our first and last encounter, he disappeared from my life like the fading of a sunset.

CHAPTER TWENTY-TWO

The story is not quite over. Naturally, when I emerged from the brush I had some explaining to do to Malone. His eyes widened, and a look of subdued astonishment drew across his features once he saw that it was me and not the Comanche walking toward him. I hoped he'd be adequately relieved at seeing me alive so that it might temper his reaction at my having to tell him that Jacquin—or *Johnny Scarface*—was free. After all, Malone had lost two comrades to the Comanche, and I couldn't know how he'd feel about my letting their killer go when I'd had it in my power to end his life—and at his own request.

Maybe Johnny Scarface hadn't thrust a knife into me. But I didn't put it past Malone to possibly finish what the Comanche had intended had our fight turned out differently. I had to take that chance when I explained to him what happened.

At first I couldn't quite make out what his feelings were. He was still grasping his six-shooter with his thumb and forefinger positioned properly. It seemed clear to me that he was prepared to shoot the Indian had he emerged from the brush rather than me. As it was, if he were so inclined he could pump a bullet into me and say it was the doing of the Comanche. Who would suspect otherwise with three of our group already dead? I sweated out those moments expecting the worst.

But instead he surprised me.

"He set out what he aimed to do," Malone said resignedly. "Know it's wrong, but I reckon no worse than what was done to him." He hesitated. "And, like the sheriff said, maybe wrong of us to be chasin' after him on Ray Colson's behalf, when that coyote and his man Stokes was the ones who caused it all." He punctuated his statement with an encouraging closure, proving to me that he *had* heard and likely absorbed the sheriff's final words. "That must be what Caldwell thought at the end." He smiled wanly. "Hard to deny a dyin' man his last request. 'Specially the request of a friend."

I was relieved, but I still wanted confirmation that he might not later regret his change in attitude.

"You were deputized," I reminded him. "Don't you feel you have an obligation?"

Malone did consider for a bit.

"No," he finally sighed. "Maybe if I was still ridin' with the Rangers I'd see it different, but that's long past."

We both stood in silence listening to distant sounds, various wildlife announcing through their chipper calls the day ahead.

Malone gave me a strange yet thoughtful look. " 'Sides," he reasoned—if somewhat reluctantly, "my hands ain't exactly clean. I just shot a man in the back."

I offered a nod. I didn't feel it appropriate to express what I felt in that regard. I could have shot Jim Stokes just as easily had I been given the opportunity, with little or no regret.

Malone furrowed his heavy brow in a frown. "Reckon somehow it all comes out even in the end."

I hadn't thought about it that way, but on reflection I had to agree with him. It began with senseless violence, and because of that there had been consequences, sometimes fair, other times not. We'd experienced both. Both the deserving and the innocent had paid a price for reprehensible conduct.

I'd tell Malone more on our way back into town. I hoped that what I'd say would lessen any guilt he might still carry over not bringing back the killer of his two comrades.

Malone spoke in a more enthusiastic tone. "Heard yuh got a coupla children."

"Yeah." I smiled. "Two girls."

He peered inside his shoulder sack. I heard a very faint but by now familiar meowing. "Think your girls might like a pet?" he said.

"Might at that," I replied.

We rode together back to Chesterfield City, the body of Sheriff Caldwell carried behind us, draped over his horse. It was an eerie reminder of a return from an earlier manhunt, the details of which were the focus of another narrative. Caldwell deserved a decent burial, as did Brad Calhern, but he'd already been laid to rest, and we decided we didn't want to disturb the ground where we'd placed him. As for Stokes, his body had drifted somewhere down the currents of the creek, and neither Malone nor I felt the incentive to try and locate him.

I'd have to inform the town council about what had happened to Sheriff Caldwell, and Malone agreed to come along to verify the story—well, as much as we were willing to reveal. Neither of us felt the community would have to worry about facing the threat of Johnny Scarface. As I'd told Malone, with the main participants dead, his trail of vengeance was over.

I didn't much care for the welcome I received from the two men with whom I'd had a previous and not exactly positive experience: Aldermen Roscoe Cutler and Amos Tyde.

"Came back with another dead one, did yuh?" Cutler said cuttingly as he met Malone and me on the boardwalk.

"Sheriff Caldwell," I said with a tight stare.

Both men gave me a peculiar look. I knew what they were thinking: second time I'd gone on a manhunt and returned carting the body of a dead sheriff.

I saw Malone's large body tense and his face start to redden.

And then he completely surprised me.

He said, "We found our man. Couldn't get him to surrender. Gambel here was forced to shoot him dead."

As shocked as I was by Malone's words I wasn't going to dispute his claim.

"That true?" Cutler said directly to me.

I started to dismount. My words were impassive. "You heard Malone tell it."

"Why don't you tell it."

"Go to hell," I said.

Amos Tyde looked slightly doubtful. "Why didn't you bring back his body?"

Again, Malone answered for me. "It's floatin' somewhere in a creek. Food for the fishes, which is what he deserves."

Cutler turned to Tyde. He made the comment, "Guess he rates no better after what was done to Colson and his daughter."

"Colson done it to himself," Malone said curtly.

For a quiet sort, I was impressed with the responses he was providing.

"Were the bodies brought into town?" I asked as I started to remove my gear from the horse.

Tyde nodded. "Funerals tomorrow." He squinted a conspicuous eye at me. "You plan on attending?"

I shook my head slowly. "Seen enough death to last me for a while. Just want to spend some time with my family."

Tyde creased his brow. "All right, I reckon." Then he hesitated before offering a peculiar smile. "We can talk later."

I didn't much care for the sound of his words, as I could guess what he and likely the others wanted to talk to me about, and, if that were the case, there was no mystery as to what my answer would be.

I tethered my horse to the hitching post, and Malone and I nodded our good-byes to each other, and then Malone started off to wherever was his homestead, and I prepared to reunite with my family. I waited a bit, though, and stood and watched the big man. I made no promise to call on him and wondered if our paths might ever cross again. I rather doubted it. We each had our own life to live, only I was a little luckier because I had people to come home to. I felt a little sad. But the memory of Logan Malone would stay with me, as had so many others who, for a fragment in time, shared with me an event, tragic or otherwise, that I reckon helped to shape me into the person I was—am—and hoped always to be.

And I carried with me a reminder, not only of Malone but also the tough but tender hearted Calhern: the little kitten that had survived quite an adventure—maybe not exactly a lucky charm, but deserving of a better life than what she had endured out on the trail.

Before I could start on my way Malone drew his horse to a halt and shouted, "Gambel."

I turned my head in his direction.

His expression was grave and he added emphasis to his words with a stiff pointing of his finger. "You make sure that kitten has a good home."

And then he smiled. Not a broad smile, but for the first time I saw him express an inkling of lightheartedness. I returned the smile and gave him a sort of salute—which he returned with more exactness, befitting the protocol of his professional background as a soldier and Texas Ranger.

He called my name again. I stopped, turned, and he gestured me over with a swift nudge of his head. Curious, I walked across the street toward him. He gave me a long considering stare, then reached into his saddlebag and withdrew a handful of money. I watched without even guessing at his intent as he thumbed through the bills and then handed me what he had counted out.

"Five hundred dollars, Gambel," he said. "Don't need all that much and figger with your family and all . . . well, you're not just entitled to what shoulda been owed yuh, but deserving."

For one of the first times in my life I was speechless. I'd used my words to work through all sorts of predicaments back in the day, though my tongue had been silenced more since I'd been with a woman of independent substance like J.C., a gal oftentimes hard to argue against.

Anyhow, it was a fine gesture, but it just didn't seem right.

Malone noticed my reluctance and said bluntly, "Look, I insist."

Maybe pride was my enemy, I don't know, but Malone had been paid fairly, and I had no right to any of the money that he had earned.

"Tell you what," I said by way of compromise. "Someday you come back into town and I'll let you buy me a beer. In the meantime . . ."

"I'll buy you that beer now," Malone offered.

I declined. "No, but I thank you. Got some people I gotta get back to."

Malone nodded his understanding. He hesitated before offering one last comment. "Someday I think I'd like to meet that family of yours," he said.

I detected a hint of wistfulness in his voice that I could understand but didn't acknowledge. Maybe our paths would cross again. But I really didn't think so. And, truthfully, I believe Malone felt the same way.

"*Adios,*" he said in parting.

I drew in a deep breath that I exhaled leisurely. Then I clutched the canvas sack protectively against my chest, petting the material to relax the excitement the tiny gray kitten named Angel was exhibiting in her struggle to be set free to join her new family, and walked with brisk strides along the boardwalk toward the former *Chronicle* building: the main floor office and printing shop surely empty now, a shell, but upstairs the home where my wife and daughters would be waiting.

No matter what might lie ahead, be it the promise of prosperity or an uncertain future, it felt damn good to be back.

And this time it was to stay.

ABOUT THE AUTHOR

Stone Wallace is the published author of twenty books, ranging from horror to Westerns, history to biographies. A communications and two-time broadcasting graduate, his career ambitions have taken him along many paths: actor, announcer, welterweight boxer, advertising copywriter, creative writing and media instructor, and celebrity interviewer. He finds particular satisfaction in writing Westerns, stepping back creatively to a time when the lands were clean, heroes and villains were clearly defined, and values were simple and straightforward. His five previous Western novels have been critically acclaimed, with his second, *Montana Dawn*, being named "One of the Ten Best Westerns of the Decade" by *Booklist*. His first novel for Five Star Publishing, *Witness Seeker*, also received positive reviews from *Booklist* and the *Historical Novel Society*.

Stone resides in Canada with his loving and supportive wife, Cindy, who is also an author, as well as a storyteller and children's entertainer.

The employees of Five Star Publishing hope you have enjoyed this book.

Our Five Star novels explore little-known chapters from America's history, stories told from unique perspectives that will entertain a broad range of readers.

Other Five Star books are available at your local library, bookstore, all major book distributors, and directly from Five Star/Gale.

Connect with Five Star Publishing

Visit us on Facebook:
   https://www.facebook.com/FiveStarCengage

Email:
   FiveStar@cengage.com

For information about titles and placing orders:
   (800) 223-1244
   gale.orders@cengage.com

To share your comments, write to us:
   Five Star Publishing
   Attn: Publisher
   10 Water St., Suite 310
   Waterville, ME 04901